D1711265

Desire of Nations
A Polynesian Novel

Scripture quotations taken from the New King
James Version of the Bible.
Book Cover: Robert Henslin Design

This is a work of fiction.
Names, characters, institutions, businesses, places,
locales and incidents within the context of history,
legend and storytelling are either the products of the
author's imagination or used in a fictitious manner.

Contents
Note to the Reader
Dedication

Pronunciation / Translation

Note to the Reader

As a Native Hawaiian, I have chosen a pen name, Ta Reo Pono—derivation of Ka Leo Pono (to speak what is right), because my novels speak of the righteousness of God, in Whom all things exist, and through Whom all things can be made right in a world gone seriously wrong.

Henry L. Williams Jr., Author, Redding, California

Dedication

To my father, Henry L. Williams Sr.
To Hawaiians, other Polynesians,
and to peoples of all nations.
Jesus Christ is our true Desire.
Come to Him.

And He has made from one blood every nation of men to dwell on all the face of the earth, and has determined their pre-appointed times and the boundaries of their dwellings, so that they should seek the Lord, in the hope that they might grope for Him and find Him, though He is not far from each one of us; for in Him we live and move and have our being...
Acts 17: 26-28

Part I

The Son Rises from the East

1

From dawn, the sun ascended higher in the sapphire dome while paddling their two-man canoe toward Kahoolawe. As trade winds pushed them further away from Keoneoio Bay on the southern cape of Maui, emerald shades of the neighbor island became more distinct.

Approaching Kanapou Bay on Kahoolawe's east end, Makoa's adrenalin rose. "Our paradise," he spat, "is now a wasteland!"

In a trance, Po'o saw remnants of a tribe wearing hammered tree bark around their waists and plaited leaves on their heads and shoulders. Standing on the shoreline, they pointed to an inland mound and beckoned him to hurry.

"Look! Over there!" Makoa yelled, bolted up then steadied himself on the canoe rails as a swell passed under them.

Po'o shook himself awake and noticed that Makoa was pointing to the same earthen bulge. Gripped by the sight of Opu Iwi, the belly of Mother Eve, Po'o fought to stay calm. "I saw them."

"Saw who?"

"Nehune," Po'o said, "my ancestors."

Makoa wiped the sweat from his brow.

Po'o's voice was urgent, "They pointed to Opu Iwi and told me to hurry!"

Makoa wondered, '*Nehune? Pointing to Opu Iwi?*'

Groaning in his spirit, Po'o chanted...

"Lord! You have called us out from the nations!
Your mercy has granted us refuge beneath the Star
of Gladness!
For generations, Your ways, oh Lord, was strong in
us, when our hearts longed for you alone!"

Makoa felt power exude from this chant.
Po'o placed his paddle down, stood, stretched both
hands toward Kahoolawe and exclaimed, "The land
of my ancestors before Nanaulu and Ulu!"
Perplexed, Makoa thought, *'I descend from Paao*
and Pili from Tahiti that arrived after the Nanaulu
and Ulu clans. If these clans and Tahitians were
second and third wave settlers, then were Nehune
the first settlers to Hawaii?'

Reaching the shore of Kahoolawe between Ule and
Halona Points, they pushed their canoe up on dry
sand.
Po'o turned to Makoa and said, "You prepared?"
"For what?"
"The Navy."
Makoa agitated, "So! Let 'em come. Enough is
enough! They stop bombing or we die!"
"Whoa, calm down."
Glassy-eyed, Makoa glared at him.
Po'o deflected, "Moolelo---what is the *story* behind
this island."
Makoa obliged, "Kaahumanu once decreed this
island as a penal colony for natives that committed
offenses. Over time, goats and cattle were shipped

7

here and stripped the land of vegetation. Dis wuz nothin' bruddah, compared to American warships and aircraft ruining this land with bombs!" He pointed south. "When Hawaii was still a territory, the army leased the southern tip to use as an artillery range," lowering his hand, "after the attack on Pearl Harbor, the navy had exclusive use here for live fire. After WWII, President Eisenhower signed an executive order to bring Kahoolawe under naval jurisdiction."
Po'o grabbed his shoulder. "Ooookay."
The diversion worked.

To Makoa, violence was an option to establish Kahoolawe as a frontier for Hawaiian independence. Po'o sought for ancient strands of a lost tribe through peaceful means.
Same convictions, but different passions forged their bonds in the crucible of political and spiritual militancy.

They unpacked fishing and other supplies then pitched camp close to their canoe.
After snacking on smoked marlin, cooked taro and bananas, discussions ensued about what their brief stay would look like.
Hours later, Po'o said, "Plenty time before the sun sets. We go climb on mama's belly."
Makoa turned to look at the distant mound, "Sounds good."

In shorts, shirtless and barefoot, they trekked up the side of the mound. Po'o was relieved when he saw no signs of damage. Reaching the top, they settled in an area that had a scenic view of Kahoolawe. Makoa sat, crossed his legs, picked up a twig and stuck it between his teeth.

Po'o remained standing. His long hair danced in the wind. In a meditative state of mind, he could *feel* travail inside Opu Iwi, as if Mother Eve was in labor. "More often than not, our lives are like this island. We endure pain until we spiral in confusion and torment. Destitute, we linger on the brink of ruin." Eyes closed, long, deep breaths; he felt the land groan with innocent blood crying from the dust. Po'o knew that what was waiting to be birthed from inside the mound would heal this silent, ancient dirge. "Despite clever remedies, the inward nagging and emptiness of our souls remain. Like wrestling with dry, scorching winds while longing for the dew of heaven to cleanse our sorrows."

Makoa looked up and squinted from the sun glare, "You and your philosophies!"

Po'o ignored him. "When the land bleeds like this from all the shrapnel stuck in its body, the flowers and plants suffer. You can almost hear them moan. The sky is earth-blue, but spirit-grey; the trees whimper over the violence of bombs."

"What you tryin' to say, Po?"

"Folly shatters the meaning of our existence. If we hail ourselves as masters of our own destinies, the noblest of our pursuits are in vain."

Makoa wasn't in the mood for another one of his rants: sin obscured the essence of being in a world forged by the ill-winds of power and ideology. "Po, you really believe this stuff?"

"Yup! Your ambition is political activism. My ambition is Jesus Christ who came to empower anyone willing to be broken to become like Him."

In the long silence between them, memories of Po'o's grandmother became lucid.
'Po'o, my poi boy, come sit on tutu's lap.'
Little round face Po'o, snot running from his nose, climbed up on her lap and rested his head on her flabby arms like he always did when it was story time.

'Now, Po'o, Nehune was already here when Nanaulu and Ulu people came to Hawaii. They all struggle for food. Not enough to eat! Nehune on Kahoolawe farmed and divided land just like ahupuaa. I dunno. Maybe they teach Nanaulu and Ulu people to farm like did. Maybe Nanaulu and Ulu people teach Tahitians to farm like dis. Somehow, somebody figured out how to make ahupuaa.'

Makoa stood and waved his hand in front of Po'o's face. "Where are you now? First you philosophize then you get lost in your head!"
Startled, Po'o blinked. "Oh, I was listening to my tutu." Faint echoes of his grandmother's voice turned his attention to the contour of land stretching to the ocean. Squinting, he lifted his hand, pointing. "Can see the pie-shaped section of land."
Turning, Makoa's eyes grew wide. "Ahupuaa!"
"Tutu Pani told me Nehune did this."

Defensive, Makoa smarted, "What? No way. Hawaiians did this!"

"If you say so." Not far from shore, peculiarly lined rocks jutted from the surface. "Notice the formation?"

Raising his left hand to shield the glare of the sun from his eyes, Makoa gasped, "Fishpond!"

Po'o gestured toward the uplands of Puu Moaulanui. "Uka is up there. Where we now stand on Opu Iwi is the Kula area, "he swung around, pointing, "down there is Kai."

Knowing about Po'o's knowledge of Hebrew and Polynesian history, Makoa inquired, "What *do* you know of Nehune?"

Po'o grinned.

Makoa knew the look in his eyes. "Don't get weird on me. Keep it simple."

Po'o was cautious. "Some believe they descend from Taranimenehune, said to be the son of Abraham."

Makoa was incredulous. "Abraham?"

Po'o reiterated, "As some believe."

"Soooo Nehune came from the Middle East?"

"An ancient genealogy points to Lua-Nuu (Abraham) who married Mihakulani (Sarah). He first had Ku-Nawao (Ishmael) by Ahu (Hagai). Then Lua-Nuu and Mihakulani had Taranimenehune, or Isaac. History becomes legends then myths, so this is debatable."

Still skeptical, Makoa scratched his head, looking perplexed.

"A census was taken on Kauai," Po'o continued, "to account for remnants of Nehune back in 1820. My family in Naalehu on the Big Island claim Nehune descent."

Makoa pressed further, "Soooo what's the connection?"

"After all these years, you *finally* interested?" Po'o chided.

Makoa smiled. "Yup!"

"When they settled here on Kahoolawe, they left behind a symbol that embodied their spiritual legacy."

"A symbol?"

"Yes."

Makoa felt a sudden warmth surge in his body. He shook it off, "Where is this symbol?"

A stern, serious look on Po'o's face. "Somewhere beneath us---in the womb of Mother Eve."

The warmth in Makoa's body became more pronounced, like radiant heat from pure light. A tear fell from his eye. The reputed lion for Hawaiian sovereignty whispered, "What's happening to me?"

Attuned to the presence of the Lord, Po'o placed a hand on his shoulder, "Jesus is the greatest of all Warriors. Cannot fight with the Chief. He is Fire. You feel the heat of His flame. Make cold hearts warm, bruddah."

Bent over slightly from the weight of conviction, Makoa looked up, "My heart," holding his chest, wincing, "is cold?"

Po'o smiled.

Makoa did the unthinkable. He fell on his knees. Wrestling against pride, he succumbed to tears.

Glossy-eyed, Po'o knelt beside Makoa, lowered his head and prayed.

Fire of the Son melts the coldest of hearts. Makoa was cold and mean. He came here to die, but Life wanted him to live. Light shone through his veiled darkness to free him.
Po'o grabbed a clump of dirt, stood up, reached his hand out and let the dirt sift through his fingers. Just then, a subtle gust of wind blew on the oblation. As the wispy dust cloud from the mound's zenith swirled, he closed his eyes, lifted his face toward heaven and shouted a conciliatory call to people on the four corners of the earth. "Man is from the earth. He is corrupt so he must be clean if earth is to be clean. Power for this renewal comes when wounded man is reconciled to healer God. The salve for this wound is the blood of Jesus!" These words were alive, powerful, and sharper than any two-edged sword that pierced Makoa's spirit. It felt like intense, divine love that bridged his internal divide.

*****

Night came. Fresh fish was netted close to shore and broiled over keawe fire. It was the end of the first eventful day on the isolated island.

Throughout most of their second day, Po'o wondered off to another place to be alone with the Lord and pray.

13

Left alone at their encampment, Makoa contended with years of anger and grief. Vindictive thoughts against the U.S. government for colonizing Hawaii were like daggers that wounded his soul. A thousand questions, lingering in his troubled mind, became a flood of painful memories. He chided to himself, *'So much for Po'o's philosophies. It's starting to make sense.'*

On the third day, they talked all morning while pole and reel fishing. They gutted, scaled, salted and wrapped fishes in ti-leaves, then stored their catch in the shade of their tent. Small shore breaks were rolling in so they decided to body surf. Throughout the afternoon, Makoa inquired more about God. In response, Po'o focused on Jesus, whom the Spirit of Truth will reveal in the scriptures if our hearts seek for Him.

By dusk, azure skies faded to greyish blue. Strolling along the shoreline away from their encampment, Po'o noticed dark clouds gathering on the distant horizon. "Can you feel that?"
"Feel what?"
"Something ominous is afoot."
Makoa hissed, "You weird."
Po'o cautioned, "Watch where we step. There may be undetonated bombs stuck in the sand."
Makoa mocked, "Whateva. Boom! I no kea if I die!" He caught himself, "Sorry. I, uh, will need time," thumping his chest, motioning as if shooing a fly, "for this anger in me to go."

"If you keep your mind on Him, Jesus will be your Peace."

After a long silence, Po'o inquired, "Do you know about the Pacific Archaeological Society?"
Makoa said, "Yes. Kyle Pahono and me wuz good friends in high school."
"Oh?" Po'o was surprised, "did you ever look into their findings?"
"Two-hundred page report and plenty hearings," Makoa huffed, "if the bombing continues, Kahoolawe's ecosystem will be too contaminated. All that research and pleading, nobody listened!"
Po'o shook his head. "Politics."
"Corrupt politicians!" Makoa grunted.
"God has a better way."
"And what would that be?"
Po'o paused, teary-eyed. "Humble ourselves. Repent for our bloodshed, immorality and idolatry." He raised his head and prayed, "You, Lord, are our only hope in this broken world."
Makoa reflected on bloodshed when Pao and Pili came to Hawaii from Tahiti and of four ancient chiefs over eight islands at war with each other for one to rise and rule over all.
Po'o added, "Man's age-old quest to subjugate others stoked the deeds of Paao and Pili. The warring chiefs of old relied on the kapu system that included strangling, clubbing and human sacrifice to enforce the law."
Makoa half-joked, "Now you're reading my mind?"
Po'o shrugged. "Time we head back. I'm getting tired."

By late evening, slivers of moonlight glistening on the water began to vibrate as increasing winds whipped the surface.

Then it rained, pummeling the sand.

Po'o was fast asleep.

Makoa roused in and out of a fitful sleep by the rhythm of rain, wind and restless waves.

At fleeting intervals, he'd lay there with his eyes wide-open, convinced that he heard the distinct cadence of drums coming from Kealaikahiki Point on the west end of Kahoolawe. He thought, *'Maybe the way the tent is flapping in the wind? The beat of my heart? Waves thumping on the sand? Drums? Gourds?'* As Makoa was falling asleep, the sound of faint, haunting screams alarmed him. He whipped the cover of his sleeping bag aside and sat up.

Sound asleep next to him, Po'o awoke. "What?"

"You heard that?"

"Heard what?"

"Never mind. Probably pueo."

At daybreak, Makoa came out of their tent to relieve himself by a coconut tree. When he turned to start a fresh fire in the damp sand pit, he looked up and froze. Anchored a hundred yards offshore was a Coast Guard Cutter.

Reaching their tent, he opened the door flap, stooped and stepped in. "Po'o, get up!"

16

Three men in uniform motored right up to the sand in a Zodiac. They got out, dragged the inflatable further up and walked toward their camp.

Commander Luke Moresi's gait mimicked the stride of ancient warlords. His blue eyes, set deep against chiseled features, peered from underneath a white, round, flat-top hat ornamented with gold lining on the black, glossy flap in the front. A patchwork of gold-colored stripes that bordered silver clover leafs in the center of each epaulet decorated his shoulders. Two military policemen flanked him and stood poised as Makoa stormed menacingly toward them.

"WHAT!?" Makoa shouted as he got close and pointed his finger in Commander Moresi's face.

"Get use to this! All the research for Kahoolawe fell on deaf ears. We wanted to negotiate. Nothing! Our resolutions not good enough! Feds don't listen until we get their attention, then they turn and push their weight around. Too late! We will keep coming back until you stop bombing our land!"

His belligerence prompted one MP to place his hand over a holstered 9mm pistol.

Makoa eyed this as a threat.

Po'o came groggily upon the scene and tried to intervene.

It was no use.

By instinct, Makoa lunged and shoved the MP. The other MP took two steps back and drew his pistol. Fearing Makoa would be shot, Po'o tried to disarm him.

"Seaman Willis! NO!!" Commander Moresi yelled. *Boom!*

17

It seemed as if time stood still. And the winds cried. In the swift unfolding of blind circumstance, another native fell in slow, agonizing motion. Fumbling and choking on blood pouring out of his mouth.

The red-tainted sand cushioned the fallen native; an audible thud followed by slight puffs of granules. Po'o lay lifeless.

Makoa shook violently and belted an ear-shattering scream. His experience of the Lord's presence on Opu Iwi was overshadowed by the unhealed rage in him that rose to a vindictive crescendo.

Staring in disbelief, Seaman Willis lowered his weapon.

Commander Moresi felt his body go rigid and his jaws lock. He resisted the compulsion to comfort Makoa, kneeling, weeping next to Po'o.

2

Many years later, people poured out from large boats that ferried them from different islands and onto the dock built at Kanapou Bay. As they gathered on the shore, excitement and laughter were mixed with optimism and anxiety.

They came to witness a significant milestone in Hawaiian land politics.

As the event commenced, there was a moment of silence to honor Po'o's death. His widow, Tiare Pani, stood behind the podium on the sand to say a few words. Thereafter, a native speaker stood and spoke briefly on the history of Kahoolawe before he introduced a high ranking naval officer behind him.

Admiral Luke Moresi stepped forward to the podium, paused to look at his notes, looked around, thanked everyone for coming, and then said, "On behalf of the Deputy Assistant Secretary of the Navy, the governor of Hawaii and the mayor of Maui, the island of Kahoolawe is being returned to the Hawaiian people."

Cheers and applause erupted.

Bound to the dictates of ruling elites, the admiral became visibly tense. "However, the oversight committee in charge of this transition has agreed that the military will remain in control of the Kealaikahiki Point area."

Hissing, sighs and disbelief.

An imposing figure in the crowd kept staring at his blue eyes. "Eh, YOU!!"

Admiral Moresi noticed that time had streaked his hair gray on both sides. People turned in Makoa's direction when, unexpectedly, he heard Po'o's voice cry from the dust, *'God resists the proud, but gives grace to the humble.'* Shaken, he remained silent.

Makoa's awkward retreat drew stares. Used to his random outbursts, Hanani gently reminded him, "Remember Christ's words."

He lowered his head.

Lifting his chin, her olive eyes pierced into his soul. "Remember?"

Shoulders slumped, he uttered, "Repentance and humility."

She rubbed his back and leaned her head on his chest.

The admiral's long pause made the crowd restless. He finally turned, cupped the microphone and muttered something to the local archaeologist who was sitting behind him with other dignitaries.

The field scientist, who held a Ph.D. degree, stood and walked up to the podium.

Stunned, Makoa recognized his high school friend. Dr. Kyle Pahono introduced himself then promptly stated, "First of all, we are excited about the return of this land to the people of Hawaii. Second, we are equally excited to witness the rebirth of an ancient land-based system."

A few people in the crowd who knew this beforehand did not anticipate this rapid development.

20

"With available funding, The Pacific Archaeological Society has planned a three-stage project that we have aptly named 'Restore Kahoolawe.'"

'Restore' held hope for pro-sovereignty attendees. "Stage One will involve the reconstruction of an ahupuaa." Dr. Pahono turned westward and gestured with his hand from the top of Puu Moaulanui, down to the midland area, and all the way to the shoreline. "That entire area is an ahupuaa."

Vague outlines of the overgrown agricultural system drew attention to breadfruit, banana, and bamboo trees within its borders. Pointing to the midland mound, he said, "Stage Two will be to excavate in the Kula area. Surface artifacts that have been discovered suggest that deeper down we may find evidence of our people's settlement."

Upon hearing this, Makoa intuitively sensed that the excavation was tied to what Nehune hid in Opu Iwi. Tiare came up beside Hanani and gave her a hug. Then she leaned on Makoa's shoulder as tears fell from her eyes. He placed his one arm around her and, with his other arm, drew Hanani closer. For years, Tiare blamed Makoa for Po'o's death. Overtime, the power of forgiveness healed their relational wounds.

In a tight huddle, Tiare searched their eyes and whispered, "Dr. Pahono knows. I told him about Nehune. He believed me. Excavation in the Kula area is a front to get *inside* the mound."

Makoa strained to keep his voice low. "A front?"

21

"Yes," Tiare assured, "finding a way inside Opu Iwi must be kept secret or their efforts could be derailed."

Dr. Pahono continued, "Of the nearly 500 sites we've researched, at least 3,000 archaeological features on Kahoolawe have been partially or completely destroyed. But this ahupuaa is still intact," clearing his throat, "ahhh, Stage Three will involve cleaning up the island up for human habitation."

A man in the crowd puffed his chest and interrupted, "Eh, we heard that it would cost a half-billion dollars to clean up the military's mess! Where's the money coming from?"

A woman chimed in, "Yeah, how long goin' take to decontaminate the land?"

He looked at them, "Bruddah, sista, I would need to be a banker and geologist to answer your questions. I am neither, so I have no idea."

Chuckles over his quick-witted response lightened the mood.

With mainland attendees in mind, Dr. Pahono explained, "In ancient Hawaii, ahupuaa borders varied in shape and size. Higher regions were called Uka, where koa trees grew for canoes, wood posts, etc. Crops were grown in the Kula, or mid-land areas. The ocean front, or Kai, is where huts and canoe houses were built. Off shore, fishponds were constructed with stones and wooden grates that allowed smaller fishes in to forage and grow until they were too large to escape."

Dr. Pahono motioned for someone to come forward. "Aloike Pani, from Naalehu on the Big Island, descends from the people who first settled here. He will oversee reconstruction of the ahupuaa. A Bishop Museum appointee and our Society will monitor their progress."

Many recognized the respected scholar of Polynesian antiquities when he stood and walked up to the podium.

Puzzled, Makoa thought, '*Pani?*' Turning to Tiare, "is he your *son*?"

Tiare was caught off guard. "Nope. Distant relative."

Aloike took several minutes to preface his speech with history to express various viewpoints. In closing, he said, "Indigenous peoples are watching with growing interest as we re-learn our ancient ways," pause, "kawa ma hope: embracing the wisdom of our ancestors will help us navigate our future."

Applause.

He smiled, half-waved then sat back down.

Dr. Pahono stepped back behind the podium. "We hope that what they learn will yield useful data. For example, did ancient weave patterns for baskets and canoe sails fair better than modern patterns in flexible, waterproof materials? If so, can these materials be improved? Rope from coconut husk rolled, twisted, and woven to rig canoes and sail masts may help engineers with the modern correlate of spider silk said to be, as a composite, stronger than steel and Kevlar. Mental star-maps to find new lands through the ancient art of wayfinding on the high seas with no navigational equipment testify to the power of human memory. This is an asset, because if technology failed, buoy-positioning transponders to map the ocean and triangulate marine navigation would be useless. Integral to their oral culture was the ability to contemplate without the constant drone of noise and distraction that permeates our modern culture. Priests were trained to memorize and recite chants, some over 2000 lines long. Many were able to memorize and recite entire chapters in the bible when missionaries taught them to read. In short, learning to memorize and recite pages of information may assist neurologists seeking to slow the onset of Alzheimer's disease, dementia and other cognitive deficits."

When the ceremony ended, everyone held hands, formed a long line and looped around until those at each end would join hands to complete a circle. Tiare had pre-arranged to set a twelve-foot, wooden pole in the center of the circle. Rope was threaded through an eyebolt on top of the pole and tied on each end of a ten-foot, wooden dowel that hung perpendicularly on the bottom, creating the shape of a triangle. Holding the bullhorn up with her right hand, she pressed the button. *"This triangle represents Lokahi. The top angle represents God,"* her left hand pointed down, *"the angle to the bottom right depicts land; the bottom left portrays man. The harmony between God, land and man means balance in creation. See how the dowel on the bottom balances on the rope looped though the eyebolt on top? That eyebolt is a closed circle that has neither a beginning nor an end. It describes eternity. God is eternal. The twelve foot pole represents the strength on which the rope and dowel rests. God is stronger than, and the lifeline to, everything. If the pole and eyebolt wasn't in place first, there would be nothing to put the rope through to balance the dowel. God existed before anything we can see. He made land, and He made man from the land."* Pausing to rest her arm from the weight of the bullhorn, she motioned for a man to step to the center of the circle.

He stood by the triangle and pulled out a knife. Raising the bullhorn, Tiare continued, *"This is what happens when the connection between God and man is broken."*

He cut the rope half way up on the left side, sending the dowel plummeting to the ground.

The demonstration was clear.

"If our relationship with God is severed, the harmony between God, man and land is severed." Many who knew Po'o and Tiare for their beliefs either agreed or went along. Native practitioners huffed under their breath. Decades ago, the Hawaiian Renaissance reinvigorated their ways of old, including homage to the pantheon of ancient deities. Out of respect, they endured her religious antics.

25

As the man faded back into the crowd, she gestured for Po'o's family members to step into the center of the circle.

Po'o's brother held a large conch shell. A nephew held a wooden, barb-tipped spear and a niece carried a haku lei, a garland, which hung loosely from her wrist.

On cue, Po'o's brother blew the conch shell in a long blast.

Tiare lifted the bullhorn. *"This sound is our cry to God for salvation."*

He blew the conch shell again.

"This sound is our cry for His kingdom to be established on the earth."

A Hawaiian practitioner remarked to his friend, "What kind of bull is this?"

Po'o's brother reached for a smaller, more high-pitched conch shell that was strung to his side, raised it up and blew.

"This sound calls for an end to violence."

A woman leaned forward, looked over at the practitioner and said, *"That's* not bull!"

The second blast was long and mournful.

"This sound is a dirge for Po'o's death."

Some in the crowd grew restless.

The third blast was strong and commanding.

"This sound is a call for the people of Hawaii to repent from our evil ways and consecrate ourselves to God."

Then Po'o's nephew lifted the wooden spear and drove the barded tip deep into the sand, followed by his niece who draped the haku lei around the upper, blunt end. Then stones were placed at the base to keep it propped up.

Tiare pointed. *"The spear reminds us to be brave when we fight against evil."* She picked up the lei, raised it above her head and turned in all directions facing the crowd. *"This haku lei reminds us of the circle of life in which struggle shapes our character."*

Some were amused; others, irritated. Still, these spiritual symbolisms were significant. For the restoration of Kahoolawe to avail, it would require humility, or their warrior tendencies would overshadow progress. If pride availed, it would unleash a war of words---if not fists and weapons. Thus, wounded natives and land would never fully heal from the hubris and cunning of men.

Seen from above, the large circle of natives looked like a garland gracing the bosom of Kanapou Bay sands.

As they sang Hawai'i Pono'i, a movement in the brush close by caught Makoa's attention. He kept looking until he realized someone in camouflage was silently watching. He abruptly broke away. "Babe?" Hanani whispered out loud.

Just then, Makoa saw Admiral Moresi walking toward him. Their eyes locked. Makoa knew it had to do with Po'o's death. He turned, kissed Hanani, and left to investigate.

A wreath of leaves masked the old man's face. He was dark brown, wrinkled and sinewy. Knitted clusters of leaves draped around his shoulders and a strip of tree bark was wrapped around his waist and between his buttocks.

When Makoa startled him, he sprang into the forest. Makoa gave chase. The aged native leapt over rocks like a gazelle, dodged fallen branches with ease, and zigzagged through a long path of trees until he suddenly jumped down a steep ravine.

Makoa skipped and jumped down the ravine and came to an abrupt halt at the bottom.

Confused, he spun around wildly until he realized the old man was gone!

3

Reconstruction of the ahupuaa progressed under
Aloike's leadership. Over the years, chartered boats
brought in food, equipment and supplies. In
addition to grant funds, large donations came from a
small group of investors that Aloike kept a wary eye
on.

One morning, someone placed a large map of the
Pacific Basin on a table to debate their origins. Few
of them gathered and contended for their descent.
Aloike said, "Now known as the republic of Sudan,
Kush was an ancient Nubian state, with its capital,
Meroe, having Ethiopian influences. Not far from
their Kush origins on the African continent is
Madagascar, where the Malagasy language is
similar to the Hawaiian dialect. Proto-Polynesian
routes possibly included the Middle East, India,
Myanmar, down into the Asiatic archipelago, South
Pacific isles and dispersed into the Pacific Basin.
This dispersion was concentrated within the
Polynesian triangle: from Hawaii to Rapa Nui to
Aotearoa."
A native historian added, "Samoa is in the
Polynesian triangle. Ancient chants and oral
genealogy speak of Hawaiian origins from Savaii in
the Samoan group, from where they dispersed,
evidenced by traditional similarities."
"Yes, but farther east from Samoa is the
Marquesas," someone else interjected, "also within
the Polynesian triangle. Marquesans relate their

ancestry to Hawaii, since their southern group dialect closely resembles Hawaiian dialect." Another person asserted, "Thor Heyerdahl theorized that people from South America settled in Hawaii." In all, they agreed, aside from Thor Heyerdahl's theory, that proto-Polynesians, originating from Africa, Asia and Europe, had reached the Marquesas, Raiatea, Tahiti and other islands in the Polynesian triangle.

*****

Aloike formed a Council on Hooponopono at Kanapou Bay where elders from each island convened. In memoriam, he constructed a stone fire pit over the spot where Po'o was killed: between Ule and Halona Points.
Hooponopono protocols were designed to reconcile offenses between the offender and the offended. Similarly, his great-Tutu Pani's words still echoed in his memories. '*The written word and the Word made flesh are two of the most powerful weapons in life against evil, my little poi boy. Same way I teach daddy. If you no learn to walk in the written word and bow at the feet of Jesus, daily, you goin' be casualty in the unseen war that wages in the earth.*' Amused that she could wax eloquent and speak pidgin all in one sentence, what stood out in his mind was this unseen war. Jesus Christ, the fortress of his youth, faded on the battlefield of academia. Voices of humanistic enlightenment contend in this arena of intellectual slugfests until youthful minds, vulnerable and impressionable, bow to their sheer

30

force of reason, and become unwitting, ideological slaves. As Aloike grew older, great-Tutu Pani would gently say, *'Daddy was on the right path. Wasting your time, boy. Your academic pursuits are carnal. The carnal mind is at enmity with God.'*
His path of native enlightenment was a journey apart from the Truth. Without the Life and Light of men, Aloike's existence, over time, became meaningless. Grasping for meaning and purpose, Hooponopono was something he held on to.

*****

Cries echoed in the rainfall and winds at night. Bending their ears to what they were hearing, Olapa said anxiously. "You hear that?"
Aloike nodded, "Yes…"

The council met under clear skies the following night. As flames from the fire pit flickered, Aloike stood, pointed west and said to the elders, "Our hearts felt sick when Olapa and I heard wailing coming from Kealaikahiki!"
Ashen faces. "Wailing?"
"Yes." Aloike responded.
Long silence.
Olapa blurted, "Admiral Moresi mentioned something about military operations there."
Their distraught faces seemed surreal in the glow of firelight. Some proposed to go and investigate.
"The perimeter is heavily guarded," Aloike cautioned.

31

Another shrugged his shoulders. "So we do nothing?"

Looking at him, Aloike slowly turned to the others. "There is something you must all know."

They listened patiently.

"Dr. Pahono petitioned the state to dig around the base of Opu Iwi," he studied their faces, "it's a deterrence to get inside the mound where a people long ago hid a message of deliverance."

One elder admitted, "I have heard they came to these islands before Nanaulu and Ulu clans, followed by our Tahitian ancestors."

"This people were known as Nehune," Aloike gazed into the flames for several seconds, "from whom I descend."

Skeptical, an elder challenged, "Nehune have been dismissed as legend."

Another elder countered, "Legend or not, a few people in the 1800s claimed Nehune descent on Kauai."

A hand was raised as a motion to speak. All heads turned toward him.

Aloike nodded.

The elder queried, "What *is* this message of deliverance?"

Brows furrowed, Aloike slowly stroked his beard. "It's some kind of symbol. When the earth travails in hopelessness, whoever finds it will find hope."

Olapa interjected, "Aloike and me suspect that finding this symbol will help us understand the wailing we heard."

Blank stares.

The same elder raised his voice, "I'm tired of kanaka sovereigntists jockeying over who is supposed to be king," pause, "if a Hawaiian kingdom can even be re-established."

Those who knew of his fierce political activism were taken aback to hear him say this. He continued, "If what you say is true, then we have nothing to lose. The Pahono's must find this symbol of hope!"

*****

Several days later, Dr. Kyle Pahono and his wife, Dana, a Ph.D. in Anthropology, greeted the council elders and gave them lauhala baskets filled with gifts.

Formally addressed as doctors, Dr. Pahono smiled. "Kyle. No need for titles."

His wife interjected, "Dana. Same reason."

Everyone relaxed.

Steamed taro and hot pork strips from the ground oven were served on ti-leaves with coconut juice in halved shells. The food was good while making their acquaintances.

After a while, Aloike looked sternly at Kyle and Dana. "Olapa and I heard screams coming from Kealaikahiki."

"Screams?" Dana nearly choked on her taro.

Olapa reiterated, "Screams."

Kyle revealed, "Admiral Moresi explained to me that what happens there is beyond his control and advised that we stay away."

This did not go over well with some of the elders.

Kyle inquired, "How often does this occur?"

"When the weather is bad," Aloike answered, "against the admiral's advice, I am compelled to go there myself to investigate."

Others threw in their support.

Discouraging this move, Kyle diverted their attention. "We finally have the permit to begin excavation."

An elder pressed, "Aloike has informed us that you intend to get *inside* the mound to look for a *symbol*?"

Kyle nodded cautiously. "Yes."

He looked around as the others nodded in agreement, "Then you have our support. May you both be successful?"

*****

Dana gazed into the distance as they walked the sands of Kamohio Bay, overlooking Puukoae Island.

Kyle sensed her unease. "Ready for this?"

"Huh? Oh..." Dana pondered silently, '*Screams at Kealaikahiki? A sacred symbol inside the womb of Opu Iwi? Two points of tension at opposite ends of the island? Is there really a connection between the two?*'

The thought of using the excavation permit as a front to get inside the mound made her anxious. Visibly agitated, she barked, "What happens if we get inside and come up short?"

Through pursed lips, Kyle ran his hand through his hair. "Not all digs are productive, sweetheart."

34

She complained, "We're embarking upon a spiritual odyssey that our colleagues would consider nuts, sweetheart!"

"I know…" Kyle took a deep breath, "Jewish scholars say that Solomon's Temple once stood on Mount Moriah, or the Temple Mount, where Muslims built the Dome of the Rock. Jews believe Abraham attempted to sacrifice Isaac there, yet Muslim scholars say that Muhammad ascended to Allah from this same mount."

"What are you getting at?" Dana prodded.

"Legends can be jewels inside a treasure chest of history."

"And?"

"Opu Iwi is like this chest. The symbol is like a coveted diamond hidden inside."

Amused by his analogy, she recalled how she inspired him to become a field scientist. Grounded in his belief in God, he came under fire from colleagues for his anti-naturalistic stance which tarnished her reputation.

"A naturalistic worldview is biased, Dana."

She looked at him and balked, "You've explained this to me before!"

Her tone made his body rigid. "I," Dana softened, "need more time to think this through."

What stood between them would eventually coalesce. Her hardline anthropology, stamped in the mold of Darwinism, flew in the face of his archaeology that proved God exists. Substantiating the existence of God among colleagues perpetuating science as god made their work difficult.

35

Kyle brushed a tear from Dana's cheek, gently stroked her hair, placed his arm around her shoulder and whispered, "I love you."

Emotions reeling, she rested her head on his chest. Indeed, his genuine love tended to her deepest needs. She smiled, reached over and kissed him. "If your motives weren't so appealing, I'd say you've lost it! But how can a smart man like you be entirely mad to believe in the God of nature?"

He chuckled, knowing that she saw all of this as a classic case of native beliefs that can lead scientists on a wild goose chase, but she'd be fooling herself if she entirely dismissed indigenous ways.

"If man is the measure of all things," Kyle postured, "then he must, by virtue of this presumption, be creator of all creation. As a creature, this is a contradictory delusion."

Dana thought, *'This kind of reasoning makes sense. Where else would this love that I feel for him come from? Is love from DNA? Are my feelings, passions and dreams bio-evolutionary, or endowed by God?'* She laughed at these thoughts---and at herself.

Part II

Ancient Settlers

4

"Careful, bebe girl!" Makoa steadied Hoku as she
stubbed her toe and skipped to keep her balance.
Walking ahead, Malia and Kawika stopped and
turned around.

Hanani looked over. "You okay?"

"Yeah." Hoku's facial cheeks, rosy from the sun,
shone.

Hiking through the quiet valley was a relief from
the bustling crowds on Oahu. After civil engineers
cleared the ancient path they were on from dud
bombs, students from Hawaii University removed
thick overgrowth. Several miles in, the family of
five settled beneath a tree to rest.

"How far?" Malia wiped her brow. Sweat beaded
down her face as she reached in her back pack for a
bottle of water. "And why are we hiking?"

Makoa grinned and said, "Because an ancient
people charted this trail in a serpent-like pattern
that's like the constellation of Drago. Devoted to
the one true God, walking this path for them
symbolically meant treading upon serpents. They
also used this trail to elude clans that came after
they had settled here."

Malia rolled her eyes. "Oookay dad, whatever you
say."

The sun-lit land flourished; its wounds salved by the
silencing of bombs. Suffused in warmth, a rich
array of botanical specimens in the valley bloomed.

Butterflies were aloft, insects buzzed; lizards slinked away.

Birds of elegant plumes colored the sky, while the Puu Moaulanui range to the east towered in tufts of white. Rustled leaves and birdsongs, attuned to wind-shaped clouds, were poetic melodies pouring from the bosom of God.

"So beautiful," Hanani sighed.

Makoa put his arm around her as he took in the picturesque scene. He pointed to pits from past explosions. "Our kupuna would turn in their graves if they saw those." Feeling anguish, prayer soothed his soul.

"You've changed since your experience on the mound with Po'o."

"Still struggle, bebe," Makoa winced, "not easy." She agreed.

God's breath swept across fragrant-flowered fields, as fertile slopes ascended to drizzle that fell softly on mountain heights.

Sparks in Hanani's eyes were like flickers of a silent flame, as if virgin rain was fire that purged rancid streams and rivers. She mused, "The sky weeps."

Makoa added, "Creation groans with storms and earthquakes, waiting for the redemption of the sons and daughters of God."

Malia, Hoku, and Kawika quietly ate and drank as they read books they brought along in their backpacks.

They hiked inland from Lae o Kuikui Point until
they got beyond Ule Point. The trail led right up to
the taro patches close to the mound on the Kula
excavation site at Kanapou Bay.
Makoa recognized his friend kneeling in the dirt.
"Kyle! Aloha no!"
He and some of his students looked up. "What took
you so long?"
Makoa shrugged, "Hawaiian time. This is my wife
Hanani, our son, Kawika, and our daughters, Malia,
and Hoku."
Standing next to a woman, Kyle said, "And this is
my wife, Dana."
Dana stood and brushed dirt from her shorts. "So, I
finally meet my husband's friend and his ohana!"
First impression of the Pahono's put Hanani at ease.

From a distance, Aloike and outer-island locals
were preoccupied with various phases of the
ahupuaa. At this site, university interns labored for
weeks to create roped-off sections of earth strata.
Students came from Micronesia, Melanesia,
Australia, New Zealand, Alaska, Asiatic
Archipelago, and the South Pacific islands.
Digging and brushing began to reveal secrets of the
past: evidence of ancient tool-makers, stargazers,
fire builders, and canoe artisans was unveiled from
around the base of the mound.
Some students penned log sheets while pouring
over scientific data. Others in lab tents were
engaged in discussion and debate while hunched
over charts. Powered by quiet generators, others

typed on laptop computers linked directly to satellites.

Detailed aspects of the Polynesian Triangle were scrutinized: 10 million square miles of ocean that connect at Hawaii, New Zealand, and Easter Island.

Kawika, Malia and Hoku were encouraged to assist the interns at the site while Makoa, Hanani, Kyle and Dana descended on a dirt pathway that led several feet down below ground level at the base of Opu Iwi.

Kyle kneeled and picked up a burnt shell from Pit 23. "Whoever built this fire, repeated Carbon-14 results show these shells to be about 1900 years old."

Hanani saw the glint in Makoa's eyes.

"When we petitioned to excavate, we weren't certain of what we'd find," raising the burnt shell, "until this evidence…"

Excited, Makoa queried, "Nehunes?"

Dana responded, "Most likely, yes. But their legacy was overshadowed by subsequent tribes. Nanaulu navigated all the way up to the Northwest region, down to California, Mexico, Japan and into the Pacific. Ulu Ohana arrived about a hundred years later. Paao and Pili, migrated from Tahiti to Hawaii between 1000-1200 A.D. This led to war and human sacrifice with remnants of Nanaulu and Ulu Ohanas."

Recalling some of the insights from Po'o, Makoa exclaimed, "Then Nehune were the first settlers?"

Kyle nodded, "Hypothetically, but we are keeping our findings from Aloike so he can stay focused on the ahupuaa."

Makoa looked puzzled. "Why?"

"We, like him, were expecting evidence of Hawaiian ancestors. Hawaiian sovereignty and land rights are tied to first settler origins. Evidence of a tribe being here first would upend this," Kyle explained, "the political ramifications of this can get ugly real fast."

Hanani gasped, "I never thought of that."

Kyle continued, "Since Tiare informed me of Nehune, Dana and I have researched this tribe. The artefactual evidence suggests *they,* indeed, hid a symbol in the mound."

Po'o's chant out at sea joggled Makoa's memories. He added, "We were still in our canoe when Po'o had a vision of Nehune pointing to Opu Iwi, this mound, and beckoning him to hurry. Then he chanted an ancient Nehune prayer to one God, not to Polynesian deities."

"Interesting." Dana said.

Hanani puzzled, "What?"

"This suggests that Nehune were monotheists. Southwest Kivu Batwas, Southern Andamanese, Northeast and Northwest Bushmen believed in one God. So did Kalinga Negritos and Pygmy groups in Asia and Africa. Similarly, Maoris, Koryaks, Ainu and Yoshua Indians acknowledged the Most Excellent Supreme, Master Above, Upholder, Cradle, Inspirer, Protector and Giver. Tribal peoples from Alaska to Tierra del Fuego hailed the Ancient One, Old Man of the Sky and the Maker of Earth."

Makoa gasped, "Wow."

Kyle added, "Polynesian myths and legends hint at etymological constructs of a singular, Divine Sky-Lord."

5

The panoramic Koolau mountain range made their Kaneohe niche a respite from populated areas on Oahu.

"Kawika!"

"Yeah, dad?"

Makoa removed thick, sizzling cuts of New York steaks from the grill and placed them in a pan.

"Take this to mom and bring out the kal-bi ribs."

The sun beat down his back as he used a stick to shift through the red-hot keawe wood to even out the fire.

Nainoa, a pro-Lahui o Pono activist, would soon arrive with several pounds of poi.

Kyle and Dana volunteered to bring macaroni salad and rice.

Aloike and Olapa would bring fresh fish from Kahoolawe.

Hanani stuck her head out the lanai window, "Honey?"

"Huh?"

"You want me to mix sauce for the fish?"

"Ohhh yeah!" Makoa rattled off to himself, "shoyu, chili peppers, sake, ginger, and garlic, green onions, sesame seed, balsamic vinegar, pineapple juice, and pureed papaya. Bam!"

"Aloike, howzit!"

"Smells good!"

"Where's...?"

Close behind, Olapa walked in the lanai with a lauhala basket of fresh fish, gutted, scaled, salted and wrapped in ti-leaves. He handed the catch to Makoa. "Get room on the fire?"

"Plenty of room."

He laid the fish on the grill and brushed on Hanani's sauce.

Aloike looked around and felt disconnected.

"What?" Makoa teased, "out of touch?"

"Feels different. Out on the ahupuaa, just land and ocean."

Makoa looked up. "And sky?"

"So focused on reconstruction, it felt foreign coming on a motor boat. We would've have sailed here on our canoe if we had more time."

"How's that goin'?"

"Koa hulls and plaited lauhala sails handle nicely," a glint in Aloike's eye, "like we're soul-mates with the ocean and wind."

Olapa interjected, "Subtle calm to storm's fury, the dread of all sailors."

Makoa looked at them. "Sounds like you guys got smacked by a storm while testing the canoe out at sea."

Aloike said, "We did."

Olapa rubbed his belly. "Poi, pig, fish, coconut and bananas on Kanapou Bay, and now kal-bi, macaroni salad, and rice. Hope our bodies can take it."

"Hope you don't constipate!" Makoa chuckled.

A short while later, the Pahono's showed up. Kyle stuck his head out of the lanai glass door and complained, "Hanani made faces when she tasted my macaroni salad."

The men laughed.

"She goin' make 'em taste better."

Olapa asked, "Eh, where's Nainoa?"

"He called," Makoa said, "running late."

Hanani cut two pineapple tops off, hollowed the centers, and filled them with pureed coconut milk and pineapple, two scoops of French vanilla ice cream topped with maple syrup and nutmeg then set them on a tray.

Malia took the tray outside to serve Aloike and Olapa. "Dad, I'll bring more for you."

"And two more for Kyle and Dana, bebe girl."

"Ummmm!" Aloike savored the island nectar.

Olapa smacked his lips. "Ahhhh. Ambrosia!"

"So, what's that you said about your body adjusting?"

Olapa ignored Makoa as he took more sips and burped.

Hoku followed with a tray of seedless lychee stuffed with chopped macadamia nuts and cream cheese.

Everyone in the backyard turned to see what the commotion was in the lanai. Hanani was chasing Kyle out of the house and managed to punch him in the arm.

Makoa laughed. "Getting in trouble already?"

Dana came to the glass door. "He asked for it!"

The popular island song resonated from a social media video on Makoa's iPhone, adding to the festive atmosphere. Food was placed on the long table on the lanai.

After prayer, everyone helped themselves.

Dana sliced into the kal-bi steak with a fork and knife. "Sooo good, Hanani. I must have this recipe."

The men tore into steaks and ribs, pausing to drink and burp.

Kyle licked his greasy fingers, turned to Dana and quipped. "Recipe? When do you have time to cook?"

"Men cook, too." Dana scolded.

Makoa chided, "Hint. Sounds like she does all the cooking?"

Kyle shrugged, "Sort of…"

Makoa stepped to the edge of the lanai, butt facing out, and farted. "Oops."

The women rolled their eyes and shook their heads.

"No shame," Kyle hissed.

Makoa smiled. "Nope!"

Ukuleles and guitars were brought out after the meal. They took turns singing while the ladies danced to several of the island songs.

Time passed.

Then Aloike heard the 6 o'clock nightly news from an open window facing the lanai. Capturing his attention, he stood abruptly and went into the living room.

Makoa took notice.

In the middle of the living room, Aloike stood, stone-still, listening…

"Glenn Miyashiro, from the Commission of Land Use, is here with us live," the reporter said, *"Mr. Miyashiro, do you have any information on the charred remains from the Kula excavation site at Kanapou Bay on Kahoolawe?"*

Microphone swings over to the state official. *"Let me first remind the public that the ahupuaa, in general, is giving us plenty of data. Re-learning ancient survival techniques is advancing applied research and development in different market sectors."*

Rephrasing the question, the reporter stayed on cue, *"Reliable sources state that the fire pit remains at the base of the Kula mound point to evidence of a 1900 year-old settlement in Hawaii. Can you comment on this?"*

Olapa entered the living room with Makoa close behind.

Mr. Miyashiro cleared his throat and shuffled. *"Until conclusive findings can be determined, I have no further comments."*

The reporter pressed, *"Can you tell us anything about how this might impact our ancestral ties from Tahiti, approximately 900 to 1200 years ago?"*

Miyashiro evaded the question.

Makoa went back to the lanai. "Guys, come inside now."

Kyle glanced at Dana. Nainoa and Hanani stood to join them.

"Well, Matt, Julie," addressing the two newscasters in the newsroom from a rectangular, digital display screen on the right, *"Evidence pointing to people settling here some 1900 years ago has raised a lot of eyebrows. This is Harvey Dean reporting live for Channel 7 News from Honolulu. Back to you Matt and Julie."*

Camera back to newscaster Matt in the newsroom. *"Jane is with Dr. Chloe Hansen, a Harvard Zoologist."*

Next frame. Jane's back is turned to the camera and facing the reputed scholar.

The muscles in Kyle's jaw tightened when he recognized her.

Camera pans to shelves full of journals and books on primates.

"Dr. Hansen, what has been determined so far?"

She answered, *"We understand that remains from the fire pit at the Kula excavation site show a settlement much older than what we presently know or anticipated. But it's too soon to verify how old."*

A precise response would disappoint the shadow commission.

Jane pressed, *"A reliable source has told us that the older settlement is dated back to about 1900 years."*

Dr. Hansen responded, *"I have not seen the Carbon-14 results from the Pacific Archaeological Society."*

First settler claims would impact Hawaiian indigeneity on blood quantum regarding ceded lands and homesteads. Jane knew it, adding, *"The Lahui o Pono group said if there was evidence of settlers before Hawaiian ancestors, it would*

49

support their efforts to establish a new government on Kahoolawe."

Dr. Hansen's thoughts raced back to the dim-lit room of obscured faces on the shadow commission as she sat fielding their questions. *"Until Carbon-14 dating can be validated, neither myself, nor anyone else, can draw reliable conclusions."*

A glove-fit response.

Camera back to Matt at the newsroom. *"We have not been able to reach Drs. Kyle and Dana Pahono, experts in charge of the excavation, or a Lahui o Pono spokesperson for any comment."*

Aloike glared at Kyle.

Tongues clicked. Heads wagged.

Kyle hunched over, rubbed his hands, thinking, *'How did this get out?'*

Hanani motioned for Hoku and Malia to go upstairs and stay in Malia's room. Closing the bedroom door behind them, she returned downstairs and whispered, "Dana."

"Huh?"

"Let them handle this. Can you give me a hand?"

She nodded and followed Hanani to the lanai.

Aloike said, "So much for an ancient Hawaiian settlement. Looks like another tribe was here first."

Puzzled, Kyle had assumed that Aloike would be upset over the political ramifications of first settler origins. "From evidence in Pit 23, yes."

Aloike scolded, "Free to roam the site, yet you withheld this information?"

"I know," Kyle responded, "we came here to tell you and everyone about our findings. How and why it hit the news before we said anything," shaking his head, "is disturbing."

Long silence.

Aloike's demeanor softened, "Then what my dad told me *is* true?"

Tensions subsided.

This got Makoa's *immediate* attention. "Dad?"

Aloike looked at him. "Po'o Pani."

Makoa sat up straight. "What? Your mom told me you were a distant relative!"

Aloike shrugged. "She *told* me to be silent so you wouldn't put any expectations on me." Thoughts of examining his father's journals after he died whisked though his mind. Though Po'o's work chronicled their Middle Eastern origins, Aloike was taught about their Tahitian roots.

As if reading his thoughts, Kyle reiterated, "In consulting with our colleagues throughout the Pacific basin, data suggests Nehune were first settlers."

"My father believed this," Aloike replied, "he said they hid a symbol inside Opu Iwi," pause, "the belly of Mother Eve."

Kyle assured, "Which we're determined to find."

Suspense hung in the air.

Aloike looked at Nainoa, leaned forward and rested both elbows on his knees. "The news mentioned Lahui o Pono."

Nainoa looked around the room. "With Kyle and Dana's findings, Kahoolawe should return to its original form of government."

51

Olapa protested, "What are you talking about?"
Nainoa didn't miss a beat. "The government of God."
Aloike laughed, "You've lost it."
"Maybe, but hear me out."
Aloike gestured for Nainoa to continue.
"Under Lord George Paulet, Britain briefly took over Hawaii in early 1843. By July of that year, Admiral Richard Thomas returned the sovereignty of the Hawaiian Kingdom to the native islanders. Acknowledging Britain's actions, King Kauikeaouli stood in Thomas Square on Oahu and said, "Ua mau ke ea o ka aina i ka pono,' or, the life of the land is perpetuated in righteousness. Righteousness exalts a nation, but sin is a disgrace to any people. This is what Lahui o Pono believes and envisions."
Aloike argued, "*Ea* does not mean life, but *sovereignty* because Britain returned the sovereign nation of Hawaii to the Hawaiian people."
Nainoa clarified, "Sovereignty is from God, from Whom all life springs, and instituted among men by God. Without the Lord, Hawaiians have nothing."
This truth pricked Aloike's soul. His knowledge of Jesus, the embodiment of Truth Who sets all men free, was tainted. Knowing that Makoa had come out of what he, himself, was struggling with, he asked, "What are *you* thinking?"
Makoa intoned, "When your dad and I were on Opu Iwi, at one point, my insides felt warm, like, from radiant light. Po'o knew because he said, *'Jesus is the greatest of all Warriors. Cannot fight with the Chief. He is Fire. You feel the heat of His flame. Make cold hearts warm.'* Then, as if by the weight

of a powerful hand, I fell on my knees and wept. Shortly after, Po'o stood. Felt some dirt fall on the back of my neck. Then I heard him shout, *'Man is from the earth. If he is corrupt, he must first be clean if earth is to be clean. Power for this renewal comes when wounded man is reconciled to healer God. The salve for this wound is the blood of Jesus.'"*

Aloike abruptly folded his arms across his chest, as if protecting his lied-to-heart from Truth that could set him free.

During the long, contemplative silence, everyone noticed that Kyle seemed restless, tense. "As work on the ahupuaa progressed, I found out developers had their sights on Kanapou Bay."

Dazed at first, then agitated, Aloike threw his arms up in the air and heaved, "Developers?"

Kyle raised both hands, "I know. Everything was fine until this."

Olapa queried, "Who are these developers?"

"You know," Kyle grimaced, "Zander and Aldwin, T.H. Avies, Kassle and Kook."

Aloike sprang to his feet and gestured wildly, "Them? Now they want Kanapou Bay! Queen Liliuokalani dealt with the same crap. The U.S. wasn't satisfied owning the lower half of the North American continent, but was bent on *'gobbling up the little islands of the sea.'"*

"It gets worse," strained look on Kyle's face, "a resort and private mansions are planned where the ahupuaa now stands."

Aloike raged. "THE AHUPUAA!?"

Hanani shuddered as she and Dana could hear him clearly from the lanai.

Eyes closed, Makoa breathed in and exhaled slowly. "To build their dream, they must destroy ours. They are not interested in what you and others have been doing for our people if it interferes with their agenda."

Aloike, fuming, lowered his voice. "Why the ahupuaa?"

Kyle explained, "Most scenic area which has been fueling their efforts to remove stray ordnance. The risk of dud bombs sticking out of the sand after a storm can shut down business overnight, or if future residents dig up shells while landscaping or gardening. Demolitions experts focused on every square inch of land around Kanapou Bay."

Olapa piped, "We watched them for years and assumed they were clearing the area because of increased foot traffic drawn by our success!"

Aloike balked, "Why, Kyle, did you keep this from us?"

"For good reason, brah. Dana, myself and Nainoa have worked hard to stop their momentum."

Nainoa nodded. "We have, *very* hard."

Kyle added, "Every challenge that ended up in the courts was thrown out. Someone bought the judges. Our case was strong, but prime location on a remote island in Hawaii was too appealing for vested interests."

No one took notice that Dana stood quietly at the doorway. She startled them, "We did not want to interfere with your success, Aloike, and we had every legal reason to believe we could win. Our lawyers were top-notch."

Unbeknownst to them, a high-stakes political chess game was being played by a shadow commission driven by something entirely different from what had been unfolding. Their historical inception framed all that they stood for and would do anything to protect. Their key, influential connections worked to perpetuate their monopoly on godless thinking that kept the masses bound to their lies.

In allowing for the reconstruction of the ahupuaa at Kanapou Bay, only to have it leveled for an exclusive paradise, kept attention away from Kealaikahiki long enough until they could *finalize* their barbaric intent.

The shadow of this body politic slithered in the midst of human struggle and spoke with viperous, two-pronged tongues. In their castle, the king, queen, bishops and knights hired Dr. Hansen as a pawn to render the Pahono's findings null and void while cooperating with local developers.

Commission members, using their ties to state media, first produced a short documentary. As narrator, Dr. Hansen cunningly persuaded viewers that data collected from Pit 23 by the Pahono's were inconclusive, rendering the non-existence of Nehune.

Thereafter, she was allowed to act on her long standing vendetta against the Pahono's and buried what she knew to be *convincing* evidence of Nehune.

Then developers were free to shut the ahupuaa down.

*****

Over the past five years, visitors from around the world stepped back in time when touring the ahupuaa. Thousands worked and learned side-by-side with the natives. Dignitaries from other countries praised their efforts. But their sweat and toil were all in vain.

Kaipo, Kaopua and natives from the outer islands had enough. They met secretly with Aloike and Olapa in their grass hut. As expected, Lopaka and Kapena showed up shortly after. Their brotherhood, initiated in the trenches of Special Forces training, was forged in the crucible of war. They were joined by three tribal activists from the mainland.

When Nainoa showed up, Aloike looked surprise but said nothing. Following his cue, no one else protested as Nainoa sat among them.

Kyle and Makoa were intentionally not invited.

Varying viewpoints were discussed, calmly at first, but emphasis on perceived injustices gave rise to heated emotions.

Seething at the thought of being removed, Kaipo slammed his fist on the mat and raised his voice, "Many came out of poverty and crime! Our health has improved by eating what we grow. Taro, bamboo and pili grass, plenty! Fishponds---full! Canoe is almost done so we can sail on the high seas using the ancient art of wayfinding. Now this?"

56

Kaopua agreed, "Yes, Kaipo. We have learned of star patterns as cosmic stepping stones. I now know that *te lapa* is underwater lightning! Who taught our ancestors that, when the stars are covered by dark clouds, to look for bioluminescent streaks from an island's volcanic activity that can shoot up to 125 miles out at sea and follow it to find land? And *hua hoa dele tai,* you know, swells that point to certain directions out at sea?"

Olapa lamented, "Here, silence has taught us to listen to the rhythms of land, sea and sky. The children play and laugh and the women sing as they work. Tilling the nutrient-rich soil connects us with everyone and everything. Passage rites of hunting, spear and net fishing have bonded the men to their sons. Lua helps the boys to assert their aggression toward each other in sport, and not against women as they age."

Long silence.

Of Choctaw descent, Greg focused on past atrocities. "Between 1831 and 1833, 15,000 to 17,000 of our people were exiled out of southeastern settlements in America so their land and resources could be used by European settlers. In three phases of removal, they marched under the watchful eye of local and state militia. In all, between 2,500 and 6,000 of them died from a winter blizzard, cholera epidemic, starvation, flooding and drowning in swamps as they traveled by wagon, steamboats and foot for some 2000 miles. Once they resettled in Oklahoma, they endured about ten years of conflict: houses torn down and burned, fences destroyed and other abuses."

James, a proud descendant of the Creek tribe, cited one historical account, "During our people's removal from their ancient lands to Oklahoma, many were being transported by steamboats. The boiler on one of the steamboats blew up, killing hundreds of Creek onboard."

Louis, of Cherokee blood, added, "Gold was discovered in 1828 on our ancient homelands. In ten years, by 1838, Cherokees were the last of five tribes to be removed. Ah, hello, I wonder why? More than 4,000 of our people died due to similar conditions described by Greg and James. Here's a heartbreaking account: Cherokees were crossing over a frozen river. Some townspeople threw sticks of dynamite to sink wagons filled with women, children, elders and the sickly!"

Lopaka chaffed. "Kapena and I endured the politics of tying our hands with stupid rules of engagement in Afghanistan. Field commanders did not have the freedom to win, but to follow rules designed to lose. Insane. Politicians should keep their mouths shut and let the generals run the battlefield. Taliban were allowed to repeatedly escape when our boys had multiple opportunities to take them out. You think this didn't piss off the soldiers!?"

Heads nodded in agreement.

Listening intently, Kapena added, "Check this one out, boys. In August of 2011, a U.S. Chinook helicopter was shot down by a Taliban RPG when it hovered 100-150 feet above the ground in the Tangi Valley in Afghanistan. Pilots in the Chinook helicopter assumed the landing zone would be cleared of Taliban. Standard operating procedure. Two escort Apache helicopters and a C-130 had Taliban in their sights and radioed in to shoot the suckas. The pilots were repeatedly ordered to stand down! STAND DOWN?" WHAT?" Many of our boys were senselessly killed, including 17 Navy SEALs from the elite SEAL Team Six. Somebody explain to me how, at the last minutes, seven Afghan commandos, who were not on the flight manifest, boarded the helicopter with NO SECURITY CLEARANCE! Just three months prior, teammates from the same SEAL Team Six killed Osaba Bin Loden. WHAT THE HELL WAS THAT!?

Lopaka questioned, "Was this to appease a Muslim outcry to avenge Bin Loden?"

The men, weary from generational and political injuries, were like wounded beasts snarling in pain. Nainoa thought about a Biblical passage in Isaiah, *'The Lord God has given me the tongue of the learned that I may know how to speak a word, in season, to him that is weary...'* He said, "This ahupuaa's restoration was an example for a mainland tribe to rethink the way they live. On their land, mineral resources have been harvested with low-environmental impact, resulting in millions to build a tribal commune in well-equipped round houses. Like yurts. Outside of city limits, they remain off-grid by using solar panels for electricity. They eat what they hunt, fish and grow, improving their physical and dietary health. They're kinda like

Mennonites or Amish, but the men hold jobs in the marketplace while their wives homeschool the children. Technology is limited to focus on living quiet and peaceful lives in prayer, meditation, ministry to widows, orphans and the poor."

Kaipo was irked. "What does this have to do with anything we're saying?"

"Plenty," Nainoa assured, "the ahupuaa inspired what this tribe is now doing. Didn't you say that everyone's health has improved by eating what is grown on the ahupuaa?" He turned to Olapa and continued, "In our noise-filled world, you and the others now know the sanctity of silence that this tribe uses to hear God."

Taken aback, Olapa said nothing.

Louis was angling for a debate. "What about colonists forcing our forefathers and mothers off our ancient lands?"

Nainoa responded, "God has made of one blood, all nations of men and He has established the bounds of their habitations. Men are expected to be their brother's keeper on lands given to them by the Lord. Struggles avail because men's hearts are gripped by greed and gain. If blood is shed, God will hold us in account, especially if we shed the blood of innocents. Olapa, if you listen closely, you can hear the cries of millions of babies slaughtered in the wombs of their mothers since 1973. Unless we turn from this heartless cruelty, sexual perversions and other wrongs, our boundaries are no longer protected by the Lord."

They were unaccustomed to hear this kind of talk. Except for Aloike who knew that Nainoa and his father carried the same burdens in their hearts for the ways of God, which is why he said nothing when Nainoa showed up uninvited.

With no stomach for this, Lopaka lunged and grabbed Nainoa by the throat. Alarmed, everyone scrambled to intervene. Kapena's swift move had Lopaka in a choke hold in seconds. He calmly said, "Easy. It's okay."
Lopaka's hazed-over eyes cleared as he let go of Nainoa, who, by now, held his throat, coughed and hacked.
Aloike knelt, put his hand on Nainoa's shoulder and asked, "You okay?"
"Yea. I'm," cough, breathe, "I'm good."
Lopaka ranted, "Who the hell do you think you are? Suicide bombers yell 'Allahu Akbar' before they blow themselves and our boys up. If God is great, then why would he allow all of this crap that's going on?"
"THAT'S ENOUGH LOPAKA!" Aloike shouted. "Don't blame God for anything. The blame is on us."
Nainoa's anger against Lopaka dissipated when he heard this, because Aloike understood that godlessness creates a void that man fills with good. And evil.
Aloike stood. "We have tried to reconcile with all parties involved. Nothing! At every turn, we came up empty!"
More chatter, complaints and name calling.

"We," he looked at Olapa and some of the elders, "will do whatever it takes to save our land. ENOUGH!"

Kaopua's heart skipped a beat. "What do you mean by whatever it takes?"

In the ensuing silence, Kaipo, Lopaka and Kapena, internally, were game for a fight.

The rest were gripped with an ominous sense of foreboding.

Memories of native splinter groups confronting the law and being subdued by force made Aloike wince. "I will continue to strive for a peaceful resolve," skeptical look, "but if push comes to shove, I will fight!"

As he looked into the eyes of equally desperate men, Nainoa protested, "No, Aloike! If the pursuit of peace is aborted, it could lead to violence!"

Aloike's empty stare was unnerving.

Nainoa looked at everyone, pleading, "Are you all willing to sow your blood as seeds for justice?"

Feeling the weight of Nainoa's words, they solemnly stood and walked out of Aloike's hut.

6

After much persuasion, Aloike and Olapa finally
agreed to meet with Kyle and Makoa at Waimanalo
beach.
Lounging on the sand, the four of them, bronzed by
the sun, were unique in stature.
The tattoos on Aloike's biceps, chest, and both
thighs wove a symbolic tale of origin, genealogy,
migration, and destiny. A band-like tattoo encircling
Olapa's muscular left bicep depicted his family line.
Makoa's stout frame bore no ink lines, only an
inward, God-breathed artistry that colored his mind
and soul.
With broad shoulders and fierce visage typical of
his Polynesian stock, Kyle, too, did not use his body
as a canvas.

They chatted easily while kal-bi ribs simmered over
the portable weber Makoa brought along. Hanani
also prepared for them an ice cooler full of rice balls
wrapped in nori, a bottle of kimchee, homemade
chocolate chip cookies full of macadamia nuts, and
two six-packs of chilled root beer over crushed ice.
As they ate, each re-lived his own childhood
memories as kids splashed, swam, and ran along the
shoreline while some rode small shore-breaks on
boogie boards.
Talk of family, friends and life lingered throughout
the day

As the day wore on, ocean and horizon hailed the sun's westward trek against a curtain of melding orange and blue hues. Beauty of the forming sunset had no effect on their strong, emotional undertow driven by the pull of human dismay.

By dusk, Olapa inquired, "So, Kyle, these cries in the wind. Do you and Dana have any answers?"
"No."
"And the mound?" Aloike intoned. "Did anyone break through?"
"Not yet. The basalt layer is difficult to penetrate."
Makoa deflected, "Nainoa told us you're hoping for a peaceable resolve, or you will fight."
"You expect us to sit idly by while they level the ahupuaa for *development*?" Aloike huffed, "you guys have a better solution?"
"A more diplomatic one," Kyle suggested, "we can petition the governor. Maybe he can convince the developers…"
Olapa interrupted, "Convince? Seriously?"

None of them knew that the shadow commission's involvement with Kanapou Bay was tied to Kealaikahiki.
Aloike pivoted back to the mound. "What you said about the mound means the symbol hasn't been found."
Eyes fixed on Kyle, Olapa's tone was desperate, "You and Dana *must find* the symbol."

*****

Weeks after, Hanani and Dana participated in the flurry of activity at Kanapou Bay. While there, a boat, far out at sea, skimmed along the surface toward their direction. Onboard, Aloike and Olapa said nothing to Kyle and Makoa as they and a few others held on to the rails. All of them wore shaded sunglasses, some still squinting from speckles of light reflecting off the water.

Solemn, they felt the sting of shameless, land-grab politics aimed at leveling the ahupuaa for a golf course, private mansions, resort and marina.

Motoring closer to shore, some on the boat grieved over what would become of the children playing among the Kai huts.

As Kyle got off the boat, Dana greeted him, "Dr. Chloe Hansen posed as a colleague of ours when she approached Fran."

Fran was a trusted intern in charge of all of the field excavation data compiled over the years. After several failed attempts to reach the Pahono's for their approval to release data, she succumbed to Chloe's assurance that it would be just a cursory review. Briefly distracted by another intern on the site, a glance turned into the theft of pertinent pages.

Overhearing Dana, Aloike, Olapa and Makoa stopped to listen. Just then, Hanani walked up, hugged and kissed Makoa and stayed by his side. Brows furrowed, Kyle surmised, "So she could access our findings and tweak the Carbon-14 results?"

"Yes," Dana nodded, "anyone reviewing it would assume Nehune did not exist."

Kyle looked at the others. "These are the altered findings she covered in her documentary to debunk Nehune's existence. Remember?"

They nodded in agreement.

"There's bad history between us, he continued, "years ago, we were invited to speak at a symposium in California. Many field scientists were in attendance. Dr. Hansen was a featured speaker. Voicing her dismay with our Society, she used the podium to slam us before we even had a chance to defend ourselves. She argued that the religions of the world were originally polytheistic before the belief in one God ever emerged. From her secular-humanist worldview, any attempt to justify the existence of one God was academically unacceptable. Judging by the condescending jeers, most, if not all, of the field scientists agreed." He glanced at Dana. "Then we took to the podium to present peer-reviewed scholarship that substantiates monotheism, proving that the belief in one God is intricately woven in the belief systems of virtually all indigenous cultures around the world. We argued against the philosophical and ideological constructs of evolutionary theory that shapes the thinking of modern evolutionists, with a growing list of reputed biochemists joining the ranks of scientists that dispute the premise of Darwinism."

Dana added, "Dr. Hansen is a reputed evolutionist. She felt humiliated by our presentation on which our scientific approach stands. When the meeting was over, we tried to reason with her and make amends. In turn, she and her like-minded colleagues that find our work an affront to their efforts vowed to undermine our Society."

"That's why all this trouble?" Makoa queried.

"In part. There's more. For example, they understand that by equating religion to mythology, science is free to fill the vacuum of our innate quest to know what, or Who it is, that lies beyond ourselves and, in effect, guides the destiny of mankind."

His chest puffed, Olapa objected, "All these problems with evolution!"

Kyle assured, "Which is why our Society exists."

In Aloike's mind, he saw himself and his father strolling along White Sands beach. Po'o's reverence for the Lord was impressed deep in Aloike. He remembered his mom Tiare sharing how she stood on the dock of Keoneoio Bay on Maui to say goodbye when Po'o departed for Kahoolawe with Makoa---and never returned. "My dad taught me that belief in Christ as the Son of God filled the void in the Hawaiian people after the kapu system ended, and evolutionists say that your work affirming God's existence is nonsense?"

Kyle assured him, "Brah, they're following a well-funded, Darwinian mantra. Better if they get a real job than being paid to perpetuate a lie. Our ancestors used the stars to find land. From what ancient source of wisdom did they learn this? Monkeys sitting around a camp fire pontificating on the constellations? Before missionaries came to speak of God, our ancestors beliefs in descending

from Papa and Wakea would have skewered anyone
who said they descended from monkeys."

Dr. Hansen's clever vendetta was the discomfiting
kind of seed that sprouts and grows then withers
into briars and brambles of politics.
Aloike and Olapa, their hopes for the ahupuaa now
pricked by this loathsome thicket, abruptly stormed
away.

*****

Makoa hiked alone to the top of Opu Iwi to sit and
think. The post-news session they held in his living
room not long ago weighed on his mind.
Shortly after, face to face with Aloike and Olapa at
Waimanalo beach to de-escalate rising tensions
went awry, leaving him and Kyle unnerved.
And what of the distant cries from Kealaikahiki
when it stormed?
Flashbacks of Po'o falling, dying, made all of the
fast-fading dreams for native Hawaiians a living
nightmare.

*****

Plain-clothed officers dispatched from Maui Police
Department docked their boat at Kanapou Bay. Led
by Officer Luna, they walked up to the Kai village.
Kaipo was agitated. "We not lookin' fo' trouble. Go
back where you came from!"

Nainoa gripped Kaipo by the shoulder to pull him away but he taunted, "Who you work for means nothin'!"

Lopaka reasoned, "You come to serve us legal notice? What is the force of an edict if it ignores *our* autonomy? Is it illegal for Hawaiians to govern themselves?"

Luna said, "I understand, but bulldozers are already being loaded on a ship to level this ahupuaa."

"WHAT?" Kaipo shouted.

Nainoa turned Kaipo around and looked him in the eye. "You need to calm down."

He did. A tear fell from Kaipo's eye. "We are at peace on this land. Look at the gardens, the huts and the tools we've made. This is our legacy for the kids."

Lopaka pleaded, "Anyone we can talk with to cancel this shipment?"

Luna shook his head. "Too much invested in this."

Aloike had been observing quietly. Officer Luna placed the eviction notice firmly in his hands, turned and motioned for the other officers who accompanied him to head back to Maui.

*****

The ahupuaa's success on Kahoolawe had inspired hope in the islands. For example, on the summit of Makapuu on Oahu, several homes, once occupied by attendees of a manned lighthouse, were vacated. Forty acres between Hawaii Kai and Waimanalo, which included acreage in Makapuu, were deemed to be surplus land that allowed for rightful heirs to reclaim before being turned over to the state. Some native families claimed this right and occupied one of the Makapuu homes. Similarly, rightful heirs living in tent cities on Nanakuli, Maile, Waianae and Makaha beaches along Oahu's west coast moved and pitched their tents in a reclaimed section of surplus land in Waimanalo, prompted by plans from non-profit organizations that raised donations and secured grants to build homes to help ease homelessness on Oahu. These heirs were vested to build their own homes with assistance from skilled labor tradesmen in framing, electrical, plumbing, etc.

Years of evictions to clear the west coast of tent cities resulted in rotating encampments. Even with ordinances in place to avoid this, homeless natives, having nowhere to go, waited for several weeks before re-pitching their tents on the same beaches. These encampment problems along Oahu's west coast were alleviated once funding was secured for this community of homes on surplus land in Waimanalo.

In addition to these surplus lands with reclamation by rightful heirs, state bureaucracies allowed for a 10% increase for applicants with the required blood quantum to move onto homestead lands. Homestead land applicants typically waited for decades. Many died while waiting. By then, their children with lesser blood quantum would not qualify for land.

But back on Kahoolawe, machinations of the shadow commission went into motion: Kula farm hands were told that taro and other crops would be discarded and cleared for a golf course. Kai fishpond stones would be dismantled to make way for a marina. Beach huts had to go, with some handmade crafts that would be set aside as exhibits for a small museum. Devastated, the majority of those who worked and lived on the Kanapou Bay ahupuaa uprooted and returned to their outer island homes.

The repercussions were immediately felt on Oahu. The occupiers in the home on Makapuu were deemed by the state as squatters. After failed negotiations with the natives to pack up and leave, police were ordered to remove them. To resist removal, the occupiers armed themselves. However, locals informed of the unfolding drama intervened before it became violent.

The domino effect reached Waimanalo: plans to build homes were interrupted. Rightful heirs stuck in their tents felt cheated. Not surprisingly, the approval process for homestead land applicants was, again, mired in red tape.

A handful of angry sovereigntists known for their life-long devotion to land rights watched all of this unfold. Rumors of a standoff led by Aloike at Kanapou Bay echoed in their ears.

With nothing to lose, they headed for Kahoolawe.

The lust for power by despots dictated this outcome. Such is the way of evil doers.

Ignore the welfare of those over whom they assert rule.

Until the ruled rebel.

Part III

Blood and Tears

7

Two Cabin Cruise boats, captained by Lopaka and
Kapena, were funded by the state to help with
evicting everyone from Kanapou Bay on
Kahoolawe within two weeks.
Curtis and two assistants were assigned by the state
to monitor the return of evictees, including
arrangements for some to return to outer islands
when they got to Maui.
Aloike and the other men tried to convince their
wives to take the children and leave while they had
time. It was no use. The women, vowing to stand by
them, forced Aloike to accept Lopaka's and
Kapena's plan.

On the first scheduled trip, Kapena left Maui early
with the same men, except Nainoa, who met
secretly in Aloike's hut. Weapons, ammo,
equipment and supplies were stored in the hull of
the boat.
Upon arriving at Kanapou Bay they hid their cargo,
gathered their wives and children and disappeared
further inland. Kapena stayed back with the
remaining evictees, friends and relatives, who
vowed to say nothing.

Hours later, Lopaka motored up to the landing dock
with Aloike, Curtis and his assistants onboard. They
were greeted and served sumptuous meals,
including chocolate macadamia nuts and Big Island

cookies, Curtis's favorite. He was told that those in hiding had returned to their resident islands.

After monitoring two weeks of round trips, Curtis appeared satisfied that everyone was gone. Assured that Kapena, Lopaka and Aloike would leave soon, he arranged for an operator to take him and his assistants on the other boat and returned to Maui to file a state eviction compliance report.

*****

Upon his return to Maui, Curtis met privately with his supervisor. "Boss. I love my cousin, but something is up."

Ted looked at home. "Lopaka?"

"No. Kapena is my cousin. He and Lopaka were in the Special Forces, so I have concerns.

Ted pressed, "What are you saying?"

"Lots of tension there. The numbers don't add up. Maybe two-thirds of them returned on the boats. By the way some of them were acting, I suspect women and children are hiding somewhere on the island."

Ted was forthright. "Then the Maui police chief should know what he might be dealing with."

Curtis looked concerned. "I hope things don't get out of hand…"

*****

Day 5. The long, hot day was spent securing their stronghold on the top of Opu Iwi. As the sun started to set, Aloike signaled for Lopaka and Kapena to leave the other men, women and children who had

74

been carrying items up to the top of the mound's hastily built fortress.

Without saying a word to anyone, the three of them went to a well-hidden area at the base of the mound. It had a ghostly feel.

Once there, they shoveled away dirt and plants that covered a 4'x 8' plywood sheet. Setting it aside, they reached into a tarp-lined dugout to remove a cache of binoculars, basic electronics, semi-automatic rifles oiled and stored in gun cases and canisters of ammo.

Wiping the sweat from his brow, Aloike seemed regretful. "I was hoping we did not have to arm ourselves."

Kapena stared at him. "It doesn't mean we have to fire a shot."

Lopaka added, "It's insurance to make sure the women and children are safe."

By early evening, when everyone was in their huts to settle in for the night, the three of them hauled weapons, ammo and equipment up to the summit of Opu Iwi.

Kapena and Lopaka returned to their hut down below while Aloike stayed behind to ponder their fate. He lay on his back for a while with his hands folded behind his head.

Gazing at the stars, he fell asleep…

…*In his dream, he sensed someone approaching him. He sat up and was spooked to see his great-grandmother Tutu Pani walk up and sit next to him.*

There was sadness in her eyes. "Boy, not safe what you doin'."
Aloike heard someone else. Turning, he saw a younger Makoa kneeling, weeping. Another man knelt next to him, praying.
He peered closer. "Dad?" Whipping around, Tutu Pani said, "Keep watching."
Just then, Po'o grabbed a clump of dust from the ground, stood, raised his hand and slowly let the dust fall. A wispy breeze dispersed the plume.
Tutu Pani gently turned Aloike's chin toward her. "Daddy's innocent blood is now mixed with the dust of this land and cries out to the four corners of the wind for people in these islands to turn their hearts to God. That day, the presence of the Lord melted Makoa's stone-cold heart." A tear fell from her eye. "Your heart has grown cold. Turn back to the Lord."

Aloike awoke, slightly shaken. Looking up, he saw a falling star.
Troubled by the timing of this sight and his dream, he sat up as the weather turned inclement while he dozed off. It drizzled first, then heavy drops. He stood to take cover in the fortress. Shortly after, rain and gusty winds pummeled the summit of Opu Iwi and the huts down below.

Then the sudden echoes of distant screams…

Awake in their hut, Olapa sprung up, wild-eyed. "Did you here that? Aloike and I heard the same kind of screams before during a storm!"

76

Nainoa, too, was awake, though his eyes were closed as he lay down with his arms folded across his chest. "I heard it."
As the haunting shrieks became clearer, it woke the men, women and children in the other huts.
Olapa braved the storm and went to each of the huts on the Kai to make sure everyone was secure. Then he returned to their hut.

Greg, James and Louis were in a separate hut, wide-awake.
Gripped by the blood-curdling screams, James recalled, "I remember hearing babies cry when I stood alone at Sand Creek in Colorado early one morning. But these cries are of another kind of death."

Nainoa and Olapa were surprised to see Aloike step into their hut, drenching wet. He was visibly shaken as he changed into dry clothes from his sports bag.
"These *cries*?" Nainoa queried.
Aloike stared at him. "Olapa and I have heard them before."
"Some kind of omen?"
"No." Aloike slowly turned away.
Olapa pressed, "Then what?"
Pondering on what great-tutu Pani said in his dream, he stared at water drops from a leak near a corner of the hut ceiling.
Olapa gasped, "Aloike, say something!"
Aloike's soul was pierced with anguish. All that he learned of the Lord from Tutu Pani, Po'o and Tiare became a torrent of light flooding his spirit. "These

77

are cries of death. We must humble ourselves, turn from our wicked ways and cry out to God for this to stop."

*****

Day 6. The sun peered above the eastern horizon. Dread lingered on the morning mist like fire that sucked the breath out of the men and women. They could feel it.
Time was running short. With the ground dry, they moved everyone back up to the top of Opu Iwi. Water, food and necessities from the huts were all in place with the women and children in a bamboo and wood fort clear behind a rock wall. From the top of the mound, their empty huts lining the beach below were in full view.

Aloike shared his dream with everyone. What he did was wrong and pleaded with them to retreat. The men wouldn't listen. Aloike focused all of his energy on what, he prayed, would be a peaceful standoff. His lifelong rebellion against the Lord left a sick feeling in his gut. He whispered, "Lord, forgive me. Help us!"
All of the men and women wanted the best, but expected the worst.

Kaipo was still angry. Shortly after midnight, he and his wife got into a heated argument. She stormed off with their daughter to an empty hut below for the night.

*****

Day 7. With the sun over the eastern ridge of Puu Moaunalui, Kapena monitored the moving speck on the horizon through high-powered binoculars. As it got closer, a boat carrying men came into view. He turned to Lopaka. "Curtis knew we were up to something. At least we had time to dig in."

After a while, men motored slowly up to the Kanapou Bay dock and secured the boat.
Anxiety on the mound turned into nausea.
The kind that makes you throw-up.
"Mommy, there's plenty guys down there?" Zachary pointed.
"Shhh…" Michelle put her finger on Zach's lips. She squinted to get a better look at two familiar figures with them on the pier.
Aloike stood next to her. "Makoa and Kyle…*what the?*" He watched as a woman walked up to them, her face half-disguised under a sun visor and shades. She removed her visor to wipe the sweat off her forehead. He gasped, "Mom?" He bent down to pick up their son. Their eyes locked. Zach's innocence pricked his heart. He drew Michelle close to him. She cried, fearing what would become of him, Zachary and the others.
They could stand their ground as long as their supplies held.
Then what?

Sergeant Chin from Maui P.D. told Makoa, Kyle and Tiare to stay back on the boat. All officers were dressed in t-shirts, bulletproof vests, khaki pants, boots and holstered pistols at their sides.

They wondered around to confirm everyone had left. With no one was in sight, Chin gathered his men in a huddle. "You boys know why the chief said to gear up. Lots of Hawaiians still pissed being evicted from this ahupuaa. It stopped progress at Makapuu on Oahu. We need to make sure that rumors are just talk. If it 'aint, and somebody got sloppy, this could be worse than what happened at Makapuu."

All of them fanned out cautiously among the hollow shacks and empty sennit lines strung across bamboo poles. Few of the men grumbled under their breath for being here on a weekend when they could be at the beach with their families on Maui.

The sudden the cry of a little girl rang out, prompting some of the officers to reach for their holsters. They relaxed when a woman and a little girl appeared from one of the huts. The child ran over and hugged one of the officers. "Hi uncle!"

"How you, sweetheart?" And you, sis, what you doin' here?"

"Kaipo lost it last night so we came down here to sleep it off."

"*Down* here?" scanning above him, "where is Kaipo now?"

She pointed. "Up there."

The figures on the top of the mound watched silently behind a thick patch of branches that covered their defense wall.

Kaipo's anger blinded him from who was escorting his wife and daughter. Friends and family being handcuffed and dragged away by police raced through his memories. Perspiration poured down his face. He grabbed a semi-automatic weapon, slipped a loaded clip in, chambered a round and yelled, "LEAVE MY WIFE AND DAUGHTER ALONE!" He aimed...
Boom! Boom!
Boom! Boom! Boom!

"Kaipo, NNNOOOO!!" Aloike's shout echoed throughout the valley.
Tiare immediately recognized her son's voice. Looking up, leaning over the boat rail, she screamed, "ALOIKE! ALOIKE!"
Makoa grabbed her by the waist, midway, as she was jumping out. "NO Tiare!"
Wild-eyed, she struggled as he pulled her safely back into the boat. "He's all I have left!"
Makoa urged, "Not now. Please. We'll take you up there when it's safe."

Kaopua and Nainoa wrestled Kaipo to the ground. The shots frightened the women and children in the fortress.
Kaipo's brother-in-law lay in a pool of blood. His partner, writhing in agony, clutched his hip and thigh as the officers scrambled for cover and drew their weapons.
"We have two officers down!" Sergeant Chin yelled in his radio. *"I repeat, two officers down! We need Medivac NOW!"*

81

Maui dispatch: *"Roger, two officers down. Contacting Medivac, over."*

Chin glared at Makoa and Kyle. *"Looks like we've lost one, but the other is holding on,"* decision for back up, *"Send SWAT, over!"*

"SWAT?" Makoa protested. Kyle held him back.

Maui dispatch: *"Roger, Medivac notified. ETA 30 minutes. SWAT contacted. ETA...45 minutes, over."*

Children started to cry in the crude fortress as tensions mounted; mothers did their best to console them.

He blared into the bullhorn. *"This is sergeant Chin! We have two officers down! Please don't shoot! I have ordered my men not to return fire."*

No response.

Left with no options, he ordered all weapons trained toward the top of the mound and signaled to bring the lifeless and wounded lawmen in.

The brother of Kaipo's wife was dead. His vest was no match for the high caliber round that went clear through his heart.

His partner's femur was splintered and his pelvis, shattered. While given first aid, Medivac was on its way.

Whoop-Whoop-Whoop-Whoop---Whiirrrrl---Whoop-Whoop-Whoop

The sound of helicopter blades cut through the air in broad daylight. It circled for a safe place to land without kicking up too much sand. Medivac paramedics secured the two officers then flew off in a sand plume.

Dispatched from the U.S. Department of Justice as a backup, Federal Bureau of Investigations agents boarded a Black Hawk helicopter on Oahu. They joined a Special Weapons Attack Team from Maui on a boat docked at Keoneoio Bay. If the crisis escalated, travel by sea minimized the risk of being shot at in the air.

FBI and SWAT joined MPD at Kanapou Bay on Kahoolawe.
SWAT Commander Sullivan said, "We have a profile on all of them,"
"And?" Sergeant Chin was anxious.
Sullivan replied, "A few minor incidents in the past with Kaipo, otherwise, we've shown no red flags on everyone else. Did you check for an uptick in purchases for weapons and ammo?"
Chin shook his head, embarrassed with this basic oversight.
Passing close by, FBI Captain Feyman was visibly perturbed. "Except for Lopaka and Kapena!" A lateral transfer from a Texas agency, he shook his head in disgust as he walked away.
Sullivan's *state* background checks did not show their training in Special Forces. In Feyman's mind, woefully unprofessional and stupid! Blinded by his own pride, he forgot that federal access revealed their military files were buried for a secret mission clearance: they were tapped for high level espionage as Wahhabi sympathizers from Arabia

because they blended in as Arabs. They went undercover when penetrating terrorist holdouts in Afghanistan.

But neither Lopaka nor Kapena had any terrorist intentions. They were focused on protecting the women and children when they refused to leave. Even if armed, Aloike was hoping for a peaceful standoff to stop development and save the ahupuaa. But Kaipo drew first blood.

This turn for the worst overshadowed any hopes and dreams for Restore Kahoolawe.

Back on the bullhorn. *"This is Commander Sullivan from Maui SWAT. An officer is dead and another seriously wounded. Place your weapons aside and surrender peacefully. Come out with your hands empty…"*

Other than the faint sounds of children crying, the mound summit was eerily silent.

Another week passed.

Hot, muggy days added to the misery of mosquito-filled nights. Failed attempts to elicit a response from the stronghold above took its toll. Random news copters buzzing overhead for live footage were irritants and ground camera crews were forbidden.

In the brutal heat and humidity, lawmen removed their heavy gear but kept bullet-proof vests over their tee shirts with their side arms. Their beachfront position was reinforced with a sandbag wall surrounding the Command Center tent.

Ongoing communications with authorities on Maui, Oahu and the Department of Justice in Washington, D.C., whittled the hours slowly away.

Idle time led to boredom. Captain Feyman, feeling laxed with an FBI agent over a card game remarked, "I was with ATF assigned to a raid in Vaco. When we got there, heavy gunfire took some of our men out."
The other agents who heard this said nothing. Apathy. Numb from the effects of this drawn-out standoff. One of them piped, "Did you guys shoot first, or them?"
Feyman looked appalled. "What kind of stupid question is that?"
"Answer the question: you guys or them?"
As if to irk him, Feyman snickered.
The long standoff left dozens of men, women and children burning in the compound inferno. Images of charred children were never shown by the media to avoid a public outcry. Many accused the Department of Justice of a cover-up and one-sided information to keep the public at bay. Media chatter suggested a domino effect within judicial hierarchies would have embarrassed DOJ and the president. Authorities overseeing the botched operations played the piper as the media danced.

Since the first, standoff day, Kyle and Makoa traveled to Maui, Kauai, Oahu and the Big Island to rally community leaders to help de-escalate the standoff. Tiare insisted on staying behind to wait and go up the mound. The men set her up in an empty hut.

After some days, Kyle and Makoa returned with a small band of elders. To avoid interference from Feyman or Sullivan, they huddled in Tiare's hut behind the line of safety.

They agreed that Bobby, from Kauai, who knew Kapena, should slip under the cover of darkness and make his way to the top of the mound. When he got up there, Aloike allowed Bobby into their fortress. Once there, Bobby pleaded with them to leave peaceably with the women and children.

They refused.

Before dawn, Bobby returned to Tiare's hut. "They're not budging."

The standoff lapsed into another week.

In Tiare's hut, she, Kyle, Makoa and the elders were restless. To their dismay, Makoa abruptly stormed pass the line of safety in broad daylight and headed for the top of the mound.

Several officers went after him.

Watching from above, Aloike yelled, "LEAVE HIM ALONE!"

Looking up, officers and agents reached for their weapons.

"LET HIM, KYLE AND MY MOM COME UP HERE!"

The elders in Tiare's hut agreed.

Kaopua leaned to help Kyle and Makoa over the camouflaged wall. Aloike reached for his mom's hand and, as she jumped down on the other side,

embraced her. Tiare wept. "Son," sniffle, "why?"
Aloike lowered his head in shame.

Kept under close watch by the men, Kaipo seethed,
"What, you guys deaf? We told Bobby we're not
budging!"
The lawmen heard the faint ruckus above.
Makoa looked at Aloike. "We've heard rumors that
you might be dug in. We came to intervene so no
one gets hurt."
Kyle added, "We tried to avoid this when we met at
Waimanalo."
Look of remorse on Aloike's face. "I know." He
was about to share his dream with Makoa, but
Kaopua interrupted, "What choice did we have,
Makoa? The law allows for self-defense if someone
forces his way into our home, right? We are entitled
to protect ourselves in our *home*land!"
Kyle reasoned, "Think of the women and children!
Bruddahs from MPD have backup from SWAT and
FBI."
Kaopua ranted, "You call them bruddahs?"
Tiare spoke up, "Some of you know that Chin is
related to Lopaka's cousin's wife. Jaden from
SWAT is the godfather of Pepe's nephew. They
have families, too, Kaopua. It's their job."

Aloike lamented when he heard Zachary crying and
Michelle trying to console him. Of European
descent, her marriage to Aloike was contentious: he
loved her but disdained what some of her land-
hungry colonists stood for. Great-Tutu Pani would
scold him that all peoples are loved by God and his

racist tendency is wrong. Her insights on the generational effects of colonization would often prick at his conscience. For example, before Captain James Cook came to Hawaii, four chiefs were at war with each other. Cook may have opened the door of westernism into Hawaii, but Kamehameha who rose to become king used Cook's armaments to defeat his adversaries. This fusion of ancient warfare and modern weapons made it a moot point to argue against colonist inception in the islands. From her broader perspective, greed infected the hearts of peoples compelled to take from others throughout history. Land-thefts by conquests is by all colors of skin; therefore, to accuse others of what Hawaiian ancestors, too, were guilty of needlessly fuels the vicious cycle of racism. She insisted that no one has grounds for racist tendencies because all people groups, guilty of sins before God, are loved equally by God who seeks to redeem us all.

Still acknowledging Aloike as the leader, Lopaka walked up. "SWAT snipers, two of them. Look!" He pointed to where two camouflaged figures were hiking up the side of an adjacent ridge.
Kapena assured, "We have a height advantage."
When Kaopua heard this, he turned to Makoa and Kyle, "Traitors! You came up here to buy them time?"
Shocked by the accusation, Tiare stepped between them and blurted, "NO, Kaopua! The snipers took advantage of the opportunity."

Glaring at Kaopua, Aloike took charge and encouraged everyone toward a workable solution without further dissension in their ranks.

Lopaka and Kapena kept a close watch on the snipers in the distant trees so they could level their field of fire. They knew it could be a diversion so they maintained a constant watch all around the mound.

SWAT Commander Sullivan and FBI Captain Feyman met alone, face-to-face in the command center tent.
Feyman complained, "Those idiots won't budge! Hawaiian jerks remind me of Native American stupids on Alcatraz!"
"Alcatraz?" Sullivan puzzled.
Feyman smirked, "Indians held out for nineteen months. When they first landed and made their silly declaration for Indians for all Tribes in November 1969, only a few insiders knew the media was informed beforehand which gave them the public support they needed. The Coast Guard couldn't keep sympathizers from San Francisco and all over the northern California Bay Area from violating their patrol zone to bring supplies to Alcatraz. My father was one of the U.S. Marshalls that finally ended their holdout in the summer of 1971.They went in fully armed and rounded the Indians up like cattle and shipped them back to San Francisco."

Commander Jason Sullivan was born and raised on Oahu, went to college on the mainland to study criminal justice, and returned to his island home. His father was a retired army officer of Irish descent who married his Hawaiian mom from Makawao, Maui. She could trace her family tree to Keopualani, the second wife of King Kamehameha who bore him the kings that ruled in the 1800s. His half-Irish, half-Hawaiian heritage tied him to the underlying issues that are divisive to Hawaiians. Being on the enforcement side during this standoff was difficult, but it was a career path that his parents supported. It ended up paying well and provided comfortably for his wife and children on Maui. He inherited his father's looks, so Feyman was clueless how his racist rants affected Sullivan. Listening patiently, Sullivan inquired, "What are you inferring?"

Like his father, Feyman had no belly for native plight. "We have enough ammo to flush those buggas out!"

Sullivan looked at him in disbelief.

Feyman was blunt, "For all we know, their provisions could last for months. Not happening, especially with the Justice Department breathing down our necks!"

Long pause.

Feyman punctuated, "DOJ don't want another Vaco!"

"What did you tell them?" Sullivan asked.

"That we have a fail-proof plan to round those Hawaiians up like Indian cattle and get them off this island."

Sullivan felt his gut tighten. "Was this plan approved?"

Feyman was mum. Sullivan pressed him but Feyman changed the subject, "Our surveillance shows a blind spot on the rear of the mound at about seven o' clock from where we're standing. Twelve-foot boulder half-way up…"

"And?"

"Position one of our guys behind the boulder."

"Diversion?"

Feyman smirked, "You got it!"

Sullivan protested, "What the hell do you mean?"

"Don't you have two snipers on the ridge right now?" Feyman asked.

"Yes." Sullivan responded.

"And their orders are to fire only if fired upon?"

Sullivan concurred. "They're for safety to make sure nobody down here gets hurt."

Captain Feyman sought to provoke return fire from the mound and report at this juncture of the standoff that the natives fired first, which would be backed by the fact that Kaipo drew first blood. His tactic would make the snipers believe that they were being fired upon and they would return fire in self-defense.

Commander Sullivan could smell blood. His jurisdiction was blatantly challenged by a federal agent following his father's footsteps: a U.S. Marshall wannabe. His father's glory was Alcatraz; Feyman sought his glory at Kanapou Bay at the expense of human lives for some kind of twisted heroism.

Feyman bragged, "Look, I'm confident they won't fight for long. We have to risk sacrificing a few of

those monkeys to get all of the women and children
out safely. Once we engage them, they should back
off quickly."

Sullivan thought Feyman had lost his mind.
Negotiating a peaceful resolve required patience,
options and clear orders from DOJ, not from some
rogue FBI agent.

It became clear that Feyman had spent time
concocting a persuasive alibi to cover his tracks if
his plans failed. He goaded, "You can try to have
me fired. I don't care what you write in your
reports."

Alarmed, Sullivan ranted, "ARE YOU NUTS?
WOMEN AND CHILDREN ARE UP THERE!"
He whacked Feyman's coffee cup off the table.
It flew against the stacked case of water bottles as
he stormed out of the tent.

FBI rookie agent Keoki Aka was singled out as the
scapegoat.

Feyman knew that to use a newly hired native from
Maui would look good on his report. Keoki fell on
hard times after he served as a Master of Arms in
the U.S. Navy and couldn't find work when he got
out. Since his recent hire, he was able to keep their
house while his relations with his wife and children
improved. He took his chances that Keoki would
follow orders to keep his job. If investigations
proved that diversion tactics were employed, with a
Hawaiian pulling the trigger, it would minimize the
outcry from natives on all islands.

"Get on the other side of the mound and take your position behind a twelve feet boulder half way up. You can't miss it."

Keoki listened carefully to his orders.

"When you hear me call Aloike's name over the bullhorn, this will be your cue to start firing into the trees up there," Feyman pointed, "two snipers are positioned in those trees, four meters up. Set your windage and elevation to nine meters, a full two meters *above* their heads. No room for mistakes."

The FBI designate flinched when he quickly realized that his orders were to shoot in the direction of the SWAT snipers from the side of the mound so they would return fire into the summit of the mound!

Sullivan radioed his men on the ridge, *"Jack and Jill, do you read?"*

"Roger, commander. We read."

"Return to camp immediately. FBI agent will be popping some zingers your way to provoke your return fire at the men on the top of the mound. Do not return fire. I repeat, do not return fire! Do you read me loud and clear!?"

"Roger, sir. We read you loud and clear."

Both snipers were confused, puzzled. Neither knew what went down between their boss and Feyman at their makeshift, central command.

Captain Feyman threatened Keoki before reiterating his orders. He knew Sullivan was staring at him from a distance. Feyman had to move fast so Sullivan couldn't thwart his plans.

"Think diversion." As he heard this, Keoki felt his head swoon as he saw his wife leaving him if he lost his job. Feyman came back into focus, "When you hear me mention Aloike's name over the bullhorn, that's your cue to start firing!"

Agent Keoki slipped to the back of the mound. As he moved steadily uphill, he felt his head pound with every step. Fighting against his conscience he stopped, bent over and puked violently. Regaining his composure, he positioned himself behind the boulder, well-hidden from the holdout above and radioed that he was in position.

"This is Captain Feyman." His voice in the bullhorn echoed across the valley. *"We don't want anyone getting hurt."*

Keoki felt a lump in his throat as he heard Feyman say, *"Aloike, can you hear..."*

He raised his rifle and aimed.

Boom! Boom! Boom! Boom!

Aloike was shocked.

He looked around to see if any of the men in the stronghold were shooting.

Confusion immediately set in.

No one moved, yet shots rang out from *below* their position.

Both SWAT snipers were already headed back to camp. They whipped around as they heard shots zip past high in the tree they were in. When they turned to look up at the summit of the mound, they saw men holding their rifles and leaning over the defense wall to see who was shooting below.

Olapa placed his rifle against his right cheek so he could use his *scope* to survey what was goin' on below. He was careful to keep his finger away from the trigger.

Bad move.

The snipers saw this as a threat since Olapa's rifle was swinging in different directions---including theirs!

Alarmed, Lopaka thought to himself *'What is he thinking?'*

Realizing that Sullivan had ordered his men down from the trees, Feyman barked another order over the radio to agent Keoki. *"Do you have a fixed position of the snipers?"*

"Yes sir. They are walking away. Looks like they're headed back to camp."

"I am ordering you to fire off a couple more rounds in their direction above their heads. Aim high now!"

Feeling immense stress, Keoki aimed high and fired more rounds, this time in the direction the SWAT snipers were moving in.

Boom! Boom! Boom!

In training protocols, if a threat is perceived, remove the threat. The snipers thought that Olapa was firing *at them!* They dropped to the ground, positioned their weapons and aimed.

Boom! Boom!

Olapa's body went limp as blood splattered from his head.

Aaaaahhh!! Michelle screamed as she witnessed his death. Badly shaken, she pleaded with Aloike, "Please. Pull back. YOUR SON NEEDS YOU! I NEED YOU!"

"Take him. And tell the women and kids to stay low."

Distraught, Tiare tried to reason with him. "Listen to your wife, son. We can't bear the thought of losing you."

"Mom. Please. Go with them." Before she turned away, he gently grabbed her arm and met her eyes. "If I die, I want a wooden cross as my tombstone." Saddened by this, she turned to join Michelle and Zach with the other wives and children in the fortress behind the wall, huddling, bracing for the unknown.

The sniper's act in self-defense followed their training protocols.

The cover up that was to follow in how the chain of events unfolded would paint a different picture and muddy any truth into obscurity.

"STOP! DON'T SHOOT!" Makoa yelled.

"PLEASE DON'T SHOOT!" Furious, he sprang up and leaped over the wall, arms flailing, hoping to end more bloodshed.

Flashbacks from the Afghanistan war raced through one of the sniper's mind. No one was aware that he was suffering from mild bouts of PTSD away from work. He hid it well. Under stress, his symptoms overcame him. If an Afghani insurgent was running toward U.S. soldiers, the rules of engagement authorized them to neutralize the threat of a perceived suicide bomber. Makoa running toward them against the backdrop of open land fit the profile of an Afghani insurgent and a real threat in his mind.

Several yards down the slope, Makoa continued to plead out loud when the sniper opened fire.

After he shot Makoa, the other sniper looked at him in shock!

As Makoa slumped over and fell, Kyle jumped up to go after him but was restrained by Aloike. "NO KYLE! WE DON'T NEED TO LOSE YOU TOO!"

Olapa's body fell close to Lopaka and Kapena while Makoa lay in his blood on the slope below.

No one on the mound would tolerate this. For them, it was now a matter of survival.

Except for Aloike and Nainoa, all of the Hawaiian and Native American men crouched in unison, some kneeled with weapons loaded, gauged their range of fire on top of the rock defense wall, took aim and began shooting furiously upon the lawmen below. Kyle, too, refused to take up arms, not in denial to defend, but out of conviction that conflicts could be settled without the use of force.

Captain Feyman's *diversion* was in full swing.

If all went according to plan, the natives would be surrendering soon.

When they heard shots ring out, FBI, SWAT and MPD dug in behind their barriers.

Forced to decide between his men or island natives, Sullivan was vexed. FBI and MPD were already engaged. His SWAT team was being fired upon so he ordered his men to engage.

Boom! Boom! Boom! Boom! Boom!

Ratat-tat-tat-tat-tat!! Ratat-tat-tat!

A few bursts of automatic gunfire rang out from the FBI rank and file below while only semi-automatic gunfire returned from above. Legal intent to outlaw fully-automatic weapons in the hands of citizens was now being proved: control and firepower advantage.

Hearing of no authorized use of automatic firepower from DOJ or from his SWAT superiors, Sullivan stayed low and crawled as fast as he could. Reaching Feyman's position, he yelled, "YOU IDIOT!"

Feyman ignored him. He wanted this standoff to end fast.

Infuriated, Sullivan crawled away and focused on minimizing casualties from *all* of the lawmen.

When he got back into his position, one of his men was shot. He laid down cover fire toward the mound as a shield while he crouched low to drag his man out of the line of fire.

A stray bullet ricocheted off Sullivan's Kevlar helmet. As he reeled from the impact, another bullet struck him behind his left ear and killed him instantly.

"Commander DOWN!" a SWAT team member yelled, "Commander Sullivan DOWN!!"

Though firearm laws are designed to restrain the common citizenry from anarchical advantages, state and federal governments can arbitrarily wield their firepower as a means to reinforce their elitist agenda.
But the natives were not anarchists.
They were threatened on their own land.
And engaged in survival.

Shots zinged past the mound, slowly obliterating the defense wall and chipping away at the exposed top of the fortress.
Children inside screamed louder and louder as pandemonium set in. Brazed and bleeding from flying debris, the women huddled desperately to protect them.

Lopaka and Kapena gawked through their binoculars at clusters of bushes on the ground along the ridge below, trying to hone in on where the snipers had re-positioned themselves.
Well-camouflaged, one of the sniper's subtle moves was enough.
Lopaka took aim and emptied an entire 30 round clip on them.
Boom! Boom! Boom! Boom! Boom!...
He had no intention of missing his targets.

Aware that Sullivan was dead; Feyman looked through his binoculars and barked, "SWAT snipers

down! Snipers down!" He flagged four FBI agents.
They picked up bullet proof shields as cover to
bring them back for medical care.
When they got there, both snipers were dead.

During the heavy exchange, casualties were
sustained on both sides.
Feyman's arrogance was taking its toll: unlike the
Indians his father loathed on Alcatraz, he didn't
think the Hawaiians and the three Native American
Indians would fight back this hard.

The disintegrating crisis worsened by the moment.
Against the no-fly zone orders of FBI and SWAT,
several news helicopters ignored their advisory and
appeared over the eastern ridge of Puu Moaulanui to
capture live footage of the action below.
News leaked that the standoff had turned bloody
and media hounds scurried to the scene.
Kapena opened fire.
Boom! Boom!....Boom! Boom! Boom!...Boom!
One of the news copters spun violently as the pilot
tried to steer it safely down with tail rotors grinding
and smoking.
Everyone watched in horror as it EXPLODED on
impact about hundred yards away!
With nothing to lose, Kapena knew media coverage
would cast them as terrorists.
If only someone captured Feyman's plans, or his
remarks about native Indians and Hawaiians on a
cell phone video.
The second news copter sustained minor damages.
Instead of evacuating a life-threatening situation,

the pilot maneuvered farther away so his
cameraman could keep filming like sniffing hounds
not easily deterred, driven by the public's appetite
for a steady diet of televised violence.

The safety of civilians now at stake, they had to act
fast. Feyman ordered FBI agents to standby with
their tear gas launchers.
"Fire when ready!"
One of the canisters went right through the roof of
the fortress where the women and children were
huddled. Launched in quick succession, the other
canisters landed in the holdout.
Bronze silhouettes scampered in the thick of hissing
billows of smoke.
Choking. Coughing.
Women and children scurried blindly.
Frenzied.
Some, in silent shock.

Shots into the mound's summit continued unabated.
Resisting the urge to stay low, some of the women
who stood out of fear were struck down: one in the
back, severing her spinal column; the other was hit
clear through her heart. After another suffered a
neck wound; her 5-year old, screaming, was
silenced when a bullet pierced her abdomen.
Greg, James and Louis witnessed their deaths.
Using their bodies to shield women and children,
Kaipo watched his tribal brothers-in-arm writhe and
shake violently from the hail of bullets riddling their
bodies. Blood splattered all over the women and
children they were trying to protect.

101

Clutching Zach in her arms, Michelle and Tiare yelled for the women to keep themselves and the children low.

Enraged, Kaipo continued firing until he, too, was struck dead.

"KAOPUA! NAINOA!" Kyle yelled. "ALOIKE IS DOWN!"

They crawled over to give aid.

When Michelle heard Kyle yell, she managed to run to her husband's side. *Nooo Nooo Aaaaahhhh NNNOOOO!"* Her ear-piercing screams rose above the sound of guns. Hot tears ran down her flushed cheeks, her face cut and bruised; the veins in her neck, strained. She knelt and held his head in her lap to comfort him and tend his wound. He hacked and choked and hacked, gasping for every breath. Then all of a sudden, there was nothing for Michelle to tend.

Aloike was dead.

Part of his right lung had been ripped out of his chest while he scrambled to find her and Zach.

As Tiare crawled to get close to her son, she watched in stunned disbelief as Michelle grabbed Zachary and leaped over the defense wall toward the direction of gunfire, wishing to die. She and her baby boy were mercilessly gunned down, hit repeatedly by a burst of rapid fire.

Cupping her mouth, body trembling, Tiare reached where Aloike lay dead, held his face with her forehead to his, and wept.

Shocked by the deaths of Michelle and Zachary, the men on the mound signaled to each other to stop shooting. One of them managed to tie a white t-shirt to the tip of a long branch: the truce was ignored. As tear gas smoke obscured the crude flag, combined firepower from below continued out of fear that the other news copter would be shot down. High caliber ammo burst through remaining sections of the wall where some survivors were trying to hide behind. Frightened Hawaiians scattered, but they had nowhere to go.

Deeply affected by the silhouette of a woman and child being gunned down, Captain Feyman decided the remaining survivors posed no further threat. He blared into the bullhorn, "CEASE FIRE! CEASE FIRE! CEASE FIRE!"
A sick feeling gripped him, like painful memories, buried deep, rushing to the fore of his consciousness. His stone-cold heart, in executing this diversion, began to inexplicably soften and warm with an inkling of remorse.

The tear gas smoke cleared slowly.
Moans rose in utter despair.
The senseless bloodbath bore dreadful images of human carnage.
Lifeless mothers were scattered.
Torn bodies of children lay in pools of blood.
Aloike, Olapa, Kaipo, Greg, James and Louis lay slain, as well as other men that secreted in to Kanapou Bay to join their ranks.

Numbed and bloodied, a few of the shell-shocked, disheveled Hawaiians began to slowly limp down the mound. Several of them crawled from leg wounds sustained in battle.

In the command center down below, lawmen knelt, heads lowered, next to the bloody bodies of Sullivan, two snipers and a number of MPD, SWAT and FBI fallen, mostly from Lopaka's and Kapena's deadly aims.
Outside, the other lawmen moved cautiously up the slope to help the wounded. Fathers in their ranks fought tears when they saw drooping arms and legs of lifeless children that lay across the arms of their sobbing mothers and fathers.
Agony.
Pain.

Captain Feyman walked slowly up to the dead woman and child. He bent slightly to turn over the mother. As she lay, face up, body bloodied, she held a young boy in her arms.
His eyes grew wide. For someone who was cold and heartless, he fell on his knees and trembled.
His younger sister left California after she finished college. A falling out with him and her parents left her bitter. No one heard from her for 12 years, though friends mentioned that she moved to the Big Island some time ago. Feyman had written her off and never bothered to find her to make amends. Thinking she might have hitched up with a lawyer from Los Angles, he couldn't imagine she would marry a native islander.

Numb and perplexed as Feyman stared at her, tears
swelled in his eyes and ran down his face,
whispering, "Mi…Mich…Michelle?"
There, in her arms, blood was coming from
Zachary's side. The curves on his lifeless face bore
the semblance of his estranged sister. He thought,
'*My nephew?*'
Grief-stricken, Feyman started to pound on his chest
as if to stop the beating of his wicked heart.
After a while, he turned to see some of his agents,
perplexed, staring at him.
Native men and women that witnessed his strange
behavior were stone-faced.
Beyond tears.

8

The air was fragrant with the scent of fresh
plumeria and pikake leis hanging on protrusions
from the bamboo fortress ruins—like pinnacle
tombstones where the slain once lay.
Brightly-colored anthurium, protea, bird-of-
paradise, awapuhi flowers and plants turned the
Opu Iwi gravesite at Kanapou Bay on Kahoolawe
into a tropical garden, a tranquil antithesis of the
bloodbath a year ago.
Volunteers took stones from the defense wall to
build steps to the summit so people, broken and
bitter, could come to grieve the loss of their kin
from last year's standoff.

Looking down on the Kai huts lay in shambles
below, Makoa brooded, "Wounds of war."
Hanani added, "Like crippled sentinels."
Touching the scar on his abdomen, Makoa
shuddered when he heard the word *crippled*.
After the surgery to remove the bullet that just
missed his spinal cord, he awoke to find Hanani at
his bedside. She stayed for his entire duration at
Queen's hospital to help nurture him back to health.
He often found himself wiping away her tears as
she mourned the dead, especially the wives and
children that stood by their husbands and men.

Next to Makoa and Hanani, Tiare, her heart
shattered, was lost in thought.

A large wooden cross was erected where Aloike had been slain. Tiare knew a woodsmith that whittled two koa logs, arranged to haul it to the top of Opu Iwi, bolted them into the shape of a cross, and mounted it in the ground.

Visible on a clear day from far out at sea, Tiare knew that someday anti-religious zealots would petition to have it removed.

Some complained that the cross, associated with Hawaii's first missionaries, was an offense. Reconfiguring the summit into anything else would have been more fitting. But Tiare insisted that Aloike's promise to his great-Tutu Pani, reiterated by his request to her before his death, be fulfilled: the crucifix of ultimate sacrifice would be his tombstone. Aloike's life was a dichotomy of Christian and Hawaiian beliefs: Christian because the teachings of Jesus Christ transformed great-Tutu Pani; Hawaiian because she was a beloved teacher of her culture's dance, song and chants as forms of worship to God. Some congregants at the church she attended misjudged her. Shameless drunkards, fornicators and philanderers accused her of mixing Christianity with Hawaiian culture.

In the past, when she lay on her deathbed, young Aloike cried at her side. He kept repeating, "Tutu, don't die," sniffle, "don't die, Tutu. I cannot let you go," sniffle. She motioned for him to come close as she whispered her dying words, *'Boy, Jesus is Light and Life to all people. Rome wen' try fo' remove dis Light, only make His cross represent hope wen' da world get moa dark. Wen he rose from the dead, it*

wen prove that death no moa sting and da grave no moa power.'
Already bitter from the loss of his father Po'o, Tutu's death disillusioned him. Aloike struggled to believe that Jesus came not to condemn, but to save, even ardent colonists that stole their kingdom. To numb his pain, he immersed himself in Polynesian antiquities. Confusion was compounded when his native colleagues throughout Polynesia suggested his belief in the white man's Jesus was a mindless quest of fairy tales. But the power of love exemplified in Tutu Pani clarified the existence of God-incarnate. Aloike's unsung fear was to believe a lie because he witnessed how the truth made her free. Poverty-stricken, she embodied selfless love toward the poor and afflicted in Naalehu. She was an admired matriarch. One to whom his promise would *not* be broken.

Makoa, Hanani and Tiare stood in the shadow of the cross. A short distance away, attendees gathered around three native priests from the Marquesas, Aotearoa, and Hawaii. They spent years of close fellowship with Po'o when he was alive. Most precious to Tiare is that they walked in the fear of the Lord and carried burdens for their island peoples.
This upset some attendees, especially those who returned to ancient ways after their cultural renaissance in the 1970s. Temples were re-built, images carved and rituals of old practiced.
Unhealed wounds inflicted by messy outcomes of colonization made preserving these vestiges of their

culture a passionate endeavor. Chants and dance to ancient deities opened spiritual gates of the past that God seeks to close among all peoples reeling in offense. If we come to Him, our wounded hearts and minds will be healed and our desire will be for Him.

Appearing in their native regalia, the priests each wore loose-fitted cotton robes beneath satin material draped over their shoulders and waistlines: Blue cloth for the Marquesan priest from Nuku Hiva, deep-purple cloth for the Maori priest from Aotearoa, and red cloth over the Hawaiian priest from on the Big Island.
The three of them stood with their faces in the wind and turned toward the cross.

After a prolonged silence, the Marquesan priest began,

"Lord, we stand beneath the semblance of the cross that you died on long ago. The shedding of your blood redeemed all of mankind till this day. Heal, oh Lord, the anger from the blood shed on this mound. May the power of your love and forgiveness mend our broken hearts."

He paused long enough to allow for the Maori priest to continue without breaking rhythm…

"Jesus our King, your love is beyond any hurt or disdain among Maoris and Hawaiians against their white brothers and sisters for what their ancestors

did in colonizing the islands. Have mercy, oh God, and heal these ancient wounds. Open our eyes and hearts to behold you as our Redeemer."

Natives who knew their history looked upon the elderly Hawaiian priest in his 70s. His long, white beard against his dark-skin looked regal and reminded them of Hewahewa and Kapihe, men of old that spoke of a people from afar that would bring a message of hope to their war-torn islands. Bent over, as if groaning in his spirt, the Hawaiian priest chanted the prayer in his raspy, deep-toned, native tongue.
Afterwards, he stood up straight and prayed out loud in English,

"Lord of heaven and earth. With you, nothing is impossible. I weep for the people in Hawaii and long for you to save us all. Forgive us, Lord, for some among us have returned to ancient gods and goddesses. Lord, I know this breaks your heart." He *stopped abruptly, shaken, wiping his tears.* "Draw *them to your love and kindness. You are Truth. Set them, and all of us, free."*

Hanani and Makoa were deeply moved.
When the priests prayed, Tiare imagined Jesus' marred visage and torn body nailed to the cross in agony for the redemption of man: blood for blood, for love and *not* for vengeance. But vengeance had taken its toll in human struggle: man's blood for the blood of men, for hate *and* for vengeance. Father gave His Son to this hate-filled world. Millennia of

110

treacherous wars could not depose the anointing upon Jesus to reconcile creature with Creator through His selfless love. Light came into a dark world, but because men love the darkness more than Light, the vicious cycle of war and vengeance continues unabated.

Meanwhile, a handful of native activists in attendance were offended by the prayers. Others openly wept. Among them, Lopaka and Kapena were grateful to be free. When they and others were brought to trial for murder, it garnered international attention. MPD, SWAT and FBI lost some of their men, too, but the death of women and children during the standoff was a stain on law enforcement that government officials wanted to amend. Jurist deliberations led to a hung jury. Because a verdict was not reached, the judge declared a mistrial. With neither acquittals nor convictions, the case was never retried because of political pressure.

No one knew that Feyman resigned to mourn. Shattered by the deaths of his sister and nephew, his penance was to sell everything he had left from a divorce. Stock investments and land he inherited after the divorce paid for Michelle and Zachary's funeral and to cover burial expenses for others. What was left of his assets and pension were put in a fund for survivors.
Left with nothing, he wondered the streets with suffocating guilt. One day, he climbed up the side of a cliff at one end of Hanauma Bay. Looking out into the ocean, he removed a 9mm from his

shoulder sack. Placing it on the side of his head, he pulled the trigger. Miraculously, the gun did not fire. Just then, a humpback whale breached the ocean surface, blew water out of its blowhole and dove back down with its tail slapping the surface. The scene was exactly what he saw in his dream the night before, followed by another scene where he sat and heard an elderly couple forgiving him for the death of their son.

He stood and threw the gun far out into the bay.

Keoki Aka was playing with his son in the water when he noticed a homeless man walking along the shoreline crag beneath the Hanauma Bay cliffside. Sometime later, shoulders slumped and head lowered, the man drew closer and walked passed them on the sandy beach.

Keoki ran up to him. "Captain Feyman?"

Looking up. "Agent…Keoki?"

They both stood there, stunned.

"What happened? I mean, why…?"

Feyman, teary-eyed, "I killed my sister and her son."

Keoki's mind reeled until he realized Feyman meant the woman and child gunned down on the mound. He remembered him kneeling, head bowed, beside their bloody bodies. After many hours, he and another FBI agent had to pry him away when it started getting dark.

Keoki had to work through his own grief after following orders that ignited the standoff into an all-out shooting match. His months-long counseling sessions to process his guilt strained his marriage and family life. He said, "There's a couple I want you to meet. Come with me."

When Feyman approached the picnic bench, Alana's heart skipped a beat when she recognized him. She and Earl prayed earnestly to forgive Feyman, but never thought they would actually be facing him. Reaching deep in her heart, she made him something to eat. Without food for several days to numb his emotions when he determined to kill himself, Feyman received it humbly, sat, and ate.

Earl walked up and, realizing who he was, became upset and turned aside.

Keoki grabbed his shoulder firmly. "Uncle, you and aunty have already forgiven him, now is your opportunity to tell him."

Nodding at his aunty, Keoki removed himself, wife and kids from the bench.

Alana grabbed Earl's hand and together, they sat across from Feyman. "We are Jason Sullivan's parents."

Reflecting back when he and Sullivan argued in the command center tent, Feyman dropped his plastic fork, covered his face, and whimpered.

Earl said, "Look up."

"I'm," sniffle, voice shaking, "I'm responsible for your son's death."

"We know."

"And you do not hate me?"

Tears in Alana's eyes. "How can we hate you if our Lord has forgiven us?" She and Earl stood, went to Feyman's side of the bench, sat and put their arms around him. "We will be attending the ceremony on the mound for last year's standoff. Come with us."

Several days later, Feyman was drunk on a quart of Whiskey when he boarded Earl and Alana's privately chartered boat. Keoki was onboard. Disheveled and unwashed, Feyman could not look at any of them for shame. Though the power of their forgiveness was his last breath of hope, guilt gripped his soul.

Upon arriving at Kanapou Bay, Alana and Earl went ahead. Keoki climbed slowly up the rock stairs behind Feyman to catch him in case he stumbled off to the side and down the mound's slope. When they reached the summit, he joined his aunty, uncle and others and blended into the crowd.

Feyman broke away and wondered about. Eyes bloodshot, the smell of body odor and reeking of liquor put people off. Many stopped and moved aside. Alana took notice when Feyman looked up and saw the cross. She felt as if a shaft of light pierced her—and Feyman's—souls.
Quivering, drawn by the power of love, Feyman staggered over to its base, bowed faced down in the dirt, and wept.
The Marquesan, Maori and Hawaiian priests knew something special was happening. They surrounded him and knelt. Then an almost tangible hush swept across the crowd and silenced them. As they gazed on, a gentle breeze blew, as if God was calling to a lost, humble soul, to souls there, and to peoples of all nations to repent.
Makoa's eyes grew wide. "Whoa…"

"What?" Hanani asked.

"I bowed down at the same spot years ago when Po'o prayed for me." Familiar with the awe-infused atmosphere on the summit of Opu Iwi, Makoa envisioned Po'o lifting his wind-blown, dust oblation.

Years later, God beckoned Feyman to repent. Weighted by awe, Makoa, Hanani and Sullivan's parents knelt. Kapena, Lopaka and the native activists, unable to resist this inward burning, fell on their knees.

Deep sobs, Feyman sat up, face muddied, drenched in tears, "Pray for the Lord to forgive me," sniffling, "I am responsible for what happened last year."

The Maori priest put his hand on Feyman's shoulder and said, "*You* must cry out to God to forgive you--- and we will pray."

Feyman pleaded for the Lord to forgive him. Many that overheard his confessions were angry, yet surprised they could feel no vengeance.

Sullivan's mother stepped up to Makoa, "God is cleansing this area from bloodshed. I can feel it."

In these passing moments, infused by an unearthly power, other attendees were left speechless. Of their freewill, however, many would reason this experience as a spiritual anomaly and resist God's mercy to turn from their evil ways. Some intuitively knew that Jesus' presence of love lit their darkened minds, kissed their souls and wooed them to Him.

Kyle and Dana could not attend because they were contending with self-righteous academics that blamed the Pacific Archaeological Society for the standoff tragedy. Getting inside the mound was on hold. Moreover, all evidence of a 1900 year-old settlement from Pit 23 was confiscated by Dr. Chloe Hansen to clear the way for development on Kanapou Bay.

Power wielded from shadow elites left islanders without the restored frontier they desired, yet something greater than their desire lay in the belly of Mother Eve. There, in the dark earth-womb, an ancient people left an unearthly legacy.

*****

Fierce, orange-red streaks glistened at dusk. The twilight waxed as the sun's glow waned. Islanders who came to pay their respects had already left, while Makoa and his family were among a group of locals that remained by the Kai village ruins for an overnight camp-out.

He and Hanani sat, alone, arm-in-arm, to watch the sunset. From the little patch of green, they were drawn to the imposing silhouette accentuated by sky-fire atop Opu Iwi.

"Like Golgotha." Hanani observed.

Solemn, Makoa intoned. "The bottom of the cross is rooted in the earth. Two sides stretch to the ends of the world and seem to be calling to the four corners of the wind."

"Calling?" Her brows furrowed.

He said, "People of every color and creed."

Makoa pondered on the semblance of sacrifice that stood, solitarily, in its rough-hewn splendor.

"Reminds me of a sword, Holy Sword, drawn from His sheathe to fight for souls."

Hanani smiled, gazing at the cross, "His Holy Sword is the power of love and humility, unlike why swords were wielded throughout history."

Silence.

"Did it strike you, bebe?" Makoa's mind raced.

"What?"

"The Maori priest?"

"About?"

"I felt this connection with him."

Hanani replied, "Oh? Well, you two look alike." She combed her long hair with her fingers, twisted the length into a bun and secured it with a wooden, two-pronged pin.

*****

Hoku shuffled in the dark for the flashlight.

"Kawika. Kawika," she whispered as she roused him out of sleep.

"What?"

"Can you please come with me? I need to pee."

Trees rustled in restless winds of eve.

Sound asleep in his tent with Hanani and Malia as Kawika and Hoku stepped out, Makoa dreamed...

An old man with white, disheveled hair appeared weak, shaky and clothed in a loin cloth. Skin weathered and sun-beaten, he knelt and used stones to chisel an image into a dark-gray wall. He was in some of kind of dank, dimly-lit hollow, except for a

small fire that cast shadows flitting to the rhythms of each flicker.
He heard the hammering of stone-against-stone and drew closer to observe what the old man was doing. Makoa stopped short. Weary and bent, the elder paused, sat, placed his stones aside, then he proceeded to rock slowly back and forth with his head lowered. Barely audible sobs shook his body until his voice ascended into a convulsive, spin-chilling crescendo. Deep, inconsolable grief, as if a helpless father watched his child die. Makoa tried to reach him, but was bound by invisible chords. He struggled to free himself so he could comfort the old man....

Groggy, standing by the bushes, Kawika yawned. He called for Hoku to hurry as he stood holding the flashlight in her direction. There was a movement in the bush close to Hoku which alarmed Kawika. As Hoku emerged, Kawika saw the face of the figure that sprang from hiding, grabbed his sister and whisked back into the dark foliage.

"HOOOKUU!" Kawika's yell from a distance woke Hanani. She jumped up, flung open the flap, and stood outside the tent.
"Hoookuu! Hoookuu!" Kawika's voice echoed from a distance.
Her heart beating rapidly, Hanani turned and flung open the door flap to wake Makoa.
"What's wrong, bebe?!" His eyes were glassy, bloodshot, sweating profusely.
"Kawika's yelling!"

Makoa whipped out from under his sleeping bag, grabbed a flashlight and ran outside with Hanani close behind.

"KAWIKA! HOKU!" Makoa yelled as he started running in the direction of his son's frightened screams.

People in camp were shocked out of their sleep. Some had flashlights while a few lit their lanterns and raced over to Hanani who turned back, trembling and teary-eyed, for help.

"What happened?"

"Makoa went after Kawika. I heard him screaming Hoku's na...." confused, she hurried back in their tent, "Malia! Where's Hoku?!"

Disoriented, Malia stared at her mother for a few seconds. Half-asleep, she knew something was terribly wrong, got up and raced outside to find the campers scurrying wildly and moving, en masse, toward where they could hear Makoa yelling for his son and daughter.

Kawika ran with all of his might and followed the sound of thrashing, whipping, twigs breaking and the scrunching of leaves underfoot as he managed to track whoever he was pursuing.

The muffled, squealing sounds of his sister's struggle drove him maniacally in the darkness: running, dodging, stumbling, ducking, leaping, jumping and landing. His chest was tight, gasping for air. "HOOOKUUUU!"

Thump!

He fell, face-first, on the ground. Someone leaped with timed precision out of nowhere, waiting in ambush to intercept Kawika to allow for his accomplice to escape.

"Lord Jesus, help us!" Makoa prayed as he ran like a gazelle without losing stride: super-adrenaline rush that blinds a father's thoughts for his own life to save the lives of his children. Holding the flashlight steady in front of him for the slightest movement, he honed in and bent his ear for any sounds. Yet only a sick, empty silence beckoned from the forest depths.
All of the sudden, Makoa stumbled over a hump straddling the beaten path and nearly lost his balance. He righted himself by grabbing a low-hanging bough.
"Kawika!" He whispered half-shocked when he saw his son's head bleeding. "KAAWWIIKAAA!" he bellowed.
Echoes of Makoa's gut-wrenching scream shattered the night.
Those about fifty yards away heard him, spread out and quickly moved toward his direction.

From the windblown, emerald-gray jungle reflecting off the lanterns and flashlights, Makoa appeared holding Kawika's limp body in his arms. Everyone was startled. One of the fast-thinking locals turned and ran back to the boat docked at the pier close to the encampment to radio for an air ambulance.

It was supposed to be an uneventful overnighter
mourning victims of the failed standoff.
Now to mourn the fate of Kawika.
And Hoku.

Night ruled by the lighted orb crossed the silence of
dawn to welcome the daystar. Jaded land and lapis-
lazuli seas radiated the majesty of Kahoolawe, yet
spiritual darkness lingered.
Maui Medivac landed a short distance away as
paramedics rushed out with medicine bags in hand.
Déjà vu.
Hanani was at her wits end, exhausted. Makoa held
her and Malia to comfort them while they huddled,
numbed, over Kawika strapped on the gurney.

As the air ambulance lifted off, paramedics worked
quickly on Kawika's head wound.
He was breathing on his own through an oxygen
mask. His pulse held.
"ER trauma. ER trauma, come in."
"This is ER trauma."
*"Sixteen year-old victim. Head wound bleeding
profusely. Started IV. Vital signs holding except..."*
the paramedic was silent for a few seconds, *"...for
cranial swelling."*
"His eyes?"
"Oscillating."
The trauma doctor at Kaisor Permanenta asserted,
*"Stabilize him for surgery. We have to cut to
release pressure on his brain."*
"Copy that..."

*****

The campers wasted no time to begin their search for Hoku.

Missing Children Organizations from neighboring islands mobilized to send help. Makoa would return soon to join the search effort, but first, he, Hanani and Malia boarded with others on the boat and was taken back to Oahu.

Everyone sat quietly, their bodies undulating with the craft's motion and speed. Teary-eyed, Malia cuddled in her father's arms. Hanani reclined stiffly next to Makoa, eyes closed, lips quivering. They tried to remain calm under the crushing weight of the unknown. For them, such was the trial of faith, when sorrow is cast to the wind and the obsession for control over the affairs of life slip away.

Surrender to God kept them from falling apart.

Makoa listened as Hanani, in her somber demeanor, whispered a psalm written by King David...

"My heart yearns for You, oh Lord,
In a dry and thirsty land where there is no water.
I have beheld You in Your sanctuary,
To see Your power and glory.
Lord, you are my God and I will seek you
earnestly."

Words that solace heart and soul.

Simple. Irrefutably wise.

From the Tanakh, a spiritual balm that soothes unspeakable madness in a mad world.

Part of the Torah, when God speaks;

And the Nevi'im, when man speaks for God;

And the Ketuvim, when man responds to God.

As Makoa studied Hanani's features, his love for her deepened. She was no coward soul, no trembler in their storm-troubled sphere. He admired her fair skin and long, silky black hair tinted with streaks of light red.

Memories of her suffering in their initial years of marriage grieved him. Against daunting odds, Hanani eased disputes to keep peace in the family. Makoa's militant activism aligned with his brash and impetuous ways. His disdain for her was unfounded; his fancies for other women, fleeting. He lived a lie by telling Hanani he loved her while betraying her with his heart.

Their children, the catalyst of their bonds, gave Makoa pause from the lunacy of fulfilling his twisted desires. Unpredictable, violent outbursts hastened their relational free-fall. Hanani fled with Kawika, Malia, and Hoku to find sanctuary with family and friends on the mainland.

Such is the torment of a broken marriage; more tormenting when innocent youth are caught in the crossfire of adult rage.

Feeling rejected, Makoa struggled against the pull and vortex of lust. But it was Hanani he had rejected. Nevertheless, she had made an unusual vow. *"Do what you feel you must. We'll be around waiting for you."* This vow of love steadied her through the hell of insidious, entangling strands that grip the heart of men teetering on the precipice of unfaithfulness.

But Love held Makoa steady, faithful, slowly untangling his miserably dark, cocoon-encased heart that swirled in an odyssey of lies.

123

Through upheaval and tumult, their journey toward marital healing was like tilling the soil of a garden withered by cold, stormy seasons of pain and distrust.

Unfertile, weed-spawned ground made fertile by forgiveness.

Makoa's Christ-empowering manhood became enriched soil into which the seed of Hanani's hidden womanhood was sown.

Cold, stormy seasons were abated by Living Waters and Son.

From this renewed garden that flourished, in Christ, they roamed freely onto treasure-laden fields where jewels were unearthed as embellishments for their marriage crown.

Bone of my bone and flesh of my flesh was the sweetest song Adam sang to Eve.

It had become their love song.

Burly with a ruffian visage, Makoa was broken, humbled.

In him was nurtured the selfsame virtues, borne in Hanani, endowed by Christ, that quieted his beastly ways.

*****

In the hospital waiting room, Makoa's heart beat wildly in his chest as he paced back and forth.

"Mr. and Mrs. Hoomalu?"

"Yes?"

"How is he?"

"Stable. You can all see him now."

Hanani's eyes watered upon entering the ICU. She walked to Kawika's bedside. Makoa and Malia held their distance so she could be alone with him. She stroked his swollen face, knelt, kissed his cheek and gently stroked his hand. He was motionless, breathing erratically. The monitors he was hooked up to sine waved and beeped.

Lips quivering, "I love you, son," sighs, tears rolling down her cheeks at the sight of bloodstains under his head bandage, "Lord, please..."

Whatever the outcome, her love for God would remain. Kawika's countenance appeared serene. Could he hear her?

Makoa eased his way forward, anxious to be close to Kawika. Then he burst into tears. His mind reeled with guilt, torn over what he put his son and daughters through when Hanani had to flee. The oldest, Kawika suffered the brunt of troubles and would tell Makoa he hated him. He cried over painful memories of the children when they were toddlers with life-filled, innocent eyes gazing into his and reaching out with helpless hands. It took years to mend deep wounds in the family. Years the cankerworm destroyed were restored by God.

Makoa sobbed. "Forgive me for not being a father to you," sniffle, "for neglecting the times when you needed me and I wasn't there."

Malia wept in Hanani's arms.

Hanani put her hand on Makoa's shoulder. "There's much," voice shaky, "to cherish what God has done."

Makoa listened, struggling to hold on to the healing in his heart wavering under great strain.

He stood to embrace his wife and daughter.
They prayed, sighed and groaned in their hearts
before the Lord.
Hanani opened her eyes to look at Kawika.
A tear rolled down his cheek.
God heard their prayers.

9

*"Good evening everyone, I'm Lisa Hodges filling in
for Matt Johnson."*
Screen over to the sportscaster. *"And I'm Joe
Meede here to bring you tonight's update on
sports."*
Screen back to the anchor. *"A child is still missing
on the island of Kahoolawe. Tune in to the six
o'clock News hour."*
Orchestral fanfare toting KGMP Channel 6 news
coverage.
Commercials.
Back in the newsroom, a digital map of an island is
suspended in the upper right hand corner of the
screen. *"Our top story tonight, police and rescue
teams are still searching for a young girl who was
abducted two nights ago at Kanapou Bay on
Kahoolawe."*
A portrait of Hoku, smiling, rosy-cheeked, flashed
on the screen.

*****

"HOOOKUUU! HOOKUU!" Makoa's booming
voice resonated. He kept a watchful pace with the
search team who had spanned out and moved west.
Eyes fatigued, he was exhausted from just several
hours of sleep in the past two days. No one came up
with any leads.
Both hands were calloused from gripping the
machete handle used to clear the thick brush,

127

hoping, praying that neither he nor anyone else would find his daughter's body.

Finally, one of the team members walked briskly over to the search organizer and handed him the first piece of evidence.

Makoa noticed the exchange and hurried over.

"That's her slipper." he felt his throat constrict.

Just then, someone else walked up with a necklace he and Hanani gave Hoku for her 12th birthday. After a quick glance, Makoa, heart pounding in his chest, nodded to affirm that it was hers.

Kyle, part of the search team, gripped Makoa's shoulder and said, "Please, rest. We got this."

Makoa replied, "We should all rest."

Good advice.

The team found a place to unload their gear. Makoa sat, rested his head on his backpack and was fast asleep.

Sudden flashbacks of pursuing the native awoke him. Makoa jumped to his feet and grabbed his stuff.

"Where you goin'?" Kyle asked.

"Back to Kanapou Bay"

"We're moving in the opposite direction, towards Kealaikahiki."

"I know."

"Getting dark, I'll come with you."

Makoa raised the maglite he was holding. "I gotta do this alone." He whisked away and disappeared around a bend of trees, drawn inexorably to where he last saw the fleeing native.

*****

The gloomy, night sky emulated the mood in
Kawika's hospital cubicle. Outside, moon and stars
were obscured in the hoary rain-mist which yielded
from its bowels a moist, cool breeze against his
window. Through the glass, Moanalua lay clothed
in blurred beacons of light.
Kawika fumbled for a break in the vague scenes
haunting his mind. As the evening wore on, he tried
convincing himself that Hoku's disappearance was
all a dream, but the throbbing gash on his head
reminded him that it wasn't.

"Son," Hanani called from his doorway.
Startled, he turned to see Hanani enter the recovery
room. "Huh? Oh, mom."
She sat on the chair next to his bed. "Lot on your
mind?"
"Yeah," confused look, "mom, what happened?"
Teary-eyed, she sighed, "You were running after
Hoku."
He made the connection. All of a sudden his mind
was alive with what happened that night. "Who
were they, mom?"
"We don't know. Dad is there with the search
teams. They're combing the entire island."
"And?"
Looking at the bloody bandage on his head, Hanani
did not want to upset him in his weak condition.
"Mom?" Kawika pressed.
"They haven't found her," head lowered, sniffling,
"not yet, son."

His adrenaline surged.

Hanani noticed the vengeful glare in his eyes and tried to calm him. She placed her hand on his arm and said, "Son, God will get us through this. We thought we lost you. He gave you back to us. We have to believe the same for Hoku."

*****

Just before the sun retired, a burst of light brightened the forest canopy as Makoa, stoic-faced, made haste with renewed vigor. Echoes of Kawika yelling seemed to reverberate within the green-hued interior. A pall befell him, just then, luminous shafts piercing through the tree tops appeared in his beleaguered mind as angelic swords defending his every step. Up ahead, clusters of ferns marked the edge of a familiar ravine.

As he descended to the bottom, muffled sounds of the forest above mingled with a strange, brooding tenor emanating, faintly, from the weed-covered wall in front of him. A closer observation revealed that it was part of an old lava flow.

"Pahoehoe?" He muttered.

Long ago, fast moving lava overlapped and piled into a heap covered in overgrowth. Some fifty yards away, he saw smooth, cooled layers of *pahoehoe* beneath the greenery that appeared as a field of cow-dung.

He listened closely as the distant, lingering tenor rose to alto, then lower to a guttural bass sound. Makoa cleared the wall to investigate where the distressed sounds were coming from. Behind the

tangle of vines and weeds, was a hollow opening.
"Lava tube!"
This occurs when a pahoehoe lava flow cools on the
surface faster than hotter material flowing beneath,
until molten mass empty out to leave a hollow,
under-ground tube.

Spooked, Makoa sensed the eerie shrills that echoed
in the tube may be connected to Hoku's
disappearance. Taking no chances, he clicked his
maglite on, stooped and went inside.
The ceiling was high enough to stand. Beyond the
beam of his light, darkness was like a gaping maw
spewing rhythmic, dirge-filled syllables from the
inner regions of its belly. He thought, *'Initiation
rituals held in dark caves. Young boys led by their
fathers into the earth's womb, rites-of-passage, only
to re-emerge as men.'*
Further down the tube he came to a dead end.
Flashing his light around, he was startled to see
more tubes going in different directions. He
muttered, "A...*labyrinth?*"
It was as if he was undergoing an initiation rite: the
deeper his journey, the more revealing the hidden
chambers of his own soul.
He thought of Theseus confronting the Minotaur in
Daedalus' labyrinth on Crete. Here, he was
confronting painful revelations of his true self that
was wounded by a lie-induced world filled with the
music of an Evil Piper and the frolic of dancers
amusing themselves to death. Another thought
crossed his mind, *'Maybe the invisible chords I felt
bound by in my dream represented these lies, and*

131

the old man I tried to help was a messenger of truth crying out'?

The quest for enlightenment often leads to serendipitous paths of revelation amidst dark journeys. Millions gloat over higher, spiritual fulfillment through mystics and galactic-sayers, or reclusive gurus in remote hermitages. Blind leading the blind into conjured Utopias where altered-states of consciousness, dreamscapes and perfect nothingness are sought. They strive to connect with universal harmony through endless, methodical, self-seeking ideations, only to discover an inner vagueness that neither intellect nor religion can make clear. So wars ensue and hate avails. Human compassion mingles with passions of destruction, ever persistent to better ourselves and the world in which we live, yet ever obsessed with folly.

Makoa knew that the labyrinth of our soul is afoul of a spiritual disease called sin, curable not by human quest, but by the blood sacrifice of Jesus who came to die for our sins.

Deciding which among the several entryways he should go into wasn't difficult. It was the hollow tube where a distant, dim glow flickered to the cadence of mournful sighs.

Reaching the end of the tube that opened up into a large cave, he froze in his tracks, thinking, *'My God!'*

An old, weary man knelt by the far-left wall of the dome-hollowed niche. His sinewy, emaciated body convulsed under the strain of muttered words. Long, oily-white strands of knotted hair rested on his shoulders, accentuated by his frayed and unkempt beard. He clutched a bamboo torch that was spliced in multiple sections on the top where a cluster of kukui nuts were skewered to each tip, the natural oils of which fueled the fire.

His mind reeled. *'My dream?'*

Not a dream, nor illusion, but a real person and the empirical assessment of the dome-niche a living panorama.

It was the scene of an archaeological treasure trove; the living imagination of every anthropologist.

Strewn along the floor were implements of survival: handmade tools, wood and coconut bowls, raiment, gourd jugs, some empty, some filled with water, hanging from protrusions in the cave, and a large stack of keawe branches next to a charred pit in the center. Wind from the outside coursed through the lava tubes, airing smoke from the pit, when used, through natural vents in the cave walls.

Human bones were piled ceremoniously to one side. Stone art decorating the lower perimeter of the inner-dome depicted an ancient, pictographic chronology of migration and plight.

Strangely, the old man rubbed his hand over one of the etchings sequenced at one end of the mural while he held the torch up for light with his other hand.

Makoa inched closer without interrupting the sage's invocation...

"Lord, You call us from nations.
You mercy make us place under Glad Star.
Many suns and moons, you make strong when us follow you.

We do wrong, offend land and not good to live on.
Us wrong is bad smoke in You sky place.
We not honor You beauty name.
Us hearts broke. We not fix broke by man way.
You fix broke You way and we do good.
You make us face low to earth and we turn from
bad.
Make us like river full to pray for You save us.
You mercy us and hear from You sky place.
You forget us do wrong.
Lord, You make us well.
And make land well."

Makoa blurted, "Po's's chant!"
Alarmed, the venerate sage turned abruptly and,
trembling, dropped his still-burning torch and
covered his eyes with his right arm.
Makoa appeared like an apparition holding a scepter
that emanated divine power. Realizing what the old
man was cowering from, he turned his light off and
lowered himself as a show of reverence.
As he drew closer, the elder collapsed from a
gaping wound on his left arm.

*****

It was close to midnight and the search crew, having
covered inland areas, fell back to Kanapou Bay
sands and pitched camp.
Kyle set his gear down at the bottom of a palm tree
and poured himself a cup-full of coffee brewing on
the Coleman stove. Fig Newton and Chips Ahoy
bags were opened for the taking. He stood there

134

sipping and munching, then walked down the beach next to the crashing surf. Bright stars in the black-velvet sky rejuvenated his soul as he appreciated how they glisten when unobscured by artificial light.

Makoa's approach from the night into the glow of lanterns wasn't cause for suspicion, since no one except Kyle knew that he wondered off before sunset. Masking his emotions as he expressed his appreciation to some of the workers nearby, he set his belongings next to where Kyle's stuff was laid, unfolded his sleeping bag, and acted as if he was settling in for the night. He grabbed a cup of coffee, strolled over to where Kyle sat and plunked down on the sand, "We go walk. Talk story."

Kyle knew something was up.

"Bring your maglite and a First-aid kit. Oh, and three "D" batteries for my maglite. I'll sit here and wait."

When Kyle returned with the supplies, they walked about a hundred and fifty yards away from camp then veered left and went into the forest.

"What's going on?" Kyle asked,

"You'll see."

When they reached the ravine, they descended down to the bottom.

Makoa went straight to the opening in the pahoehoe wall, stooped, and motioned for Kyle to follow him inside.

A field scientist, he was used to exploring caves, aware that they weren't entering just any cave, but a lava tube.

135

His resolute stride in the long, winding corridor piqued Kyle's curiosity. They came to the clearing where multiple tubes spread out. Makoa said, "Check out the way the tubes connect."
Kyle responded, "Rare, but it happens."

A bright flicker could be seen at the end of the tube leading to the cave. Makoa stoked a fire pit with keawe branches stacked close to the pile of bones before he left to signal their return route.
Memories swarmed Kyle of the Lascaux caves in France and how Inuit's access their igloos. "This lava tube reminds me of an umbilical cord."
Preoccupied in thought, both were unfazed by this accurate comparison.

Kyle stopped, transfixed, feeling like he lapsed back in time as he saw the old man reposed by firelight. Makoa's voice resonated in the natural acoustics of the dome. "He's lost a lot of blood."
Perplexed, Kyle said nothing.
"I washed his wound and used a tapa tourniquet to slow the bleeding. Told him I'd returned with someone he could trust."
Makoa had placed the wounded elder on a lauhala mat and bundled tapa together for a pillow under his head. He stood to dip a half coconut shell in a gourd filled with water in husk netting against the wall. Kneeling, he lifted the elder's head gently and tipped the rim of the shell to touch his mouth. Weak from loss of blood, lips quivering, he sipped.
"Who is he?"

136

"I chased him years ago when I broke away from the circle we formed on the sand after the ceremony with you and the admiral."

Kyle was chagrined. "Chased? You never mentioned this!"

"Saw him peering from the bushes. Thought I was seeing things. He knew I was approaching, so he ran. I pursued him till he disappeared at the bottom of the ravine outside. This is where he came."

Kyle was thinking of how some locals, fed up with modernity, seclude themselves in the verdant landscape, emerging when rain, hunting and herbs are lacking. A few go back into their forest hiatus.

Makoa said, "We talked for quite a while."

"Talked?" Kyle looked surprised.

"I mostly understood his ancient tongue."

Kyle queried, "Nehune?"

"Yup."

Makoa checked his breathing and pulse. Kyle knelt and opened the First-aid kit to clean, salve and bandage his arm.

Emaciated, the old man weaved in and out of consciousness. Short in stature, his eyes were sternly affixed. Strong Polynesian features lined his visage with subtle, Asiatic semblances. How could he have survived after two centuries of colonial intrusion?

"What did he say?" Kyle asked.

Makoa studied how the reflections from the fire-pit flames cast shadow and light along the contours of Kyle's face while trying to formulate his own thoughts. "I frightened him when he was reciting in

broken English what Po'o himself chanted when we
first came here."

"What?"

"I know. Blew me away. After he calmed down, he
began to explain that he had a vision where he saw
me coming into the cave. He had also witnessed me
shove the M.P. who escorted then-Commander
Moresi. Watched in horror as the other M.P.
stepped back, drew his weapon and killed Po'o!"

Kyle listened intently.

Makoa continued, "His name is Tevake, from
Kauai. Makes sense 'cause Po'o knew that, long
ago, his descendants were brought from Kauai to
Kahoolawe."

Silence.

"I asked him about Hoku," fighting back tears, "as
he was fading, he said I must find her."

Kyle interjected, "Which means," Kyle reasoned,
"she's still alive."

Hope-filled glare in Makoa's eyes. "Yes."

Kyle pivoted, "Tevake will have to look like he got
lost fishing or something."

Makoa unzipped the dark blue neoprene bag he kept
with him and removed his discolored t-shirt, worn
puka shorts and slippers to put on the elder. "Papa."

Stirred from his rest, Tevake winced in pain.

*****

"Who's this?" Denton asked.

"Fisherman," Makoa lied, "Kyle and I were walking
along the beach and found him like this. Looks like

138

he slipped and tore his arm on the reef when he was
casting his net."

Suspicious, Denton thought, *'Why would any local
from the outer islands be on Kahoolawe net fishing
at this time of night---in clothes and slippers too big
for him?'*

Kyle acted along with the unrehearsed scenario.
Both knew to keep his identity hidden. Word of his
true identity would rouse the authorities;
interrogations would frighten him into silence.

As head of the search effort, Denton Maene was a
Paramedic by trade. He removed the bandage on
Tevake's arm to assess the extent of his injury. One
look at the wound, he shook his head. "I dunno
what you guys telling me, but this no look like he
slipped on a reef. Somebody ripped him open with
some kind of jagged weapon!"

Northeasterly trades were calm, which meant that
crossing the Alalakeiki channel at two-thirty in the
morning to get Tevake to Maui General was low-
risk. Loss of more blood could send him into shock.

When the ahupuaa was progressing, the land
seemed to heal, forgiving of Po'o's death. Last
year's bloody standoff on the mound inflicted a
deeper wound that God sought to heal in the
Hawaiian community.

Hoku's abduction added to the suspense.

Now Tevake, growing weaker from his serious
wound, died on the way to Maui.

"DEAD?" Makoa shouted.

139

"Freak winds. Huge swells. He was too weak to endure the crossing." Kyle explained regrettably after receiving the bad news.

Makoa was indignant. Finding Hoku relied on what Tevake knew. With a fierce resolve to find his daughter, he stared crazily at Kyle.

Makoa would need his help in a way they never dreamed.

Part IV

Revelations

10

Several years passed.
On Kahoolawe's west side, Kealaikahiki Point remained off-limits by the military. Why it was kept secret would soon be known.
Meanwhile, on the east end, mansion-like homes on the midland slopes of Kanapou Bay blended with the verdure. Within view of these homes, the island's architectural centerpiece, Club Mez, was luxuriantly sprawled along the shoreline.
With the ahupuaa gone, handmade tools hung in a small museum tucked neatly in the lobby next to a gift shop.
Modeled after elaborate themes of outer island resorts, Club Mez featured waterfalls, multi-colored flora, palm trees, an artificial cave with a wet bar, tropical fishes and dolphins that graced the aquariums next to an Italian-tiled swimming pool that was separated by glass. Statues of old-world personages lined the concrete pathway with bright flowers on the perimeter.
The fishpond rock wall was removed to make way for a recently built marina now docked with expensive yachts and sailboats.

Further up from where the homes were built, the once manicured taro, bamboo, pili grass, and banana patches in the Kula area were cleared for an eighteen-hole golf course. On the same grounds at the base of Opu Iwi, the excavation site was filled in, seeded, and decorated with coconut trees!

On Opu Iwi's summit, the cross remained as a memorial to the slain. It was left undisturbed until it came under scrutiny for removal. As expected, some agitated mansion dwellers complained that their free-spirited, naval-gazing consciences were pricked by the crucifix.

Despite native outcry, a few wealthy residents ignored the agreed quota of felling rare koa trees in the Uka forest, using what they wanted for home interiors. One went even as far as to have her house built entirely out of the prized wood.

Environmentalists persuaded the state government to intervene and declare the koa trees a protected species.

The U.S. Navy returned Kahoolawe in obeisance to the shadow commission's timed schemes. The existence of Nehune could not be discovered—*yet.*

Meanwhile, marionette developers, strung by the commission, sought to temporarily stimulate the Asian/U.S.-led Hawaiian economy.

Those who bask in hubris manipulate and control the masses.

Have power, suppress the people; even it if meant oppressing them.

Have money, tempt the people; even if it meant selling the Hawaiian soul.

*****

Kawika's release from the hospital was a miracle.

Random bouts of amnesia and anger with his brain trauma injury took time to heal. Fervent prayers that rose to heaven fell back to earth like a healing balm. Still, tears availed with Hoku's bleak whereabouts. Family and friends accepted her disappearance and encouraged their family to come to terms with. Regardless, Makoa and Hanani made frequent trips to Kahoolawe. An anonymous stranger had arranged for them to use his personal Zodiac, as if he knew the puzzle in Makoa's memory would be pieced together. But each time they approached the west side of Kahoolawe to search for their daughter, a patrol boat steered them away from the shoreline.

Kawika's past account of how Hoku was abducted jogged Makoa's thoughts and sent chills down his spine. Circumnavigating Kahoolawe in the Zodiac was an opportunity for recall. He mused silently, '*Where could she be?*' Just then, the chiseled image in the cave came to mind. Sensing a connection, he blurted, "Petroglyph!"
Gazing at the south face of Puu Moaulanui, Hanani turned. "What?"
"Tevake pointed to the petroglyph representing some kind of future deliverer…"
She concluded, "Then maybe the petroglyph *is* the symbol of hope, and the cave *is* the opu of Iwi?"
Makoa thumped the side of head, "The belly of Mother Eve!"
She whispered a prayer.
He said, "I need paper and pencil!"

Rounding the bend that led into Kamohio Bay, he turned the Zodiac around and headed back full-speed to Kanapou Bay.

As the salt-air coursed through his silver-streaked hair, Makoa felt his spirit surge. He only had a glimpse of the stone-etched figure among the pictographs on the cave wall.

At Club Mez, Makoa asked, "Paper and pencil?" The older, Filipino lady behind the cash register at the restaurant was cordial. She and a handful of locals who worked there, the golf course and marina were accommodated with living quarters close by, with scheduled time-off spent back home on Oahu. She left for a moment and returned with several sheets of paper. Then she opened her purse on the shelf under the counter and handed Makoa her eyebrow pencil---and a sharpener.

He smiled. "Mahalo plenty!"

As he was walked, a janitor was pushing a trash cart out of the kitchen backdoor. Makoa noticed empty paper tower rolls in the bin. "Excuse me," pointing, "can I have a couple of those?"

He handed Makoa two cardboard rolls. "No problem."

*****

Makoa told Hanani of his cave dialogues with Tevake and the pictographs on the wall. But she wasn't sure where it was located in the forest lining the golf course.

Before descending down the ravine, he observed how the mound could not be seen. "If your guess is right, it never dawned on Kyle and I that we were in Opu Iwi. Look around you. It's nowhere in sight! Almost as if the outside entrance and inside tubes are meant to throw people off-course."
Makoa cleared the lava tube's entry, stooped, clicked his maglite on and motioned for Hanani to follow.

Ahhchooo! Mold along the walls made her sneeze.
"You okay, bebe?"
"Ah huh." *Ahhchooo!* Sniffle.
They stopped where other lava tubes fanned-out in different directions. "Look. Wild, yeah?"
Hanani gasped, "Wow! Which one?"
He swung the maglite down the familiar tube.

Coming to the end of the tube, the dank and smelly dome in the thick darkness sent chills down Hanani's spine.
Makoa flashed his light beam around until he found the same bamboo torch right where the old man left it. Just as he expected, the kukui nuts on the tip were oily enough to re-light.
Hanani held the maglite while he lit the torch with a match.

Enamored by the ancient mural as Makoa moved the torchlight along the cave wall, she swung the maglite to the right and cupped her mouth. "Human bones!?"
"Maybe the only proper burial place," he guessed.

She shuddered.

"You can turn it off. This torch is plenty light."

Holding above his head, he moved around then abruptly knelt on one knee. "Here. That's it!"

Hanani puzzled, "I've seen many petroglyphs, but this one is different."

She held the torch as he placed a sheet of paper over the chiseled image, angled the eyebrow pencil and pressed gently in broad, diagonal strokes until he colored in the page. The outline of the petroglyph was clear enough to decipher for someone who understood Polynesian rock art. He made another copy, rolled both sheets up neatly, and tucked them separately in the two empty paper towel rolls.

*****

Rocky Ikaika lived high up in Kealakekua. The bay where Captain James Cook landed over two centuries ago was in clear view from his reclusive lanai. A spelunker who explored many caves on the Big Island, he knew most symbolic meanings of petroglyphs.

Dana and Hanani waited in the living room as they marveled over the glass cases that lined Rocky's living room walls. Each case displayed artifacts that he and his friends collected from caves on the slopes of Mauna Loa, Mauna Kea, Hualalai, and Kilauea. Their husbands joined Thomas Kitani in Rocky's backroom study to analyze rock art from all over the world to compare with Makoa's petroglyph tracings from the cave wall.

147

Coming out of the room, Thomas insisted that Kyle and Makoa hang out with their wives while he and Rocky fix food and drinks in the kitchen.

They brought out a large platter of ahi sashimi, soy and wasabi sauce, smoked marlin, shrimp and broiled eel sushi and placed on the living room table, including bottles of cold, grapefruit Juice squeeze.

After stuffing his mouth with sushi, Makoa pointed to Rocky's collections in the glass cases. "How long took you to collect these?"

"Over 20 years." Rocky focused on unrolling Makoa's tracings from the cave on an adjacent table. "You said it was part of a pictographic mural?"

"Yes." Makoa replied.

Fascinated, Rocky stated, "In the late 19th century, my great-great-grandfather was a colleague of Abram Fornanter. He collected and analyzed petroglyphs in and around the Pacific basin, including the Mesopotamian region, Africa, Madagascar, India, Burma, and the Asiatic archipelago." He paused to look closer at Makoa's tracings, looked up and noticed the looks on their faces. "What?"

Thomas smiled and said. "For years, I've been studying the cultures in the areas you just mentioned, including Fornanter's work. He collected information on Polynesia between the 1830s and 1870s. Perceiving that colonization in Hawaii would erase native legacy, Fornanter mastered the Hawaiian language then archived their migration into several books. He discovered our

148

origins, legends and chants may have some correlation to biblical accounts and characters. Others during his time suggested that these correlations were influenced by missionaries."

"Small world," Rocky mused, "my collections have been our family heirloom passed all the way down to my grandfather. When he died, my dad and I cleaned his house in Puna before it was sold and we found all this old artwork. Many were actual rubbings right off the rocks. All were carefully annotated with dates and places. When I found out that my dad was planning to donate these to the Smithsonian Institute, I convinced him to keep them."

Thomas pointed, "So what do you think about Makoa's copies of *this* petroglyph?"

Rocky rubbed his chin then shrugged his shoulders. "Never seen anything like it. Best if we go back to the cave to see how this fits in context to the mural."

Dana fidgeted. Kyle turned to Rocky. "We're banned from the island."

"I know." Rocky responded, a sly grin crossing his face, "an anonymous caller contacted me several days ago. He was pleasant enough so I stayed on the phone to see where our conversation would lead. Never left his name, but he knew much about you and Dana. Said that Makoa and Hanani have been making good use of his Zodiac?"

Everyone was taken aback.

Hanani sensed, "He's probably aware that Makoa and I have been searching for…" She choked back tears. Makoa squeezed and rubbed her hand.

After a brief silence, Kyle asked Rocky, "Anything else?"

"Yeah. He said that you and Dana's ban have been lifted. Why he called here to inform *me* about this? Odd that he knows about me and you guys. How did he even get my phone number?"

Kyle guessed, "The way all of this is adding up, I have a gut feeling he knows where Hoku is."

11

Light, shadows and vibrant colors wove into the Aotearoan tapestry. Near a grove, Clifford Beck observed a butterfly slowly pumping its wings on a pink rose. From its grueling, metamorphic struggle, it leaped onto the air like a gymnast of the wind. He pondered, '*Protagoras's divinity of numbers cannot dictate how it is set aloft after rebirth. The complexity behind each flutter is greater than machines that propel science to lofty achievements. In cellular and genetic sciences, man cannot create but only duplicate and manipulate cells and genes.*'

Mary Beck found Cliff cocooned in an Oahu orphanage. After adopting him, she brought him to the ancient homeland of Tangata Maori. In this southern hemisphere, the pink rose reminded him of a marae, Maori longhouse, and his plight like the butterfly that found refuge where roses bloomed. An archivist at Te Puna Matauranga o Aotearoa (National Library of New Zealand), Mary became interested in a reputed Maori scholar. From his anthropological perspective, Polynesians emerged from Caucasoid, Negroid, and Mongoloid groups. Their move to Wairarapa on the north island of Aotearoa evolved into pursuing Maori land and cultural rights. Her mastery of their language and devotion to his work captured their hearts and minds.

In his youth, Cliff excelled in Maori artisanship. He built a collection of intricately carved model canoes made from indigenous woods.

Marae elders were entertained with his lucid imagination: stars were pinholes of a greater light on the other side of the night sky; ocean was liquid air for fishes; trees danced to wind songs; birds swam on a two-dimensional plain, ascending and descending like humpback whales; animals were toy bipeds and quadrupeds with wind-up motors that the Toy Maker above wound each morning. People were mannequins in motion.

A child prodigy, Mary supported his endless inquiries toward fact-finding in books until the Internet made research easier. Her insight on Maori plight kept him rapt. They spent sleepless nights pouring over articles and journals strewn across his desk and room. She had a way of probing his thoughts and knowing when to ask him the right questions. Despite their closeness, he was affected by her bitterness toward what missionaries had done to global tribes in general, and to Maoris in particular. Mary would often rant, "As we looked to heaven, the land beneath our feet was stolen."

In his 20s, Cliff spent time in Te Ope Kaatua o Aotearoa (New Zealand Defense Force). Haka was part of their morning exercise routine to get their adrenaline going. It was a natural way for him to be in the element of ancient warriors: track and ambush opposing war parties; act as scouts to protect tribal bounds.

In his 30s, Cliff's lifelong interests shifted toward world religions, born in part out of Mary's intriguing style of relating legends as gem stones lost in the troves of global belief systems. He made it his quest to find and arrange these gems according to legendary patterns. To his surprise, he realized these patterns told the story of creation from one Creator known by many names. In particular, he discovered that Ngati Kahungunu iwi, a tribal group in Wairarapa, held beliefs about creation that was strikingly similar to the biblical creation accounts spoken of by the missionaries--- the same religious zealots his mother blamed for ruining cultures. Instead, it was a core of greedy, land-obsessed perpetrators that took what they could by force.

Able to travel abroad, Cliff took note how different world cultures reflected similar beliefs. His journeys through the matrix of religions led to devoting his life to the simplicity of Christ. Love was born in the likeness of men, came in the form of a servant and learned obedience through suffering. It blew him away that Christ would empty Himself to come and lead us back to the Father. It felt like His Light, long obscured by dim clouds of confusion, broke through and lit the dark corridors of his mind and soul.

Upon returning to Wairarapa, he became deeply involved in Maori plight. A self-designed facial tattoo punctuated his identity with the Ngati Kahungunu iwi. He eventually devoted himself to the work of reconciliation that focused on making amends with north island natives offended by colonial Christianity. What he learned during his travels abroad prepared him to contend for the hidden gems of biblical precepts in Aotearoan antiquity. A culture labeled by missionaries in the 1800s as pagan.

When he returned from his travels, the clash of worldviews between him and his mother was sometimes tense, but never heated. He loved and respected her too much.

Years passed. Mary fell ill in her eighties. While hospitalized, a bright light appeared in her room from which a voice spoke. She never revealed what was said. But it was with such gentleness and love that she turned her heart back to the God of her parents who came to Aotearoa from South East England as missionaries.

On her deathbed, Cliff leaned closer as she managed to stroke his right cheek with her hand, "I love you, my little butterfly."

Stung by the death of his beloved mother, the dream of a deathless paradise where she now lived drew Cliff closer to Christ.

Most of his friends sought him out and stood by him through his year-long mourning.

Needing change, he traveled far north in the Pacific and settled in an Aina Hina townhouse on the east side of Oahu, Hawaii. Like-minded Maori's in Aotearoa introduced him to Hawaiians whose conciliatory efforts aligned with his.

All nations of men came from God, and their habitational bounds have been established by God. Cultures that emerged in geographical habitats inherited an ancient edict that some of their ancestors from an antediluvian world knew: the knowledge of good and evil bound people in a continuum of death and destruction until their knowledge of the Light and Life of Jesus Christ would free them.

While living on Oahu, he learned that his biological father was still alive. His voice echoed in Cliff's mind as he turned into the Waimea Bay parking lot. He stepped out of the car: bronze, broad-shouldered statuesque in a 6'2" frame in slippers, T-shirt and shorts. A sleek, swirling tattoo down the center left of his face did not distract from his natural good looks, strong chin with a greying goatee, and salt n' pepper hair pulled back in a ponytail.
From pictures he acquired over the years through family contacts, Cliff identified his father mingling with his sons, daughters and grandchildren around two picnic tables while sitting next to a silver-haired matriarch: the step-mother he neither knew nor met. When the elder looked up to see Cliff, a flood of painful memories gripped him. Dispelling years of shame, he held his head high, stood quietly and moved toward his abandoned son leaning against the car, head contemplatively lowered and arms crossed.
In his late seventies, Henry Hoomalu's gait was calculating: slowed and timed by a back injury that

had become progressively worse. His close cropped, kinky hair was stark white against his dark skin. Tears rolled down his cheeks. Just three days ago over the phone, Cliff reiterated his forgiveness over past hurts, wanting only to cherish what years his aging father had left to live.

Coming out of mourning, Mary's life of love and sacrifice for him and Maoris made Cliff realize the beauty of living. Choosing not to forgive his father who abandoned him at youth would rob him of this beauty, of precious moments that could be possessed, now, instead of wallowing in resentment, bitterness and accusations.

Cliff saw his biological father approaching. He stepped forward to embrace the aging patriarch.

His body wracked with sobs, Henry kept repeating, "Forgive me, son."

"I forgive you, pops," Cliff consoled, "it's all good now, no worries."

Makoa and his siblings were expecting their brother that was adopted at youth. Watching their father hug the stranger in the parking lot, they knew it was Cliff. Most of them had mixed feelings while the two approached.

As Cliff drew closer to the picnic site, Makoa's eyes lit up. "You're the Maori priest at the ceremony!" Cliff smiled. "Yes!"

"I felt this connection to you…"

Cliff looked puzzled.

"Never mind, *brother*." Makoa reached over to hug him, "welcome home."

Cliff intoned, "What happened on that mound, gosh, the women and children."

"I know."

Studying Makoa's features, "I don't remember seeing you there. You look a lot like dad. Nice to meet *you,* brother."

Henry interrupted, "Cliff, this is your stepmom, Esther."

He reached over to hug her and said, "Soooo nice to meet you, eh?"

Esther smiled. "I love your accent." Unpretentious and good-natured, she was loved by the entire family.

After greeting his step-brothers and step-sisters for the first time, many of the children came up to Cliff with wide-eyes, curious stares and nervous smiles.

Hanani handed Cliff a large plate bulging with two scoops of rice, beef teriyaki, cold daikon, two scoops of macaroni salad and two cans of chilled Root beer.

The day went smooth.

Lively talk and laughter.

Light breezes. Warm air.

Cliff appreciated their hospitality. Felt like he was alive again.

Reconciling with his father Henry was priceless. No value can be put on mending a broken soul; no measure of man heals what love and forgiveness can.

The guys played guitars and ukuleles while several of the women stood to hula. Tonya was a close friend of their family. As she stood to dance, she moved and swayed, then unexpectedly grabbed Cliff's hand to join her. Esther and the women teased and cheered as he grinned when Tonya winked at him. Proficient in the haka, he clumsily followed her hula footing.

He dated in the past, but remained single during the time he mourned. Busy with life, marriage was always in the back of his mind. The site of Tonya rekindled this desire.

Wrapped in a pareo around her swimsuit, she was a pretty haole from the mainland. Cliff found her attractive. Everyone giggled as the two exchanged glances.

The kids ran, chased and tumbled. Some cried from rough play; others lay down until they were fast asleep.

After a season of sorrow, Cliff was moved with joy.

After sunset, most family members packed up and left. Cliff said his goodbyes to Henry and Esther and promised to visit them.

Makoa stayed back with his family and asked Cliff to hang out with them. He hung a battery-operated lantern on a coconut tree while Kawika and Malia put stuff away in the car as Hanani spread blankets over the blue tarpaulin and tidied up.

Turning to Cliff. "Coffee?"

He smiled, "Sounds great, eh."

She brewed Chocolate Macadamia Nut coffee on the public grill. Kawika and Malia got out a bag of Marshmallows, wooden skewers, Hershey bars and a box of Graham crackers.

"And what might you two be up to?" Cliff asked.
"You'll see," Malia smiled while she roasted a Marshmallow over the fire until it bubbled, turned crispy brown then placed it between Graham crackers with blocks of Hershey candy, and handed the *sandwich* over to Cliff.
"What do you call this?" He inquired.
"Somemores. Can't just eat one, gotta eat some more."
He smiled and ate it. "It's good with the coffee, thanks."
Makoa said, "Wait till you taste the Banana flavor."

The moon hovered in silence as sparks rising from the grill melded with the glitter of white specks in the heavens. Makoa and Hanani reclined.
Cliff lay on his back with his legs propped up and hands folded behind his head. "Awesome Lord who spoke the stars into existence."
Makoa inquired, "Tell us more about Wairarapa."
Kawika sat with his legs crossed to listen as Malia, looking up, contemplated the cosmos.
Cliff obliged, "I would join with Ngati Kahungunu iwi there to worship the Lord on a ridge that commands a breathtaking view of the sunrise. Awe-inspiring, you know, to watch the star-studded horizon glow as if the Creator slowly opens the lid of our sphere so His light can infuse the earth."
Malia quipped, "I know what you mean, uncle."
She recited...

"Sun, abandoned to the horizon,
Bows to the bliss of night

And whispers to the moon,
 'Sing, orb, of the diamond-black veil.
 Utter a luminescent tune
 As I, this day, have sung
 A melody of warmth and light.
 Together we shall worship with the stars
 And, again, bring glory to our God.'"

"Did you make this up?" Cliff asked.
Malia nodded shyly.
Hanani reached over to hug Malia. "Poetry helps ease the pain of losing her sister."
Kawika leaned toward Hanani as she rubbed his back.
"Our youngest, Hoku, has been missing for three years," Makoa said.
Cliff was solemn. "I'm sorry to hear this."
Makoa urged, "Please, continue."
"On Sundays, we meet with Maori who feel out of place at modern churches in Wairarapa."
"In maraes?" Makoa inquired.
"No, in homes. Maraes are sacred places specific to Maori culture. If we're invited to a marae by Maori elders to speak of Christ, then yes."

*****

Sunday morning on Oahu was calm. Surf report on the radio mentioned 10-12 feet waves on the North shore. Before they got out of the car, Cliff joined his brother and family to pray for Hoku's return. Sometimes it felt like a dagger in their hearts.

Makoa's dreams of her made the pain of the blade unbearable.

Kawika and Malia went ahead with Hanani to the Lighthouse church building located on the old Kamehameha IV highway as Makoa and Cliff lagged behind.

Cliff looked at Makoa. "In my travels, I've sat and listened to people from different cultures. Many of them believe in one supreme God," serious look, "some of their stories are similar to what's in the bible."

Makoa added, "We were with a friend on the Big Island who mentioned that Hawaiian legends correlate with biblical accounts."

"In Wairarapa," Cliff continued, "we sit with the natives when they share what they believe."

Makoa chimed in. "Reminds me of Paul at the Areopagus on Mars Hill. He referred to the inscription *'to an unknown God'* on one of their monuments as a way of speaking to them about Christ, the Son of God."

"I was thinking of the same thing," Cliff said, "listen to this transliteration of the Te Matorohanga chant from Ngati Kahungunu iwi…

'Io dwelt within the breathing space of immensity. The universe was in darkness, with water everywhere. There was no glimmer of dawn, no clearness, no light. And He began by saying these words that He might cease being inactive, 'Darkness become light possessing darkness.' And at once, light appeared.

161

"'Io then looked to the waters which encompassed Him about and spoke a fourth time, saying, 'You waters of Taikama, be separate. Heaven be formed.' Then the sky became suspended. 'Bring forth Tupuhorunuku.' and at once the moving earth lay stretched abroad.'"

"Like Genesis," Makoa mused.
Cliff went further, "Have you heard of the Nehune tribe?"
"Yes!"
"Legendary first settlers to Hawaii. They were the children of Tarani that hid a symbol in Opu Iwi."
Makoa finished, "The belly of Mother Eve! A friend, Po'o, and I paddled our canoe from Maui to Kanapou Bay on Kahoolawe to protest military bombing, but he was more interested in searching for this symbol. He died there. Since then, Drs. Kyle and Dana Pahono excavated around the base of Opu Iwi to get inside."
Focused, Cliff rubbed his forehead trying to piece things together, "their ancestral father was Lua Nu'u, or Abraham."
Makoa chuckled, "Yes!"
Long silence.
A thought came to Makoa's mind. "The Te Matorohanga chant reminds me of another lost lore."
The look in Cliff's eyes spoke of finding yet another gem stone in the trove of legends. "I'm listening."
Makoa recited…

"The Word spoke from the hallows of Divinity
Into existence, vast, invisible realms.
Behold, a great mystery that man cannot
understand,
Beings, stars and moons issued from
The Life of the Word.
Then the Word spoke and Earth was
Suspended in the womb of darkness.
The Word was Light before the sun.
Then earth waters were divided when land became.
Then all living things on earth sprung forth.
Four-footed and two-footed creatures;
All that slithers and crawls and swims and takes
flight.
Man came from the land and woman came from his
body.
Breath and soul came from the Word.
Then Evil, that eyes cannot see,
Deceived man and woman to believe a lie—
To be like the Word.
Death became, because creature cannot be Creator,
Creation groans to be free from this lie.
So the Word became human to deliver all peoples
From Evil that eyes cannot see,
To make creation His song and joy as it was
In the beginning."

The Te Matorohanga chant and fragments of this
ancient lore were bringing two spiritual halves,
shared by half-brothers, into a divinely appointed
whole.

*****

163

Minutes before service started, Makoa and Cliff sat next to Hanani and the kids. Cliff looked perturbed when several women dressed provocatively as they walked into the congregation. Makoa saw the look in his eyes and leaned over. "I tell Hanani that true beauty is her gentle and quiet spirit which is precious in the sight of God."

"Sounds familiar."

"1 Peter 3."

"I knew that," Cliff teased, "when it warmed after the sunrise in Wairarapa, we'd bask in our malos, but if women showed up, we'd keep our cloaks on out of respect. The look-at-me selfie culture exerts a lot of pressure on people to expose themselves beyond their personal dignity. I appreciate how the Mennonite and Amish women dress."

Makoa agreed. "What people wear can send the wrong message."

"Speaking of the wrong message, what do you think about people who profess Christ as Lord yet are in favor of LGBTQ and abortion?"

Makoa replied, "That came out of nowhere."

"Well?"

"These sins are clearly addressed in the bible."

"Yes," Cliff said, "a gay friend was undergoing conversion therapy to break free from his homosexual lifestyle. In the middle of his sessions, the state banned this therapy. Fortunately it worked. He married a woman and they're a beautiful family today. Confused by the ban, others who were receiving the same treatment returned to homosexuality under pressure from gay activists.

Another friend was an emotional mess after her abortion. She wanted to warn congregants in her church not to kill their babies but was told by leadership that pro-abortion members would be offended. I mean, how can they learn about why Sodom and Gomorrah were destroyed and still embrace LGBTQ, or told that Jesus came to give us life yet believe that killing another human being is okay?"

Makoa alluded, "I heard a black preacher say that if you feed people garbage, they think that ideological sewage in culture is fine."

"That's bold," Cliff paused to phrase a response, "the stench of lies will mask the fragrance of truth until people think the stench of their sins smell like pikake flowers."

"Did you just make that up?"

Smiling, "Uh huh."

"Reminds me of Po'o being all eloquent."

Cliff got serious. "Remember the sins of the Nicolaitans that Jesus hated?"

Makoa responded, "Didn't Nicolaus decide to be celibate as part of his devotion to Christ?"

"Yes, but he was unable to control himself, so he justified sex with other women. He believed that God's grace would save your soul no matter what you do with your body, sexually, and with other fleshly vices. How can women suffocating with guilt for killing their babies, or gay men and lesbians wanting out of their lifestyles ever heal if they're listening to misleading teachings on God's grace?"

Makoa added, "That same black preacher said that people, in the footsteps of Jezebel, eat at the table of demons and delight themselves with evil that is set before them."

Seminary trained, prim, proper, the haole pastor in a flora-printed shirt preached a sermon that focused on the House of God. He contextualized their sanctuary within the framework of America's founding history:

"Two ministers in the 1800s were nestled in a quaint Victorian home in Virginia. Both sat beside a fire place after dinner while being served tea by one of their wives. One minister commented on how the Indians somewhere in the forests beyond the open fields from where he could see outside the living room window, were foolish savages to brave the cold and hunger while they reclined in the warmth, safety and provision of their colonial home.'
'The correlation? Security and fulfillment of God's people within the four walls of the church from a savage-ridden, sin-filled world on the outside…"

When the service was over, Cliff excused himself and stood to leave. Hanani saw the disturbed look on his face.
After mingling with friends, Hanani stepped into the foyer and saw Cliff talking with the pastor.
Whatever was troubling him was being aired.
"Hi, I'm Cliff, Makoa's brother."
The pastor greeted him with a firm handshake, "Please to meet you."

"Do you have a moment?"

"Sure."

Cliff gathered his thoughts. "The emphasis you placed on church buildings as the sanctuary of God?"

"Yes?"

"It does not fit in the context of some cultures." The pastor looked perplexed. "I'm not sure what you mean."

All too eager to explain, Cliff launched into a subtle tirade as he pointed upward. "Their sky is your ceiling," gesturing, "your walls are, for them, the mountains. Carpets are plush valley floors. Rolling hills are lecterns and jutting rocks are pews. Thunder and tremors are sermons in earth sanctuary. The symphony of dawn resonates in creation that was sung into existence."

Unaccustomed to these tribal views, the pastor listened respectfully.

Cliff ranted, "It is said that the dust of the ground is cursed. Man is made from the dust. Our sins against the Creator means our bodies return to the dust. The doctrine of cursed dust equates to no respect for lands. Tribal caretakers of mother earth see the land cursed with pollution and congestion. Instead of rock spires, skyscrapers are like modern temples where corporate deities in pin-striped suits gloat in their glory among the clouds and sneer condescendingly on the people below. Masters of what has been taken by force. A restlessness avails despite global efforts of peace. Man was never meant to toil in vanity and be idle in purpose. His connection to the land is now an exercise in futility.

The soil is defiled. He hunts for sport, not for food; he strives for commanding heights and reaps the demise of his soul." Still wounded from confrontations with ministers, he railed, "Many church sanctuaries are whited sepulchers full of dead men's bones!" His speech slowed, "The living dead have turned the sanctuary of earth into a crypt."

Rattled, the pastor stared at him for a moment. Cliff anticipated an intellectual fisticuff or some kind of biblically tactile rebuttal. But the haole minister sighed deeply. "I never saw this through another set of eyes. Thank you for helping me to see."
Caught off guard by his humility, Cliff was dumbfounded.
The pastor reached over and gave him a long, firm hug. Cliff felt the pastor's sincere remorse passing through him like a fiery rebuke!
The chasm between the morning sermon and his past offenses by ministers was bridged by the love that flowed out of the pastor's heart.

Makoa and his family were waiting in the car.
Cliff got in. Aloof. Shamefaced, he searched his soul regarding those with whom he was accustomed to be at odds with, or offended by.
When his convictions were challenged by religious folk, through sermons or otherwise, he became contentious.
Like his mother, Mary.

The preacher's humility disarmed his pride. He had encouraged Maoris to live with love and reconciliation.
In deed.
Not just in word.

12

The centennial commemoration of the January 17, 1893 overthrow of Queen Liliuokalani took up a large section of the Honolulu Star Bulletin's front page.

Placed side-by-side were old photo insets of the last reigning monarch and the first Republic president, Sanford B. Dole.

Troubled by Makoa's impending trip, Hanani browsed uninterested over the coverage. Walking down the stairs when the phone rang, Makoa picked up the receiver.

"Hello?"

"Makoa?"

"Eh, Cliff, what's up?"

"Did you see today's newspaper?"

"Hanani just gave it to me."

Cliff asked, "You up to it?"

He knew that returning to Kahoolawe made Hanani feel anxious.

"Might be a good idea," Makoa said.

She was eavesdropping by the way she sliced papaya over the kitchen sink. Almost cut herself as her nerves twitched; then her abrupt manner of digging out the black seeds.

"Cliff?"

"I'm here."

"I'll call you back."

Makoa gently placed his arms around her waist from behind. Hanani cringed and jerked her shoulder.

"Bebe, you've always been intrigued with the monarchs?"

No response.

"It might do us both some good."

He turned her around and drew her into his arms. She succumbed and leaned her head on his chest as he stroked her hair.

*****

Clear skies made for their pleasant drive to the commemorative event.

"Feel like I've hit a brick wall," Cliff said, "made a fool of myself in the church foyer, eh?"

"That was months ago," Makoa reminded him.

Cliff rambled, "Good intentions are bad if driven by pride. Orators of holy writ tend to ignore what privileges them to speak. Being what they expound; living what they believe. I misjudged him, you know, the seminary type?"

Hanani teased, "Or misjudge anyone that doesn't see things your way?"

Humbled by her perception, he sheepishly admitted, "Ummm, yeah."

Humility was in the pastor's eyes when he apologized for his unintended offense against what, in Cliff's tribal views, are held sacred. A soft answer turns away wrath, and Cliff realized that he was swift to speak and slow to hear. He should have been swift to hear and slow to speak, but the demand to be heard deafened him. If anything was in demand, it was the taming of his tongue, the one anatomy of man full of poison that stings his soul. Cliff's tone was solemn, "I can be brash, impetuous, but I have purposed to remain a student. If I assume to have mastery over everything, I can no longer learn what others can teach me about anything." Makoa shook his head. "Guess it's in our DNA." Cliff looked puzzled.

"Brash and impetuous." Hanani interjected.

"Oh." Cliff smiled.

Makoa added, "Typical of warriors without a war."

"Yeah, honey, you need to get a grip." Hanani teased.

Pricked by what she said, Makoa thought, *'Yeah. A firm grip because I feel like I'm on some kind of collision course.'*

*****

On January 13, 1993, the centennial observance started with a 9:30 am gathering at the Royal Mausoleum at Mauna Ala in Nuuanu Valley, the resting place of Hawaiian alii. Entombed rulers lay in state and immortalized in memory.

When the crowd dispersed, they all drove a short distance to join a throng of sympathizers and spectators on the Iolani Palace grounds.

For the next five days, re-enactments of historical events were scheduled in proper order that led to the dethroning of Hawaii's last Queen on January 17, 1893.

By noon, the blowing of a conch shell signaled the official opening of ceremonies.

Approximately 2,000 people surrounded the bronze statue of Queen Liliuokalani situated between the Iolani Palace and the State Capital. Christian and Hawaiian prayers implored Divine beneficence upon all that was to transpire and to honor the legacy of the Queen.

Four large bamboo torches were lit and placed on both sides of the Queen's statue in remembrance of the fire-burning kapu established by Iwakauikaua, an ancient law inherited by the Queen through her parents. Then the torches would be transferred to a site near the statue of King Kamehameha I.

One-hundred torches were lit in front of Iolani Palace. Then a 100 hour vigil began--each hour for every year that the Kingdom of Hawaii had been occupied.

Dignitaries from Tonga, Cook Islands and Vanuatu were present, as well as representatives from Switzerland, France and Australia. City and state officials came, along with reputable organizations and musicians.

Sentiments ran deep among all who visualized a monarchy without foreign governance.

Speeches on the passing of 100 years were enthralling, adding emotional gravity to the ex-Kingdom's illegal overthrow. The sobering rhetoric appeased many who listened. Those unimpressed with empty words were at least held spellbound by the eloquence of political demagogues; of well-spoken, duplicitous, intelligentsia.

173

Under island shades, shadows disappear. But there is a Light where no shadows exist and where the hearts of men are revealed. In what light man has been given, he often chooses to grapple in shades of unreason. If the light of reason eludes his mind, he commits to vain philosophies to address his purpose for being---defined by ideas like Darwin's evolution or Nietzsche's god-superman; ideas that influenced a world power that rose from the foundations of Rome, Greece, London, and Jerusalem: a nation flexing its *'In God We Trust'* supremacy. This same God has left a witness of His truly Supreme Self, and decrees by which the American Constitution was modeled to uphold the God-bestowed equality of all people with certain, inalienable rights. Any speeches equating the inalienable rights of Native Hawaiians within the context of American Constitutionalism, would, by the end of the planned observances, fade from memory, because the United States has no intention of returning Hawaii to the Hawaiian people.

Represented by an armament-clutching eagle and a sun-rayed statue of liberty, this body politic with noble beginnings had become, overtime, rife with corruption. Hubris, fed by power, was encased in a white, multi-pillared, Greek-like pantheon edifice, distanced by a Hagia Sophia-like dome and complemented by an Egyptian-like obelisk. Might it be that those who hold the reigns of American rule perceive themselves as gods and goddesses?

On January 14, 1993, the second commemoration day, the royal standard of Queen Liliuokalani was raised on the Iolani Palace grounds for the first time in 100 years. When the flag was affixed during her reign, she sought to overturn the Bayonet Constitution forged by devious politicians that sought to limit King Kalakaua on significant political fronts. Nevertheless, the Queen desired to reinstate equitable decrees for natives, including their voting rights, and to stem the influential tide of foreign economics.

Pre-meditated maneuvers by her own Cabinet members, most of whom had pretentiously showed the Queen their support, had turned on her.

Shortly after, she implored her people to return to their homes peaceably and quietly. Had she encouraged them to fight, casualties could have re-established her rule.

For a short time.

In the rising, colonial tide, brief resistance from ill-equipped natives would have been overwhelmed with well-armed forces across the sea.

Warm sunrays gracing the palm trees greeted the crowd at the Iolani steps. They anticipated the regally-dressed, Queen Liliuokalani look-alike. When she appeared it was like history came alive. Her startling resemblance in jewels and flowing gown, the Iolani Palace backdrop, the royal horses and carriage, mustachioed dignitaries and costumed attendants were an all-too realistic step back in time.

She stood behind a microphone.

Long pause.
From the pages of Queen Liliuokalani's journals,
the actress waxed eloquent as she recited the words
from memory.

In essence, the Queen was manipulated by
Provisional government puppeteers to play the
puppet-villain. Refusing to be exploited by them,
she was summarily dethroned and locked in a room
of her own palace for eight months to wither her
stolen reign away. During her exile, she wrote songs
that would become the lyrical cornerstones of
Hawaii.
Self-appointed megalomaniacs understood the
stage-setting out in the middle of the Pacific. The
logistics of one warship and a battalion of soldiers
at their beck and call dictated how the show would
climax. When the curtains first opened to the
audience on Capitol Hill, Hawaiian monarchs were
shown to be the antagonists in an island paradise.
Land and sugar barons paraded out from behind the
scenes to rescue Hawaii.
Then the curtains closed.
And the unseen stage would forever be changed.

Hanani was choked up.
Feeling the vitriol, Makoa resisted and prayed to
remain steady. He focused on the Lord whose
innocent claim of being the Son of God was judged
as criminal. Religious hierarchs blinded by self-
righteous fervor signaled Rome to have his back
ripped to shreds, beard torn, slapped, punched,

thorns shoved into his skull, stripped and hung to die.

He thought of the actions of Cliff and close friends who strove to mend the gross inequities of those who had used the form of godliness to take God out of the God-fearing ways of cultures.

He remembered missionaries that brought relief to people engaged in tribal blood feuds. Jungle wars were averted by their peaceful negotiations. They labored to improve health and safe welfare while living alongside former adversaries. They gave, and continue to give, their lives in the name of love.

With these thoughts racing through his mind, the drama before him unfolded: of greed-driven moguls that relinquished their nobility for the ignoble dollar.

Innuendos and epithets volatile enough to incite a riot resonated throughout the crowd.

Hanani felt uneasy, scared. She clung to Makoa.

Cliff remarked, "None of this was intended to provoke anger."

Expressions on some of the actors seemed strained, either by the stress of exacting performances, or because they could feel some natives seething with anger. Some were wishing they didn't rehearse for the parts. But here they were, posing as impostors of the past.

The black suits they wore a hundred years ago on Iolani Palace grounds were symbolic of the death of a Kingdom. Ample, well-groomed disguises with lavishly combed beards. Savvy hunters that stalked through the thicket of Machiavellian malfeasance,

indomitably patient, postured to pounce upon
unsuspecting prey.
Kill-frenzy hunters sought the prey's brood:
Hawaiian generations.
And the prey's lair: Hawaiian lands.
They wrote Hawaii into history.
A dark history they ritually dressed for.
In black.
By the stroke of pens upon fallacious documents
that never legally dissolved the Kingdom of Hawaii.

"We are not American!
The native speaker shouted on stage. She was a
renowned figure in the islands who led an
outspoken Hawaiian Sovereignty group with other
political activists.
"We will die as Hawaiians!"
It was like someone had come up to Makoa and
slugged him in the gut. Vexed by seeds of
discontent, her proclamation over the podium
sickened him, because it rode upon the crest of
hidden animosities that force upon mind and soul
bonds of unspeakable grief.
Sympathetic with her hurts and frustrations, he, too,
grappled with perplexities that accounted for his
people's sorrows. Makoa's own tension between
two worlds was one of divided loyalties: a thesis of
nativism, an antithesis of westernism and a
synthesis of both that often clashed while trying to
find his identity and sense of belonging.
Days transpired. History re-lived was healing for
some, and open wounds for others.

Finally, on January 17, 1993, the fifth and final commemoration day, 100 torch bearers that began their procession from Kawaiahao Church ended their 100 hour vigil.

Carrying the flames of Iwikauikaua, they marched at night through Iolani Palace grounds to the statue of King Kamehameha I, where the fire would be transferred from descendants of Queen Liliuokalani back to King Kamehameha, symbolizing the call from the last monarch to the first monarch. For Kamehameha to step forward once again from the dustbin of history and assume his kingship, unbroken from his founding till her reign, and stream forward for the people of today to rule with *Ua mau ke ea o ka aina i ka pono*---The life of the land is perpetuated in righteousness.

Throughout the vigil, hand-held torches cast a dim glow on somber faces.
Conch shells were blown, followed by the beating of pahu drums.
Island breezes mourned as the wounded earth's heart beats for the breaking of a new dawn.
Haina ia mai ana kapuana---Let the echo of our song be heard.
The sound of drums took Makoa way back on the morning Po'o was killed.

The bittersweet procession began at the bronze sculpture of Queen Liliuokalani, then from Kawaiahao Church, pass Iolani Palace and ending at the warrior-image of King Kamehameha. These remaining vestiges rose from the natural habitat as

179

imposing monuments used, historically, as strategic platforms to end the Kingdom of Hawaii.

Hawaiians, other Polynesians and peoples of all nations long for the Kingdom of God that Jesus spoke of. He rules by love when executing righteousness and justice. Contrarily, once men and women taste of the fruits of money, sex and power from the tree of temptation, their fallen nature of hate, unrighteousness and injustice will taint their rule. People are tempted when they are drawn away by their own lust. Lust conceived brings forth sin, and sin, when it is finished, brings forth death. When this happens, it is, principally, incumbent upon the ruled to remove them by whatever means. If not, the sickness of corruption, like an open, festering open sore that befalls rulers, will infect the masses with misery.
Resistance and rebellion throughout history are blueprints to right wrongs. Wars and rumors of wars linger. Unsolved resolutions are swords of Damocles dangling by strands of hair. Wherever these swords fall, death and destruction follows because evil in men's hearts propels the vicious cycle of empires rising and falling.
Jesus is the true Desire of nations. He said that what men hold in high esteem is despised by God, and what God holds in high esteem is despised by men. His Kingdom on the earth will heal violations of ancient boundaries. The generational consequences are redeemable, in Christ alone, so unity between brothers and sisters can commence and be forged in the bonds of love.

Jesus calls to weary men and women of every tribe and tongue.
His burden is light and His yoke is easy.
Come to Him.

*****

Several days after the ceremonies ended, Thomas Kitani and his wife, Marie, flew in from Puna on the Big Island. They stopped over on Oahu before heading to Ottawa, Canada, for an Indigenous People's Conference hosted by Cree and Sioux nations.
Makoa and Hanani were glad that they and a friend, Jill Caines, whom they brought along, could stay for a few days in their Kaneohe home before leaving.
Jill was a God-sent descendant of Wahunsenacawh, the father of Matoaka--better known as Pocahontas. Lakota elders in Montana held her work with indigenous peoples in high esteem.
Her efforts were brought to the attention of Thomas while he was on a lecture circuit in Canada a few years prior. Jill's vacation in Hawaii, her life-long dream, was for a planned rendezvous with Thomas and Marie.
Elias Harwell, a well-known Native American Indian with the Canadian Parliament in Ottawa and a colleague of Jill, had promised her to meet with Thomas and other Native leaders to discuss reconciliation between native and non-native peoples.

Distressed over the ceremonial re-enactments, Makoa was tired of his inner struggles and desperate to heal from his painful past. "Thomas, I need your help."

Hanani, Marie and Jill were present.

Thomas was caught off-guard. After intensive dialogue with Makoa, he concluded, "Your search for God is blinded by philosophy and intellectualism."

Thomas' counsel was seasoned with grace, whose own life's example of well-doing had put to silence the ignorance of foolish men.

Hanani least expected any of this to occur. Having grown weary of Makoa's highs and lows, she welcomed his healing. Wallowing in ideas and opinions of man had taken its toll. Despite the pain that pricked her scar-ridden heart, her love for him remained. She confided to them, "I remember a vision two years ago. Makoa was striving for significance. Feeling worthless, rejected, he fought with the side of himself that believed a lie and struggled to face the truth."

Makoa wasn't humiliated, but receptive to his spiritual dilemma. "Tell them, bebe, about Tiare's vision.

"When praying," Hanani shared, "she saw Makoa with his legs crossed. He had no shirt on and his head was clean-shaven. Disturbed, he kept rocking back and forth trying to quell the agony in himself, repeating over and over again, '*My soul is naked, even as my head is naked. My soul is naked, even as my head is naked…*'"

Long silence.

Then Jill spoke. "When our thoughts are like the tempest, our hearts are blinded by dark clouds. God's peace in the midst of our inner storms will calm us if we are naked before Him in mind and soul."

Makoa looked at Hanani, then Thomas and Marie. The expressions on their faces affirmed the wisdom of Jill's words.

*****

The windblown surf of the restless sea reflected Makoa's inner emotions. He crestfallen gaze was distant. Empty.

Hanani walked closely by his side. Streaks of orange-brown and yellow-ochre seaweed colored Nanakuli's white sands.

The sun was low in the sky, ready to set. Their slow, steady strides left imprints in the gritty turf, much like how sorrow is impressed in the grit of the soul under the weight of sin. But unlike how imprints in the sand are altered by wind, rain, or rising tide, the impress of a burdened soul is unaltered by the weight of life's miseries, though weathered by fleeting moments of joy.

Hanani stooped to pick up a stone from the sand and held it close to Makoa's face. "Babe, look. This is symbolic of what you've learned," pause, "the idol of knowledge."

Her observation silenced him.

"Sweetheart," Hanani pressed, "look out into the ocean."

He heard her but lowered his head. She gently lifted his chin and again prompted him to look sea-ward. "How beautiful and majestic are the deep waters! Yet, we only see a portion of all that really is. The ocean is symbolic of God's wisdom in depth and expanse. All that the earth contains is a mere droplet in His eternal springs of knowledge. This stone is only a grain."

She weighed insignificant, heady pursuits against a deeper understanding of nature; misguided wit against unfathomable truths.

Reaching an open hand to her, Makoa motioned for the stone.

Hanani held the stone over his open palm for a brief, deliberate second. Staring into his eyes, she dropped it.

Clutching the stone, he walked toward the shore's edge, fell on his knees and stretched his clenched fists to the sky. Not as a gesture of defiance, but of surrender. As he remained there for a while, Hanani quietly knelt beside him and looked beyond the white, rolling crests.

"Lord," Makoa prayed, "I offer this stone. Rid me of this idol. Empty my mind, my heart, to receive all of You."

He stood abruptly, ran knee-deep in the ocean, and flung the stone far into the waves. Anticipation of its plunge would herald a new beginning.

Death by immersion.

Its rippling effect blended with the blue-turquoise sea, as one who is abandoned to the unimaginable vastness of love.

Makoa heard a screech and looked up to see a Hawaiian hawk circling high above them. He whispered, "Iokaha."
The prophet Isaiah wrote of how those who wait upon the Lord shall have their strength renewed. They shall walk and not be weary, run and never faint, and they shall mount up with wings like eagles.
Are not hawks kin to eagles? Accipitridae.
The Hebrew God of the Bible is spoken of as having outstretched wings under which the weary find refuge and are safe. It seemed that he and Hanani were finding similar respite below different wings.
Io is acknowledged by Ngati Kahungunu iwi Maoris. To Kanaka Maoli of Hawaii, Io is akin to a hawk. Did Hawaiian and Aotearoan forefathers worship the same God as did Hebrew patriarchs, but through different eyes?
To Hebrews of old, Yahweh was the one and only God. What do indigenous peoples of the world say about Yahweh?
Overwhelmed by cultural similitudes, eyes shut; he raised his head toward the heavens. Suddenly, he was in a vision:

Sky-bound, free from earthly encumbrances and mounted with the wings of an eagle, he was carried by the breath of God and soaring alongside the

185

hawk in a fuchsia-imbued dawn. The feathered-one
spoke, "You are free. Be bound no more."
Time and space were absorbed into an everlasting
twilight soft with magenta hues that bade him to
settle upon the ethereal, pristine terrain below.
Alighting upon a field of unknown colors, he felt
rest and peace.

Hanani saw the calm on his face while he stood
unbecomingly still.
He opened his eyes and wiped the tears rolling
down his cheeks.

Shortly after, they walked further down the beach to
sit and watch the sunset. The orb's plummet was
languorous, its effulgence now only a glow where
the clouds converged to mirror its fire, to reflect its
dying breath into the night's grave until its
resurrection at dawn. The cycle of earth seasons:
Spring, Summer, Fall and Winter; birth, life, death
and burial---only to be reborn and to begin the cycle
once more.
Gray and dark-pink billows altered the shape of the
half-immersed star until a strange phenomenon
began to appear. Makoa beheld a non-illusion,
shaped not by years of toil, but by a higher
command.
The setting sun was like a ziggurat, a pyramidal
temple-altar used by ancient civilizations, having a
built-in stairway and a flat summit designed as an
altar to the gods. Priestly mediators of old implored
sky deities to intervene in human affairs by

descending to the bottom of the stairway into the midst of man.

Idols and images, placed on the summit of a ziggurat, were given homage through prayers, rituals, and sacrifices.

Knowing this made Makoa cringe as he pondered, *'Lord, what does this mean?'* Enlightened, the waning, fiery ziggurat represented an intellectual temple.

Temple of the mind.

On the ziggurat's summit, idols of earthly wisdom, and images of envy and strife: sensual, fraught with confusion and every evil work. Needing neither idol nor image to affirm, wisdom from above is pure, peaceable, gentle, easy to be entreated, full of mercy, good fruits, impartial, non-hypocritical and yields fruits of righteousness in peacemakers.

No matter how grandiose an intellectual ziggurat may be, or how impressive the idols of earthly wisdom may appear on its summit, it can never fill the longings of man.

And the cries of a desperate heart.

Part V

The Symbol

13

Makoa leaned on the rail of the redwood deck at Dr. Kyle Pahono's home in Aiea Heights. Built on the side of a mountain, they had a sweeping, birds-eye view of Hickam Air Force base down below.

"You ready?" Kyle sipped his coffee and watched two F-15 jet-fighters loop around and vector in for a landing. His heart ached when Dana was on a lecture circuit. In the collage of tropical plants lining the deck, white, stephanotis flowers bristled in the sunlight and reminded him of her pikake perfume.

"I can feel the drama building."

"I feel it, too." Makoa turned to sit on one of the deck chairs.

Kyle sat right across him. "Rocky will meet us there," he paused, "Hanani cool with this?"

"Yup." Makoa scratched his head, leaned back and folded his arms. "While I was with Tevake in the cave, he said that the Lord brought me to him in answer to his prayers. Then he motioned for me to bring my face close to his," pause, "he placed his right hand on the top of my head and *blew* in my mouth!"

Kyle jerked his head up and stared at Makoa.

*****

Zigzagging through the backside of the golf-course under the cover of darkness, they reached the bottom of the ravine. The cave would be kept a secret as long as they got inside the lava tube undetected. Kyle and Rocky knew that scientists would horde inside the dome like bees in a hive if its existence was known.

Kyle removed a compass from his pocket. "We're moving in the direction of Opu Iwi."

Once in the dome hollow, their flashlights revealed much on the wall.

Moving slowly around the perimeter, Rocky marveled, "Reminds me of the Birdman tribes from Rapa Nui that carved thousands of petroglyphs and left paintings in lava tube caves on Rapa Nui."

Kyle agreed. "Some have mistaken the Birdman tribe with the tribe that carved the Moais stone heads."

Etchings of full-sail canoes, stick figures, oceans, survival tools, weapons, and crude-looking animals mystified Rocky. "They hammered their message in stone so it would not be marred by smoke from their cooking fires."

Kneeling at the end of the mural, Makoa ran his hand over the petroglyph. "What do you guys think?"

Rocky knelt, rubbing his chin. "Hmmm…"

Kyle walked up and said, "Christians lived in Roman, Greek and European catacombs, most notably the Derinkuyu underground city in Anatolia. Many left evidence of their allegiance to the Jewish Messiah."

Rocky scanned the mural with his flashlight, and then retraced the petroglyph with his finger. "This is new to me. Judging by these shapes in the mural, looks like dissected pieces of the petroglyph are encoded at migratory intervals, anywhere from what seems to be generations depicted in themes. Like repeated ideographs."

Kyle recalled, "Me and a rabbinic genealogist friend attended a gathering of Christians and Messianic Jews in Jerusalem. The keynote speaker mentioned ideographs of Yeshua encoded in the Torah."

Rocky's thoughts raced, "A series of tubes lead to this cave, like it *connects* to their legacy."

"Meaning?" Makoa asked.

"Like an *umbilical cord* that kept them tethered to this mural in a *womb.*"

Makoa shivered. "Kyle mentioned this when we last came here."

"You all have pieces of the puzzle."

Startled, they whipped around.

"Who said that?" Defensively poised, Kyle, Makoa and Rocky stood abruptly.

A silhouette of someone stood by the cave's entrance.

Makoa raised his flashlight. "What the…?"

Nervous silence.

As the deep-tanned haole man stepped out from the shadows, he looked like castaway with long, sun-bleached hair and beard. A Roman-like toga made of tapa cloth was loosely draped over his well-defined body. A thin sennit rope slung across his chest held a small gourd that hung on his right side. He appeared dignified; his facial features, angular. And his eyes were deep blue.

191

"Admiral Moresi!" Makoa exclaimed.

Kyle was confounded. "You're barely recognizable. What are you *doing* here?"

The Admiral's piercing gaze showed no hostility as he drew closer to them. "I knew you all would be coming, so I followed you here."

Rocky recognized the voice on the telephone. "So *you're* the anonymous caller?"

He looked at Rocky. "Luke Moresi. Retired Rear Admiral, U.S. Navy," turning to Makoa, "I am here for a purpose." Wasting no time, he pointed to the petroglyph on the wall behind them. "This *is* the symbol of hope spoken of in Nehune legends." Luke allowed some time for this revelation to sink in.

Tevake's prayer echoed in Makoa's mind; Kyle and Rocky needed time to process.

Luke turned to Kyle, "All along, you and Dana tried getting in from the outside, until you," pointing at Makoa, "found Tevake here."

Luke knelt on one knee and drew in the dirt with his right index finger. It was the outline of a fish, for the Fisher of men. The Greek letters I, X, O, Y and E were drawn inside, which stood for: Yeshua Christos, God our Savior.

Rocky stroked his chin, puzzled. "Greek letters?"
Luke answered, "For reasons locked in antiquity,
Nehune adopted traces of Greek culture."
Kyle enjoined, "Which may have included a
Phoenician lineage, renowned for their deep-ocean,
navigational skills."
Luke leaned over and said, "Whatever their ancient
migratory route, Nehune hid these Greek letters in
this image." He traced over the petroglyph. "The O
is its head, and the I is this line that runs down the
center."

"The Y, superimposed over the I, was placed
upside-down, at the bottom of the I, to depict legs."

"The upper part of the X completes the V-shaped torso, and the lower part of the X is superimposed" he traced over the legs, "over the upside-down Y."

"The E is superimposed over the I line down the center of the torso, is elongated and curved on each end to depict outstretched arms, but still distinguishable as the letter E."

"The two halves of the outline are that of a fish." He
pointed to the head-half of the fish depicted as its
right hand, and the tail-half of the fish depicted as
its left hand. "It represents how the body of the
Fisher of men was torn and sacrificed for the
redemption of mankind."

Kyle came to the logical conclusion, "Which
confirms we're *in* Opu Iwi. I imagined the symbol
of hope to be something other than this petroglyph."
Makoa raised his hand and ran his fingers gently
down the etched figure. "And *this* represents the
Desire of Nations. He will bring healing to our
people and land!"

A sudden wind and powerful presence of an unseen,
Holy fire could be felt in the cave.
As quickly as it came, it left.

"What was that?" Rocky's eyes were wide.
Awed by the moment, no one said anything.
After several minutes, Luke said, "I need all of you
to listen very carefully to what I am about to tell
you."
They nodded.

195

"In 1920," Luke began, "a military scout team was sent out to clear Kahoolawe from outer-island squatters. They came upon hundreds of natives and were stunned by their vastly constructed village with a mature eco-system that flourished from the slopes down to the ocean, much like the reconstructed ahupuaa at Kanapou Bay. They eventually learned that a tribe, known as Nehune, had been confined to Kealaikahiki for several decades. Military officials had strict orders to remain silent.'

'Shortly after the Japanese attacked Pearl Harbor in 1941, parts of this island were designated for bombing exercises. Field commanders were ordered to steer clear of Kealaikahiki. Nonetheless, Nehune were fear-struck by the way the ground rumbled from strange thunder they perceived to be coming from 'fire-sticks mounted on sea and air-borne chariots of the gods.' They resorted to human sacrifice to appease the wrath of these gods. Only during heavy storms, no one knows why. This is when the sounds of beating drums and screams can be heard from Kealaikahiki.'

'By 1953, the navy had jurisdiction over all Kahoolawe for military use. My dad, a Chief Petty Officer close to retirement, was assigned to keep Nehune confined to Kealaikahiki. When I joined the navy as an Ensign, I worked myself up the ranks and managed to follow in my father's footsteps.'

'Once in position, I dug-up background information on a closely guarded secret: the existence of a Shadow Commission. Powerful, wealthy men had banned together in the late 1800s. From its inception, their true agenda hid behind a complex web of lies to protect this tribe. The Commission remained in-tact, adding hand-picked members from various spheres of influence to hone their craft and schemes till modern times. Though privileged to be Nehune's guardian, I was ordered to keep Hawaiians focused on Kanapou Bay while overseeing surveillance and 24/7 armed patrol around Kealaikahiki. Allowing the reconstruction of the ahupuaa was a deterrence from Nehune's existence at Kealaikahiki.'"

He looked squarely at Kyle and said, "When you and your wife uncovered evidence of Nehune in Pit 23, commission members were informed and they became furious! Word trickled down to level the entire ahupuaa. The resistance led by Aloike that followed shocked everybody, including me. Those who died on the mound brought flashbacks." He paused, lowered his head, breathed deeply, looked up and continued, "It reminded me of our holdout on a hill when I was in Vietnam. We were outnumbered by Viet Cong forces: pinned all night, low on ammo and a high body count, rescue finally arrived the next day.'

'Since retiring as a Rear Admiral, I was determined to interfere with this commission's agenda. They will stop at nothing to achieve their objectives. As an example, the media stunt by Dr. Chloe Hansen was carefully crafted by the commission so they could control the evidence from Pit 23 at the base of Opu Iwi. Allowing the development of private mansions, Club Mez and a marina would not only buy the commission more time not only to deter away from Kealaikahiki, but also to bury the evidence of Nehune once and for all!'"

Kyle, Makoa and Rocky looked like deers frozen in a headlight beam.

Luke gave them time to process. Studying all three of them, he set his gaze on Makoa and said, "Tevake knew why Hoku was taken."

Wild-eyed, Makoa's heart burned. "She is...*alive?*" tears welled up in his eyes, "where is my bebe girl?"

Lowering his eyes, Luke stepped forward and, looking directly into Makoa's eyes, gripped his shoulder firmly, said, "Hoku lives among the Nehune people."

Makoa broke down and wept.

14

Makoa stepped out of the car as his friend drove away. Whisking through the front door, he startled Hanani. "Babe!"

Kawika ran downstairs, "Dad, everything okay?"

Malia saw her father from the lanai and opened the glass door. "Dad, you're home."

Hanani hugged and kissed him. "You're *smiling*? Whaaat *happened* while you were there?"

Makoa looked at them. "Hoku is ALIVE!!"

"What?" Hanani sighed. Bent over, shaken, she fell on her knees, sobbing. "It's been three years. She's *alive*?"

Makoa sat and held her in his arms. Kawika and Malia joined in as they huddled on their living room floor, crying, laughing and thanking God.

*****

Deeply affected by what he learned in the cave, Rocky returned to the Big Island. Nehune descendants were a problem for first settler origins. Political activists would chaff once they knew of this since it could seriously undermine progress for their land rights.

*****

Kyle stayed at Kanapou Bay to resolve many unsettling questions. To his surprise, the retired admiral was a groundskeeper at Club Mez to keep a low profile.

By mid-afternoon, it heated up to the 90's. Luke brought two cold bottles of Aquafina to the end of dock on the marina. Kyle was waiting for him. The couple hanging out on their sailboat within earshot finally left.

Luke was free to speak. "Before he retired, my dad trespassed *onto* the village grounds and was apprehended by armed mercenaries. It was under tight security, including the airspace to avoid aerial sightings. After my dad served his time, he managed to live with the tribe, as long as he remained hidden and kept his distance from perimeter patrols. He was eventually found out, interrogated, tried and stripped of his retirement rank. He knew too much, so they wanted to punish him. He lost everything."

Kyle held his questions.

Luke gulped down more water as he thought about what would compel men to form the Shadow Commission in the late 1800s, and why they were bent on keeping Nehune hidden from the world.

"You're an archaeologist that believes in God and not in evolution," he questioned, "Tell me, what was the impact of Darwinist science in the 1800s?"

Kyle wiped the sweat from his brow. "In a nutshell, science created chinks in the pillars of religious institutions. Human origin was owed to a Creator. By the mid-1800s, Charles Darwin theorized that man evolved through natural selection. This was a window of opportunity for anti-religious atheists to debunk theism. In addition, racist ideas cast darker-skin tribes as uncivilized, compared to light-skin, civilized societies." Looking at his arms, Kyle teased, "I guess I could blend in with Neanderthals."

"And here I am," Luke chuckled, "blonde, blue eyes with my hair and beard looking like, well, remember the caveman stomped by the brontosaurus at the end of the FedEx commercial during Superbowl XL?"

"Yes! Hilarious!" Kyle laughed so hard that he farted.

Without missing a beat, Luke took a swig of water and burped.

Time passed. Luke thought about the woman he still had feelings for. Pouring water on his head to cool off, he thought, *'Could I fall in love with her again?'*

Kyle jumped in, swam around, remained waist-deep in the water and folded his arms on the dock.

Small talk. Not much. Both needed time to think.

Luke fidgeted and sighed deeply.

Kyle glanced at him, "Must be heavy?"

"It is. The human sacrifice part."

"Yeah, you mentioned this in the cave," Kyle recalled and added, "bones we've uncovered in strata from different parts of the globe were, in some cases, were evidence of human sacrifice in ancient societies."

When Luke returned from Vietnam in 1974, the Roe v Wade case had become law the previous year. He was deeply affected when his niece died after aborting her first child. His sister blamed the U.S. Supreme Court for giving her daughter the legal option to kill her child, and then lose her life from the brutal procedure, and worse, for opening the floodgate of death upon America. Luke drew close to his sister on her journey to heal from this deep wound. With this running through his mind, he said, "I've had much time to think through their human sacrifice over the years. I can't get it out of my head that it is no different than babies being aborted today. Injecting saline into the amniotic sac to burn babies alive in the womb is akin to binding a victim with cords to a bamboo altar and setting him or her on fire. On the village grounds, this altar is set up inside a rectangular enclosure, a temple. Outside, there is a large flat stone. It, too, is an altar used to enforce village law. On it, infants have been slain in proxy for priests or chiefs of influence; women died for eating the wrong food; men caught in the shadow of Vanatu were stretched out on the flat stone and had their heads bashed in. Next to the flat stone is a tree where men have been forced to stand with their backs to the trunk, had a cord placed around their throats and strangled to death by a native pulling from behind."

Kyle was visibly shaken. "Modern abortion *is* the same as their ancient sacrificial methods. Abortion is legal murder. Politicians and intellectuals who defend killing unborn babies as women's rights entirely dismiss the right of these defenseless babies to live. G.K. Chesterton said '*the problem with intellectuals is that they have educated themselves into imbecility.*'"

Still troubled by his experiences with Nehune, Luke continued, "I mean, what is the difference between the priests ordering the men to hold victims down on the flat stone, then bashing their heads in as one form of punishment, and partially removing babies from the womb to puncture the back of their heads with scissors then suctioning their brains so their skulls collapse? Think about it, politicians, media and the largest abortion agency are like these priests holding sway over abortion doctors to perform the modern sacrifice of killing babies."

His hackles raised, Kyle looked him square in the eyes. "No difference! And to think that lawmakers and pundits defend these murderous acts against our most vulnerable innocents. Imbecilic madness!"

Both paused to reflect on the murder of babies in the womb, masked as a human right.

Kyle broke the silence. "Makoa heard drums and someone screaming when he came with Po'o. Olapa and Aloike explained they heard it too when Dana and I came to meet with the council elders. But why only during high winds and storms?"

Luke shrugged. "Don't know."

Kyle dipped his head in the water, brushed his hair back, folded his arms on the dock again and scanned the landscape to frame his thoughts. "Your mention of victims being burned on an altar of fire reminds me of the ancient middle-east. Children were cast in the fires to Moloch in the Valley of Gehenna."

The screams of a victim writhing in hot flames echoed in Luke's haunted memories. "I was there only once when the head chief ordered this gruesome act. I knew the person, which made it very difficult. That early eve, when dark clouds filled the sky, the atmosphere felt ominous. Suddenly, Tevake appeared out of nowhere to plead with the villagers to return to God. When spotted by Nehune priests, they gave chase but a blinding, torrential downpour shielded his escape. Human sacrifices on this altar, the flat stone and tree kept villagers in fear, submission and control--- something they knew Hawaiian chiefs used to manipulate commoners when the kapu system was still in force."

Kyle questioned, "Was Tevake hiding in the cave when Makoa found him?"

"Yes," Luke affirmed, "it was his secret refuge. For years, he came out only at night for water and food he gathered from the forest. During my time there, he boldly confronted the chiefs several times. When they tried to apprehend him, he was able to escape. One time they set up an ambush and wounded him badly, but again he broke away and fled."

Kyle gasped, "That's when Makoa found him bleeding from his arm."

Luke nodded, "Yes."

Kyle sighed. "I need time to pray. The Lord alone can unravel all of this making-my-head-spin stuff."

"Sure. Bungalow comfortable enough?"

"Very." Kyle replied as he got out of the water, stood, dripping, and gestured with the shaka sign. "I'll bring papaya and pastries from the restaurant and meet you here tomorrow morning at 8:00 am."

Luke responded, "Sounds good. I'll bring coffee."

*****

The following morning was cool as the sun crept higher in the sky.

"One thing I miss when Dana and I are traveling is this." Kyle dug into four, deseeded papaya halves with his plastic spoon.

Smiling, Luke agreed. "Always better when fresh picked."

"Exactly."

After a while, their talk turned to other serious matters. "Over the last few years," Luke said, "Hawaiian activists have fought vigorously to block the building of a missile silo on Niihau. Commission members convinced military brass that Kealaikahiki would be the perfect site as part of their continuing scheme to bury evidence of an experiment that went bad in the 1800s."

"1800s...*experiment?*" Kyle puzzled.

Luke replied, "With Nehune. It's complicated. You'll find out soon enough."

Kyle reflected on how his friends in 1990 protested geo-thermal development in the Wao Kele O Puna rainforest on the Big Island, some of whom chained their necks to the fences set up in the area. They were anti-development and pro-land. Similarly, anti-silo activists were unknowingly pro-Nehune. Shutting the ahupuaa down at Kanapou Bay and replacing it with a haven for the affluent was one thing. The commission's scheme against living heirlooms at Kealaikahiki Point was another.

Luke inhaled deeply, "Arrangements were made several years ago. Hawaiians trained by Papa Mau in wayfinding have been teaching Nehune to build and sail double hull canoes from Kealaikahiki."

"To where?"

"That will depend on Nahiena."

"And she *is*?" Kyle cocked his head.

Luke revealed, "Tevake's wife."

15

The powerful arachnids that hired Dr. Chloe Hansen watched as their web of lies slowly unraveled. At this point, it was beyond her control. Timing was essential: one wrong move, Nehune would be prematurely exposed to the outside world.
Should the lost tribe be exiled---or not?
At least she could trust the ex-admiral to mediate their impending exodus.

Luke Moresi and Chloe Hansen had a short-lived romance that ended when he sought to protect Nehune and she, after joining the commission, was assigned to assimilate them into the modern world.
She was a beautiful Eurasian local-born girl raised in New York. Her white-collar upbringing and island heritage qualified her for the task.
Still looking like he came out of the sixties, his dark tan, shoulder length hair and full beard was complemented with jeans, suede loafers, and a button up floral-print shirt. He agreed to meet at her suite with a commanding view of the Ala Wai canal further inland from the Waikiki beachline.
Meandering toward her large office window, he watched paddlers in single-hull, six-seater canoes skimming up and down the canal to prepare for the annual Molokai to Oahu canoe race that drew many entrants from around the world.
Chloe asked, "What did you tell them?" She felt uneasy that he might have revealed too much.

He glanced at her from the corner of his eye. "What they needed to know."

"Needed to know!" she raised her voice, "I don't need them getting in my way! And this *other* guy, who is he?"

"Rocky. No worries about him."

"In my line of work no one is to be trusted. You're my only exception."

Luke assured her. "He went back to reclusive his life in Kealakekua."

She hissed.

"Makoa is Hoku's father. With Kyle's help, we have a better chance of getting her out alive."

The mention of Hoku made her wince. Regaining her composure, she inquired, "*Dr.* Kyle Pahono?"

Luke nodded in agreement.

The Shadow Commission wanted Nehune to disappear, but Hoku's unexpected abduction hindered their moves.

Luke said, "The silo is a poor excuse to force them out of their homeland. Besides, they have no specific destination."

Chloe rebutted, "Why not Niihau? It's the least modernized and," she shrugged, "they'll blend in, right?"

"Have arrangements been made for this?" Luke pressed.

"As a matter of fact, yes," Chloe assured him, "Niihauans agreed to work with us."

Luke was taken aback. "Do they know *who* they will be working with?"

She ignored him. "Nehune have two months to prepare before they set sail. That's all you should be concerned about."

He turned to look out the window again and fixed his gaze on the movement of the canoes.

She stared at him, conscious of his visible disgust over the way she sought to further her career by agreeing to mediate for power-mongers on the commission, and her vendetta to impede any progress made by the Pacific Archaeological Society. .

Late for an appointment, she stood up to leave.

"I've heard about a symbol located somewhere on Kahoolawe. Do you know anything about this?"

Luke glared at her, turned, and walked out of her office.

*****

To blend in with Nehune natives, Makoa and Kyle wore malos for several weeks in the hot Maui sun to tan their buttocks. They spoke in Hawaiian, part of the linguistic spectrum of Tongan, Samoan, Maori, Tahitian, etc. In this matrix of Polynesian languages, Makoa understood most of what Tevake said in the cave.

Makoa was on edge the whole time. He had plenty of time to think about Hoku living with Nehune for three years. Did they hurt her? Was she healthy? When he tried to imagine how she looked like as a young woman, he would tear up.

During this time, Luke arranged for Mau, a master Wayfinder from Micronesia, to teach Makoa and Kyle some canoe building skills before entering the village grounds. While training alongside Mau, they were surprised to learn what happened in 1976, the year known for the rebirth of the Hawaiian culture. A never-before-built, double-hull canoe, named Hokulea, was constructed to retrace their lineage from Hawaii to Tahiti and back. Mau, a native from the Carolinian island of Satawal in Micronesia, was asked to teach Hawaiians how to navigate the high seas using the stars, sun, moon, swells, currents, winds, etc., to find land. The lost art of ancient wayfinding needed no navigational instruments to traverse the open ocean.

Its maiden voyage, scheduled to be launched from the Big Island, included haole researchers. Hawaiians possessive of Hokulea as a symbol of their cultural pride demanded that only island natives should be onboard. Through negotiations, a compromise was reached for haoles and Hawaiians to sail and learn alongside each other. Sadly, tensions among several of the crew members culminated into a fistfight. Once they all reached Tahiti, Mau refused to guide the canoe's return trip. Disgusted, he flew back to Micronesia. Left stranded on Tahiti, the crew was forced to use navigational equipment to sail Hokulea back to Hawaii.

The peaceful twilight could not lighten their mood as they motored all the way from Kanapou Bay. When they finally reached Waikahalulu Bay at night, Luke's gaze was fixed in the direction of Kealaikahiki as they disembarked from his Zodiac. He was dressed the same way they first saw him in the cave.

210

Approaching the outskirts of the village, Makoa noticed the silhouette of a Coast Guard cutter under moonlight.

Luke saw him staring and said, "Random surveillance. They're assigned to escort the flotilla under the guise of canoes from different parts of Polynesia to commemorate Hokulea's maiden voyage. News articles and the media will push this alibi one week before they launch."

"What about the border guards?" Kyle asked.

Luke chuckled, "I convinced the commander that his men were jinxing launch efforts. By some Divine providence, he actually complied and pulled out." Taking a deep breath, he turned to Makoa. "Before I go in, there's something I've withheld from you."

"What?"

Hesitant at first, Luke said, "Nehune chieftains dispatched two warriors to find a sacrifice that would insure the success of their launch. I pleaded for them to release this person to no avail." He would have been bludgeoned to death for interfering, but they esteemed him and his father as descendants of their harvest god, similar to how the British Captain James Cook was perceived upon his arrival in 1778. Luke added, "Since this will not occur till shortly before the launch, we have time to rescue…"

Curious why Luke was telling him this, Makoa felt his gut tighten. "Find a sacrifice?" pause, "rescue…Hoku?"

Kyle's heart race as he looked over at Luke, who, still grappling for words, finally said, "Yes."

Makoa's body went numb. His thoughts spinning wildly, he grabbed Luke and threw him to the ground. The bearer of bad news is sometimes the victim of the hearer's rage. A combat trainer in Vietnam, Luke could have easily deflected his deft move.

Kyle shoved Makoa aside. "Knock it off! He knows what he's doing."

Makoa stared at Kyle, "Did *you* know?"

"*Not* about Hoku." Kyle assured.

Luke got up slowly and dusted himself off. "It's okay. He should be upset." The muscles in his jaws flexed as he looked Makoa squarely in the eye. "It was for Hoku that I couldn't tell you this earlier."

"For her?" Makoa calmed down.

"I couldn't risk you interfering. They believe their survival hinges on offering a sacrifice. Any suspected interferences would have—and will-- bring her to a swift end."

It was time for Luke to return. With all of the raw emotions passed them, he laid out a strategy to rescue Hoku.

Makoa and Kyle agreed it was a good plan. They stayed low and watched through the tall brush as Luke disappeared into the Nehune village and waited until he returned with a group of Hawaiians as cover.

When they did, Luke introduced them to the group. "They arrived yesterday as additional help so Nehune haven't had time to determine who's who. This is it. We'll go back in together. Just follow

212

them into their huts. I'll give you word where
they're keeping Hoku as soon as I can."
Kyle was concerned for Luke's safety. "They may
suspect that you planned her rescue."
"I'll worry about that if it happens."

Part VI

Sacrifice

16

"Hello?"

"Dana?"

"This is she. Hanani, is this you?"

Distressed, Hanani paused to gather her thoughts.
"Yes."

"Are you alright?"

"They've been gone for nearly a month!"

Dana had to compose herself. She had been worried
too. "I know. Kyle tried to prepare me for this."

Hanani returned, "So did Makoa, but we've heard
nothing," teary-eyed, "nothing!"

Dana felt her stomach tense up in knots. "Rocky
called me several days ago to inquire about them. I
didn't know what to say."

Hanani painfully recalled why Rocky returned
home. He didn't want anything to do with what was
going on at Kahoolawe. Nor did he really explain
why.

"I feel like Kyle downplayed their risks." Dana
confided.

Hanani agreed, "So did Makoa!"

"I'm tempted to inform the police," Dana
suggested, "but Luke was adamant that we don't."

*****

As the first morning light pierced through the
threshold of their hut on the Kealaikahiki village
grounds, Kyle observed how the main entry faced
east, in the direction of the rising sun. Stepping

cautiously into the stillness of day, they marveled over the village layout. Natural resources abounded. In the upper regions, they saw groves of koa trees that were being used not only for house posts and images, but also for the twelve double-hull canoes progressing rapidly towards completion in the canoe houses lining the Kai shoreline.

Kauila and ulei trees grew wild and were used for spears and a variety of handmade tools. Kyle thought about war, evidenced by the type of wood they were growing. He thought, *'Were Nehune arming themselves?'*

Olona was also being grown for cordage used for their fishing lines and nets.

Kyle marveled, "Feathers from mamo, elepaio, iiwi, and oo birds were used to make colorfully ornate cloaks bound together by olona thread and worn only by ancient Hawaiian chiefs."

Makoa nodded and added, "You smell that?"

Inhaling deeply, Kyle said, "Sandalwood!"

Not far from the koa groves, the prized iliahi, or sandalwood trees, flourished. Used for bathing and storing tapa cloth, the rare wood's fragrance wafted through their nostrils.

The mid-slope verdure was covered with medicinal plants, and abounded with wauke and mamaki for clothing and linen purposes. Kukui trees, the source of oil form the nuts used for bamboo torches added to the fields of pili, kalo, ti-plant, bananas, yams, awa and gourds. Toward the seashore, coconut, milo, and kou trees grew. Pohuehue were plentiful.

If encased in a massive dome, botanists would see this verdant paradise as a self-sustaining biosphere, much like what Captain Cook saw during his 1778 arrival in Hawaii.

*****

Things got worse since their phone conversation two days ago. Dana pressed one of Luke's known confidants and found out that the lives of their husbands were at stake. In accompanying Luke, it was a deadly risk to bring Hoku and themselves home alive.

Sipping her mocha cappuccino frappe at Marie Calendar's in the Windward Shopping Mall, Dana studied Hanani's countenance, now strained by Makoa's whereabouts. Her marriage to an intimidating brute mellowed by the power of love was threatened by his unknown fate.
Dana, too, felt the strain. Kyle meant everything to her, more than her career and prestige and the status that her rich, over-possessive parents tried to make her believe as one born into privilege. Her husband's down-to-earth simplicity taught her to think and feel otherwise.
Hanani lost her appetite. She finished drinking her double-chocolate latte, but the cheesecake she ordered with it was barely eaten.

Visibly troubled, Dana leaned over the table and lowered her voice to tell Hanani what she knew about Hoku.

Sacrifice?" Hanani shouted and pounded the table. Everyone in the restaurant turned to look at them. Dana buried her head in her hands.

Hanani's trembling fists were clenched so tight that her knuckles turned white.

A young couple eating at the table next to them kept staring.

Hanani strained to maintain composure. "Who told you this?"

Massaging her forehead, Dana looked up. "Someone close to Luke."

Tears poured down Hanani's face. "Makoa said Hoku was alive...but not for this!"

Dana assured, "Had Makoa been informed of the reason for her abduction, he could have foiled plans to get her out. Luke didn't want to take any chances. He understands all too well that interruptions in village protocols could be catastrophic. Especially because their survival depends upon..." she stopped mid-sentence.

Hanani put her right hand up. "I don't want to hear it." Lips trembling, she began to sob.

Dana waited until she calmed down. "Luke left me a contact at Kanapou Bay. She was instructed to answer our questions since it *is* our husbands who are there with him to bring her home. As we spoke, it was clear that she does not want us on Kahoolawe."

A sudden resolve overcame Hanani. She sat straight up in her chair, smeared mascara and all. "Malia is out of town with her uncle Cliff. They're on a tour with Isle Breaz. Kawika is busy with work."

Dana knew what Hanani was implying.

218

"Anyone you know who can take us there,
privately, on a boat?"
Dana took out her cell phone and dialed 555---.

*****

After over a month of being among Nehune at
Kealaikahiki, Kyle and Makoa learned most of their
Polynesian dialect. Pig, taro, taro leaves, banana,
coconut, coconut milk, kava, limu, herbs, and fish
were plenty for their hard labors.
For the past two years, Hawaiians and Nehune fell
twenty-four 60-foot koa trees from the upper forest.
They helped Mau chip koa logs with adzes, pausing
at fifteen minutes intervals to sharpen the edges of
the basalt tools against harder stones.
Holes were bored in patterns along the top portion
of the hollowed-out koa hulls. Separate pieces of
wood were carved, then, with the use of bone,
sennit was threaded through the holes to sew these
pieces on the top edges of the canoe. Smooth stones
from the beach were used to sand the rough-hewn
logs and planks. Breadfruit sap was applied over
joint or crevices for water-proofing. Kukui nut oil
was massaged into the wood by hand in the final
stages of completion.
Hundreds of paddles, twenty for each canoe, had to
be whittled, shaped, and smoothed out of koa wood,
used also to shape long steering paddles mounted on
the rear of each canoe.
Women spent painstaking hours each day sitting
and hunched over piles of lauhala leaves until they
plaited twenty four sails, along with pounding tree

bark into enough tapa clothing to keep them and their children warm at sea.

Old men rolled coconut husk on their thighs into tight strands that were braided together for needed cordage. Some whose hands were bent by arthritis still labored with incredible skill when braiding the outer skin of coconuts to produce rope for the sails, hau-wood masts, and the platforms that joined the hulls together. Yards and yards of strong netting were knitted and strung across the rear of each canoe.

The canoes Nehune help build alongside their Hawaiian counterparts handled well when sailing out at sea during test runs. Mau was confident that each double-hull canoe was seaworthy.

In addition, gourds were hollowed to store and preserve ti-leaf-wrapped food, miscellaneous supplies, water, seeds, plants, roots, etc., during their ocean crossing.

*****

Luke Moresi asked Makoa to join him and a friend in his hut. When all three of them were seated, Luke introduced Makoa, "This is Kalani, Tevake's son." The surprised look in Makoa's eyes was expected. Luke continued, "With the sudden death of Tevake, he's in charge of securing their departure. He knows what you and Kyle know. If the head chieftain knew Kalani was here, they would kill him."

Kalani studied Makoa for a while then spoke in broken English, "Our tribe, my father was last priest

220

of Lord. He pray for our people come back to God. He pray for someone take over if he die." Kalani pointed at Makoa. "You take over."

Puzzled, Makoa looked Luke.

Kalani continued, "When he almost complete symbol on cave wall, he pray and weep for people. Then he see you spirit in dream come to him." Makoa's eyes grew wide as he remembered his dream when he stood in the cave and approached Tevake.

"When you find him in earth time, he breathe in mouth."

"Yes!" Makoa said.

"He pass on you to bring Nehune back to Lord. You first learn forgive bad people, like he forgive bad people try kill him. Po'o and Aloike die so they not do this. You carry father work so people learn forgive."

Makoa was perplexed.

Kalani's fixed gaze on Makoa was like a flickering flame hoping to be rekindled. "Po'o family come from Nehune. My father work make Paao and Pili bad be forgive. He work make Hawaiians learn forgive bad people take land that make people of land poor."

Po'o's efforts among island natives earned him respect to help with conciliatory protocols to unshackle generational hate, some of which were used in Rwanda when Hutus and Tutsis agreed to reconcile after the devastating genocide in the 1990s.

Shrugging his shoulders, Makoa inquired, "Paao and Pili be forgiven? For what?"

Kalani explained, "Tahiti they come, do bad to Hawaii. Blood spill on land, make land not good."

Moved by this, Makoa looked at Luke and said, "Shedding innocent blood breaks the harmony between God, man and land. If shed before fulfilling intended destinies, life in the blood will cry out in death. Silent cries of innocent dead across defiled lands were lives meant to bring good on earth. Those that should have been, but are not, have left a void in humanity."

Luke never heard anything like this before. Being versed in the art of war meant to kill or be killed, at sea, on land, or in the air against perceived enemies. Reconciliation was the domain of diplomats and ambassadors.

Kalani continued, "Po'o not meet father. They see future people follow God, not do bad. Do good, pray with face low to ground. Good prayer medicine, heal bad. Prayer to God. He heal land."

Makoa's eyes brightened. "Po'o believed that Kahoolawe would be a place of refuge where people come to humble themselves, turn from their wicked ways, seek God's face and pray for Him to forgive their sins and heal their land."

Kalani responded, "Father explain Aloike mean know Son. Olapa mean life to land. Aloike, Olapa mean know Son bring Life to land!"

Makoa became tense as he recalled what Hanani told him of their deaths while he was in the hospital. Kalani looked down and noticed Makoa's clenched

222

fists. "What in heart, not good. Bad if rule you.
Must learn forgive all time."
Given the weight of his vision-experience of the
soaring hawk when Hanani was with him on the
Nanakuli sands, Makoa was painfully aware that
Kalani was right.
What transpired after their meeting in Luke's hut
was almost as if Power moved in a Divine
continuum that orchestrated forthcoming events.

*****

Kawika knocked gently on her bedroom door when
he heard her crying. "Mom? Can I come in?"
Lost in thought, Hanani didn't answer.
He grabbed the door knob. Unlocked, he opened it.
"You want to talk, mom?"
Reaching for a tissue on the night stand, Hanani
blew her nose, cleared her throat and shakily said,
"No."
Kawika stood in his father's stead. Since Makoa left
for Kahoolawe, he stayed close to Hanani. He
thought of how she stood at his bedside when he
was in the hospital recovering from his head wound.
He went over next to her, sat down, and placed his
arm around her. "I love you, mom."
Hanani placed her head on his shoulder. She was
proud of her son. After a brief pause, she started to
convulse, cover her mouth, and began to cry.
"Is it dad?"
"He and Kyle," sniffle, "are with someone who's
trying to rescue Hoku."
Kawika looked puzzled.

223

"Hoku and dad are in danger."
The words rescue and danger triggered Kawika.
Holding Hanani's right hand, his grip tightened.
Now of age, he was capable of fulfilling the threat
on his hospital bed to avenge his sister. The scar on
his head reminded him of Hoku's abduction. As he
watched Hanani weep, anguish opened the
vindictive scar on his heart. Not just to avenge
Hoku, but now his father.
He hugged her tightly. "It'll be alright, mom.
Remember how you tried to console me?"
Sniffle, "Yes."
Kawika stood abruptly. The way he left the room
reminded Hanani of how Makoa would leave home
long ago to attend meetings for land rights. It went
deep into the core of her being as she felt cold chills
run down her back. Feeling a sense of urgency, she
stood and reached for her iPhone on the dresser to
call Dana that they needed to move fast.
Destination: Kahoolawe.
To find Hoku, Makoa and Kyle.
And pray for God's intervention in what Kawika
had set his mind to do.

*****

Sweet sixteen. For Hoku, it was bittersweet.
She was a beautiful young woman with her
mother's long, flowing, red-streaked hair.
Hoku reminded the older villagers of stories spoken
about half-white beauties in the 1800's that foreign
gentlemen sought to possess.

They perceived Hoku's appearance to be touched by light, part-divine, descending into their midst as a daughter of the sun.

For three years she dreamt of Kawika hard on her trail as she screamed and flailed while locked in an iron grip and flung over the shoulder of her abductor. In the same dreams, Hoku could hear her father yelling for her and Kawika from far away.

Forced into their world against her will scarred her. She spent the initial months among them deep in thought, often reflecting on what Makoa and Hanani taught her as she was growing up about God, and the passion to live for His glory. Nehune girls her age wondered about Hoku's glossy-eyed, distant stare, but said nothing.

Eventually, she adapted and acquired the village customs and speech. But her involvement was only what was expected of her, nothing more other than an incognito existence.

Over time, however, her trust in God became more resolved. This is when she began to intimate with the people: their hopes, desires and passions.

As she grew to love and care for them, despite their reason for bringing her here, her destiny was in God's hands.

*****

"Daddy," Hoku whispered, fighting back tears. Makoa placed his finger gently on her lips, "Ssshhh."

This time, he stole into her shack when no one else was around. Their first encounter was nearly a

225

disaster. She noticed how a stranger tracked her movements. One day, while she sat alone gazing into the evening calm, Nehune men spear fished, knee-deep, in the village kai pond. Makoa quietly came up beside her and knelt down. She turned and shrieked. Several of the fishermen hurried over. Realizing it was her father, she persuaded them to leave. Now here he was again, alone with her.

Makoa said, "Friends of mine, Kyle and Luke, are here with me."

"I know Luke. I have seen him in the village. He can be trusted."

"Yes, he's been keeping watch over you." Makoa proceeded to describe Kyle so Hoku would recognize him. "They have charted an escape route for you. I will secure you loosely to the altar, and when Luke arranges for the right timing, Kyle will carry you away to safety."

Hoku searched his eyes. "But dad," pausing, she shuddered, "if I am rescued, it only means that..."

By now, Makoa understood their protocol: if her sacrifice blundered, then he would become the proxy sacrifice.

She feared for his life, but saving her outweighed any thought for himself.

Since being in their village, Makoa's prayers for Nehune filled his heart with compassion for them. Their storytelling and respect for creation moved him. Other than the dread of human sacrifice, life for Nehune was simple and free.

This was their world, soon to be shattered, neither by conquistador-like colonists, nor by scientists infatuated with gorilla theories, but by the intrusive

226

eyes of cameras---and the informational storm that would sweep across media networks.

17

Waning hours of the day lingered on the twilight mist. As the high priest, Kalani concentrated on the gibbous moon he had seen in a dream. It was a years-long sign for God's intervention, according to what his father, Tevake, prophesied.

Nehune priests were troubled by eerie billows of grey hovering high above their village. Vanatu, too, felt unnerved. As head chieftain, he sensed that his control over the villagers was in jeopardy.

Grimacing over the troubling weather, he complained, "Sky angry."

Standing next to him, Kalani said what Vanatu wanted hear, "Moon speaks. I get priests. We wait."

The ritual hut was situated within the perimeter of the temple grounds. Kalani and the priests entered in for an all-night vigil. Though Kalani was delighted by the sign of the gibbous moon, the ill-mood of the eve indicated that the virgin offering was unacceptable to the Lord God to whom all of the apostate rulers of darkness submit. From what Tevake taught him, Kalani knew this. While the other priests implored evil deities throughout the night for guidance, Kalani secretly prayed to the God of heaven to lead his people.

It never occurred to Vanatu and the other priests that the unsettled sphere had, for them, long been creation groaning because of their bloodshed. This time, by divine decree, human sacrifice would no longer be tolerated.

In the wisdom of a living creation, when the land becomes offended by evil deeds and groans under the weight of sin, God alone determines when to offset earth's harmonic balance into a series of dire outcomes.

During the all-night vigil, bursts of light lit the horizon, followed by violent rumblings and blustery winds. After long, grueling hours, the other priests became impatient because they did not receive any direction from vile, unseen beings. Meanwhile, Kalani tarried for the Lord to clarify his dream three years ago in which he saw the gibbous moon precede the star Arcturus in the constellation of Bootes. After its three year suspension in the northern celestial hemisphere, it would lead the constellation of Coma on a journey.

As the priests stepped out of the hut early in the morning, their angst was visible, but Kalani was at peace. Passing beyond the temple gate, they all knew the chiefs looked bewildered because of the night's tempest. They became anxious when one of the priests said, "Not receive direction."

When Vanatu heard this, he, too, seemed baffled. Accustomed to word from sinister dictums in the past, this unprecedented event meant he had no direction in what to do.

The fate of the virgin sacrifice now hung in the balance.

Luke signaled for Makoa to bind the long-awaited sacrifice to the raised platform on the bamboo altar in the middle of the temple ground. Hoku's voice crackled as she stared anxiously at him through watery eyes. "I love you daddy…"

Makoa's heart broke as he wrapped cordage around his daughter's trembling body while the villagers looked on below. Kyle was among them, visualizing how he would quickly climb up on the bamboo pyre, grab Hoku, and flee on the same path that led to the village, then to Luke's Zodiac covered with branches and leaves at Waikahalulu beach for their final escape.

Bending low toward her, Makoa whispered, "I love you, too, bebe girl."

She knew Kyle was poised to intervene, but her confidence was shaky over Luke's plan to thwart any attempt by the warriors to slay and burn her father as a result of her rescue.

As a sun child, virginity made her pure: an untainted offering meant, in the minds of Vanatu and his minions, an unhindered launch into the unknown.

Hoku pleaded under her breath, "Lord, help daddy! Do not hold this sin against the people."

Mercy is better than sacrifice and obedience more than burnt offering. This brave teen chose to obey the burning in her heart to pray for God's mercy instead of cursing her oppressors.

Alika, the head village strongman, had to act fast. He would not tolerate grooming Hoku for three years, only to be stumped by no direction that jeopardized the control of Vanatu, his chiefs and priests.

Irate by these strange occurrences, Vanatu took matters into his own hand by calling the chiefs and priests into a huddle just outside the temple walls. "Sky angry. Demand sacrifice NOW!"

When he said this, a burst of lightning permeated the air all around them. Seconds later, thunder rocked the sky. As if his demand was punctuated with a rebuke from God.

Shaken, some of the village young clung to the legs of men and women.

Kalani was appalled when he overheard Vanatu's desperate plea.

The villagers, too, were confused and fear-struck.

From the way the dark-hued clouds hung low, rain would soon spill in torrents. But this time it was meant for intervention, and not for innocent blood to be shed.

Vanatu ordered Alika and his strongmen back into the temple where Hoku lay bound. Alika felt the tethered branch bundles stacked under the altar was not enough. He commanded, "Much wood!"

Two villagers ran and added more bundles for a hotter flame to ensure the virgin would not be delivered by rain.

He shouted, "Fire!"

Numea ran up to the inside of the temple wall, grabbed a mounted torch, whisked back to the altar and waited for Alika's signal.

*****

Kawika and his friend moved relentlessly through the thick of the forest. With every step, he could hear Hanani plead *'Son, please don't try to rescue Hoku and dad, it's too risky.'*

Whoever got in Kawika's way was worth the risk: it was either them or his family. His friend, trained as a sniper in the military, came to help.

They paused to make sure their 30 round magazines were locked and tight on their AR-15s, pulled the slider bolts back and chambered their rounds.

Kawika looked up. The sky seemed like it wailed, sending a chill down his spine that made him shiver and hope this did not portend a gloomy outcome of his motives.

Looking through their own pairs of binoculars, they noticed minimal activity around the huts. Scanning the scene up ahead, it appeared that the majority of villagers were standing outside a large, rectangular-shaped area with bamboo walls, apparently forbidden from entering in.

They climbed a tree to get a better view of what was going on inside the walls and, adjusting their binoculars, saw feather-dressed chiefs, one of whom stood out for his regalia, and priests clad in togas gathering around a tower-like edifice in the center of the rectangular construct.

Among them, Kawika recognized the well-built native that held a torch. Numea stood next to the pile of branches beneath the tower. He turned to his friend and said, "You see that ripped dude holding the torch next to the pile of branches?"

"Yeah."

"He's the one that grabbed my sister and ran!"

Feeling the sting of vengeance in his heart, Kawika
scanned upward with his binoculars to see a
platform at the top of the tower-altar. He instantly
recognized his sister bound by cords, "Hoku!"
His friend turned his binocular upwards and
spurted, "What the hell?"
Unbeknownst to them, standing next to Numea was
Makoa---the proxy sacrifice for Hoku if anything
went wrong.
Adrenalin formed beads of sweat on Kawika's
forehead; his friend was anxious and emotionally
charged.

Bent on rescuing his sister, Kawika instructed his
friend, "Take out Numea. I'll go for the guy who
looks important."
He meant Vanatu.
They pulled on the shoulder straps of their rifles,
slid their weapons down their left arms to raise
them into position, fixed their separate aims at the
hearts of Numea and Vanatu through mounted
scopes, gripped the gun stock handles with fingers
beside the triggers and…
…*Boom! Boom!*

The sounds of their weapons were muffled by the
sudden boom of a blue lightning bolt that crackled
from the storm clouds into the center of the temple
next to the tower-altar. Bound to its platform, Hoku
screamed. Fear-struck, Vanatu, the chiefs and
priests fell back. Outside of the temple, the villagers
ducked.

The timing of deafening boom startled Kawika and his friend.

Kawika fired at Vanatu and only grazed his shoulder. Just as his friend felt his right shoulder jerk from the recoil, Makoa stepped into his line of fire to shove Numea aside as he was lowering the torch to the cluster of dry branches on Alika's signal.

Lowering their rifles, they grabbed their binoculars to see what happened: Kawika and his friend knew something was wrong: a native fell limp, while Numea and Vanatu were still standing.

*****

Struggling in the ferocious winds through rugged bush that led to the village, Hanani began to gasp, heave, bow over and dropped to the ground. "*AAAAAHHEEEE!!*" She screamed fitfully, "Something just happened to Makoa! *Aaahh*...something terrible happened to my husband!"

Hanani wailed and flung uncontrollably as she muttered the same words over and over as if she had suddenly gone mad. Dana, confused and scared, tried to solace her grief-stricken friend.

*****

Makoa managed to grab the torch out of Numea's hand, but with his fatal wound, the torch flung from his hand and onto the branches.

Stoked by winds, the dry fuel burned quickly.

234

Feeling the heat of the rising flames, Hoku filled the air with blood curdling screams! Struggling to free herself, the sennit cords with which she was bound loosened immediately.
Just as Makoa planned.

The rain.
It fell with vengeance.
But the fire continued to rise beneath the virgin.

Kawika instructed his friend, "Wait here while I climb down to investigate."
"I'll keep an eye on you through my binoculars." His friend said.

Kawika burst out of the forest, passed the village, and toward the temple walls. Running, he held his rifle up and fired random shots in the air to clear the path leading to its entry.
All too familiar with the power of a fire stick, the natives dispersed, en masse.

Just then, Hanani and Dana emerged from the forest: fair-skinned, exhausted and drenched.
When the villagers saw them, they were afraid.
Looking wildly at each other, they stopped and knelt in the mud and heavy rain.
With the fire burning beneath the altar, Vanatu, Numea, Alika and the others, thinking Makoa was struck by lightning, left the temple ground for fear of their lives.
Once outside of the temple walls, Vanatu raised his hand for the others to stop. Surprised by the

villagers kneeling in the mud, he knew they were awed by the women standing there: one whose red-streaked hair clung to her porcelain skin; and the other with greenish eyes recessed in a cherubic face behind golden strands.

Kalani's prayer for clarity of his dream had bowed to a sequence of events timed precisely by the Lord. Christ heard the cries of parents whose daughter was about to be the victim of a death ritual, and the cries of innocent natives seeking reprieve from their oppressive plight.

Seeing the high chief and others leave, Kawika made a beeline to the tower-altar.
The rain fell heavily, dousing the stubborn fire.
Out of nowhere, he saw Kyle scurrying up the crude construct where Hoku was numb with fear.
Focused on his sister, Kawika paid no mind to the man who lay face down in the mud.
As soon as Kyle helped Hoku down, she fell into Kawika's arms and nearly fainted. Weak, she glanced over his shoulders and saw, through half-dazed eyes, what had become of their father.
Regaining her strength, she broke away from Kawika and fell upon Makoa as blood gushed out of his chest. "Daddy...DAAADDY!!!" She screamed, convinced that Numea slew him with a bone dagger.
In shocked dismay, Kawika realized what went wrong. "NOOOO!!!"

The rain slowed into a gentle drizzle carried by softer winds.

Brother and sister wept aloud over their father's body.

Kyle watched in stunned silence.

Hanani and Dana stood next to the large, flat stone and tree of blood outside the temple walls that Luke explained in detail to Kyle. Why there standing next to the stone and tree frightened the villagers. Were these heavenly deities here to cleanse what were used for blood and defilement? Was this a sign? If so, what would the significance of this sign be?

Luke was concerned that Hanani and Dana came to Kahoolawe against his counsel. Wondering why the natives were kneeling before them, they both looked at Luke for a response.

Mistaking them as angels, Kalani faced the fair-skinned women and tore his toga. As their acting high priest, the other priests followed his move. The chiefs, too, ripped their garments until they were ragged and disheveled. As a show of guilt, they put mud on their heads.

Vanatu, and the warriors surrounding him, remained standing.

Alika, blinded by rage, stood defiantly and ran.

Kalani pleaded, "Hold us not wrong." He believed that penitence would avert a similar, thunderous fate on him and his people.

Taken aback, Hanani and Dana said nothing.

Nehune held Luke to be a descendant of a harvest deity, and Hoku as a sun child. They only heard of fair skin, green eyes or golden hair as divine attributes in their legends and chants.

Vanatu concluded that sun had come with moon. Lightning and thunder hailed their earthbound journey to rescue a child of the sun. He hailed, "Sun! Moon!"

From Tevake's teachings, Kalani thought their appearance from heaven might signal a glorious destiny for Nehune if they turned from their wicked ways.

Tormented by the echoes of Hanani's warning, Kawika stood up, threw his rifle in disgust, fell back on his knees, pound his fist in the mud and cried out, "Nnnooo! NnoooOOO!!"

Kyle stared at him, puzzled.

Kawika wailed, "I convinced my friend to come and help. I told him to aim for Numea. I did this! I killed him! I killed dad!"

Hoku continued weeping, too stricken with grief to hear what Kawika was saying.

Sorrow, tears and confusion within the temple walls were the antithesis of silent reverence on the outside.

Hanani and Dana could only guess at Kalani's behavior that prompted the others to follow suit, while Vanatu's feathered regalia remained in-tact. In what was unfolding, this was a sign of bravery, or defiance.

Luke walked quietly toward them. Not bowing when he approached them was, in Nehune's minds, consistent with his perceived status.

At this juncture, Vanatu, concerned only for his own hide, knelt and abruptly clung to the fold of Luke's clothes, stopping him in his tracks. He muttered, "We not know why Sun and Moon come!"

Having dealt with him in the past, Luke was skeptical. He noticed the blood streak on his shoulder where Kawika's shot had grazed him. Vanatu was obsessed with holding on to power. Except for the warriors, he ruled the lower caste villagers with a heavy hand.

When he turned to look at Kalani, Luke saw wild, bloodshot eyes that bore the strain of fatigue and perplexity. Kalani pleaded with Hanani and Dana, "We not want die. Not hold this bad with Hoku against people."

Luke looked up and caught Hanani's piercing gaze. Dana, ever the scientist, mused over the broken English of the chiefs and priests, unaware that Luke's dad snuck tutors into the village long ago at the request of the chiefs to teach them and the priests the English language.

Dana leaned over to Hanani and whispered, "Judging by his regalia, that man clinging to Luke must be the high chief. Notice how he did not tear his clothes like the others?"

Luke called out to Hanani and Dana and, gesturing toward Vanatu, said, "He and the others have assumed that I am a descendant of a harvest deity, and Hoku is a child of Sun---your child, Hanani!"

"Me?"

"Yes, you."

Appalled, Hanani shook her head in disgust.

"They all think that you, Dana, as Moon!"

Dana looked perplexed.

Makoa's bloody, lifeless body was straddled across Kawika's arms when he stepped outside of the temple gate. Kyle was beside him, stone-faced. Hunched over and weeping, Hoku followed slowly behind.

Sobbing, Kawika placed his father gently on the ground. Hanani ran up to them and knelt next to Makoa. Trembling, she covered her mouth and wept.

Speechless, Dana wondered how Hanani knew that something happened to Makoa on their way here. When Hoku came up beside her, Hanani's grief was mixed with joy. All the villagers watched in silence as Sun wept over Makoa and with her child. Afraid that the torrential rains were tears that flowed from Hanani's eyes, what would she do to them for taking Hoku?

A sudden shriek came from the forest canopy as Alika ran toward Hoku with a stone-head weapon. Bent on killing the intended sacrifice, he yelled, "She DIE so we live!!"

Kawika pulled out a hunting knife strapped on his ankle and stepped in front of his mother and sister. Kyle stood next to him, poised.

Alarmed, Hanani stood to her feet. Kawika said, "Mom. He's talking about Hoku! Stay behind me and Kyle."

As Alika drew closer, Hanani's mind reeled. With her husband gone, she was not about to let anything happened to Hoku. Full of adrenalin, she pushed passed Kawika and Kyle, glared at Alika and yelled with all of her might, "YOU WILL NOT KILL MY DAUGHTER!!"

The sky flashed and the crackle of a blue thunderbolt struck Alika dead!

Nehune were shocked, breathless at her swift retribution for Alika's cold defiance and murderous intent. Calling down thunder from the still-dreary clouds frightened them.

But it wasn't the power of Sun. It was Power greater than the sun and moon; greater than stars and universes. It came from heaven as a sign that the shedding of innocent blood would no longer be tolerated.

Hanani turned and shouted while the people were still reeling from Alika's dramatic demise.

"WE ARE NOT SUN AND MOON!"

Dana, Kyle and Luke were caught off guard. The timing of her defense for Hoku followed by a lightening spear thrust into Alika from the sky was leverage for survival, but this admission could prove fatal!

Hanani stood firm with Hoku at her side and repeated more emphatically, "I am *not* Sun and she," pointing to Dana, "is *not* Moon!"

241

While chiefs and priests were stunned, confused, Vanatu seemed pleased with this. Commoners looked at each other with wild, dashing eyes. They turned their gaze toward Luke. What would he say? Knowing the risks, Luke said, "I am not a harvest deity. I allowed all of you to believe this to keep Hoku alive!"

The villagers understood enough to know that they were no longer in danger. Though stumped, they slowly but steadily seemed relieved.

Luke became nervous. Dana and Kyle braced themselves. After Hawaiians found out that Captain James Cook was not a harvest deity, a series of events resulted in his death in the shallows of Kealakekua Bay. They were at the mercy of Vanatu who could turn on them quickly.

If Hanani and Dana were not Sun and Moon, and Luke the descendant of a harvest deity untrue, then who were they?

Who was Hoku?

And why, upon their sudden emergence from the forest did the storm slow to a drizzle and the winds calmed? Was the heavy downpour shortly before their appearance intended only to douse the sacrificial fire?

Kalani stood slowly. The priests, chiefs and commoners followed. Relieved, he seized this opportunity to turn Nehune back to the God of their fathers. Looking at Hanani he said, "Not Sun?" Turning to Dana, he continued, "Not Moon?" Hanani and Dana nodded in agreement.

Out of the corner of his eyes, Kawika saw Vanatu nod at Numea and the other warriors. They promptly turned and left.

"Your legends say you are descendants of Tarani." Hanani said.

Vanatu became visibly angry. If they revealed what they knew of this legend, he risked losing control. Keeping the people ignorant was an effective deterrent from their legacy.

Rays of light suddenly encompassed Hanani, Dana and Hoku, not unusual when sunlight pierces the clouds after heavy rains.

The timing of this confounded everyone, especially Kalani. In the ray of light from the visible sun he, alone, saw a brilliant angel descend with a sword in his hand and stand not far from Hanani, Dana and Hoku. He struck and shattered the large flat stone. When he struck the tree, it was set aflame.

Kalani watched in awe. He and Nehune, all of whom were shocked, witnessed a portent of what would become of the earth because of evil and the shedding of innocent blood.

When Kalani bowed low to the ground in reverence to the Lord, Nehune fell to their knees in fear.

Rage blinded Vanatu from the significance of the flat stone being shattered and the burning tree. Fixed on Kalani cowering before the two women and child in radiant glory, Vanatu grew more enraged. Kalani was the fulcrum of religious rituals and human sacrifices. As acting high priest, he was expected to damn these humans who were now disclaiming the status of their deity.

Once their blood was spilled, Vanatu could hold on to power.

The massive, heavenly being watched as the warriors came out of their huts with crude weapons of wood and stone.

Risking certain death, Kalani bravely raised his voice, "My father Tevake tell me we belong God and worship Him alone!"
"KILL HIM!" Vanatu ordered.
The Spirit of the Lord opened the eyes of Numea and his men. Horrified, they watched as the angel stepped forward and stood there, holding a sapphire sword that glistened in his hand---the same color of the thunderbolt that killed Alika.

Dropping their weapons, the warriors kneeled with their faces to the ground. Cowering warriors was unthinkable. They enforced Vanatu's decades of rule over these puny-minded villagers. Perpetual servitude at his beck-and-call made their island haven a castle, privileged with the opulence of tropical fare.
Seeing that all was lost, Vanatu picked up one of their weapons to kill Kalani. The angel of the Lord intervened and struck him dead.
Like the flat stone and tree, no one but Kalani saw what hit Vanatu as he fell, face down.

Suddenly, the atmosphere surged with an unseen Fire that burn in the souls of men.

From the greatest to the least among them, the power of His presence pierced their hearts.

Then the Spirit of the Lord opened all of their eyes. Everyone fell prostrate as the Lord appeared next to the angel. His face shone like lightening and His eyes were blue flames. Known as the Voice of prophets, Wisdom of sages, and Ancient of days, a deep, abiding calm was in Him, like seas stilled after a fierce tempest, with an uncompromising holiness that affirm His justice and righteousness. Jesus said, "No more bloodshed. All of you must endure what is to come. Be faithful and follow Me." His voice pierced through their language barrier, causing all of them to clearly understand His words. The brightness of His glory radiated out from Kealaikahiki. Even the wealthy at Kanapou Bay stopped what they were doing when they sensed that something powerful was happening at the west end. Some that had been searching for truth were gripped in their hearts by the distant resonance of His words. The Light that shone in the west shined in them on the east end to follow Jesus Christ, the Son of God. All of a sudden, this deep sense of what they achieved and possessed meant nothing. Little did they and everyone at Kanapou Bay know that their opulent enclave on the midland slopes, above the luxuriant sprawl down below, would soon be no more.

The shattered stone and burning tree at Kealaikahiki signaled the impending judgements of God throughout the earth for the shedding of innocent blood and for evils hailed by the wicked as good.

All that mankind has built according to his visions
of self-glory, would soon be no more.

Nehune remained prostrate from the intensity of
Christ's presence. A few of them gained the
courage to look up when they heard His voice.
After the Lord spoke, He and the angel disappeared.

Part VII

Shadow Commission

18

As head of the Shadow Commission, Dr. Dawkins Gould was a well-respected zoologist in ivy-league circles. Mainstream intellectuals hung on his word when he pontificated on human evolution. He looked at Dr. Chloe Hansen and smirked, "Sir Carlton Lyell was a colleague of Charles Darwin. Like the Galapagos Islands, he and his team of scientists saw Kahoolawe as a natural laboratory. This mid-Pacific ecology was a perfect location to *test* the theory of evolution."

Chloe puzzled, "Test?"

In her late fifties, Dr. Julie Glen was seated at the round table. A behavioral ecologist, her red outfit blended with the red-gold symbol flag that hung on the wall behind her. She explained, "They convinced authorities to round up a sample-group of Nehune from Kauai in the late 1800s and put them on Kahoolawe. Once there, they were closely studied for decades to see if they would re-adapt to their ancient ways."

Other well-dressed elites were seated in the dimly-lit room.

It was their protocol to keep the lights low and the room sterile from micro-cameras or electronic bugs. It always made Chloe uneasy when summoned to convene with these erudites that were unknown to the outside world. She wasn't even aware that their names were fabricated.

An island girl, she felt some pride when she responded, "Similar to what was accomplished in five short years on the ahupuaa. Hawaiians proved they could re-assimilate ancient methods to achieve self-sufficiency in all aspects of survival. In so doing, they discovered multi-disciplinary applications in modern science and research."

Economist Davis Chan smirked, "I know. I saw the data. Impressive. It aligns with what Dr. Pahono articulated at the signing ceremony, and more."

Puzzled look.

He leaned over and smirked, "Our scout, Dr. Hansen, was in the crowd."

"Oh."

Davis added, "Certain industry sectors are already using some of this information to increase infrastructural efficiencies."

Chloe felt some remorse but was careful not to show it. "Since the ahupuaa and Kula excavation site were shut down, I have all data and findings under lock and key. Some of the information was published in a few industry journals. We can glean through the unpublished archives that may be deemed suitable for research and development in other market sectors."

Curious, she glanced at Julie first, then the others. "Were Nehune *able* to re-adapt to their ancient ways?"

"All too well," Bonnie Dale answered. Bright, pretty, young and reckless, she was the commission's media liaison when spinning their agenda. In her quick-witted, innocent kind-of-way, her on-air presence was calm and persuasive.

Her curiosity piqued, Chloe pressed, "And this proved *what* about testing the theory of evolution?"

Everyone looked in the direction of Dawkins. He piped, "Chimps, gorillas, orangutans and homo sapiens are in the same hominidae taxonomy."

Chloe quipped, "I know."

Dawkins mocked, "This longitudinal study that Julie looked into revealed their instincts to be more chimp, gorilla and orangutan-like, and less homo-sapien. Their ability to appear civilized was only to the extent that they assimilated western behavior on Kauai. You know, monkey see, monkey do?"

Chloe looked dead-serious. Some of the members couldn't hold their giggles.

"When returned to a remote isolation," Dawkins continued, "they de-assimilated from western behavior and, by instinct, behaved more like the lesser-evolved primates that they are."

Chloe felt her gut tighten with this twisted line of reasoning. People forced into remote isolation against their will have been known to survive, even thrive, as did the Nehune. It had nothing to do with being lesser-evolved primates. Recent encounters with Luke compelled her to regret working for them. The love she felt for him when they first met, and the brief time they were together never left her. Status and pay were more than she ever dreamed, along with enviable perks and globetrotting. But the aching in her heart made none of this matter. In her sleepless, fitful nights, she became acutely aware of how entangled the Shadow Commission was with high-placed players.

Their mantra was from a dark script replete with the cursive of power-mongery and strange, hubristic creeds of feigned innocence cloaked in weird science.

Even the slightest, far-away look could cue them that her loyalty was starting to wane. Appearing to be onboard with what he just explained, she asked, "And the end *goal* of this study?"

A professor of world religions, Phillip Bolten took a sip of his coffee, leaned over and smiled, "To determine if their monotheism would remain intact in their primal state of existence," another sip, "surprisingly, it did."

Confused, she inquired. "What does *monotheism* have to do with any of this?"

"Everything. You see, Dr. Hansen, this is a problem for us because it aligns with billions that believe in one God under the banner of Christendom."

She could hardly believe her ears.

He continued, "Ed Tylor theorized that polytheism preceded monotheism, and therefore, concluded that primitives believed in multiple deities presiding over the forces of nature. Apart from the monotheism of one supreme God, their systematic practices and rituals immortalized multiple deities."

Chloe remembered Luke explaining that Nehune believed in one God when they first settled Hawaii, before the pantheon of gods and goddesses from Tahiti crept in.

Highlighting another aspect of their madness, Phillip said, "Sir Carlton Lyell's data detailed Nehune savagery, the kind of documented proof scientists needed to substantiate their work."

Chloe probed, "Proof?"

Phillip glanced at the head of the Commission. Dawkins interjected, "Proof that Nehune were, and remain, inferior segments of the hominidae taxonomy."

Feeling the urge to shake her head in disgust, Chloe resisted.

Shifting to a related topic, Phillip added, "Missionaries brought with them a book."

She thought, *'Why is he mentioning missionaries?'*

Phillip looked disgusted. "Hawaiians called it Papala Hemolele. Biblical creeds affirm the belief in God that *made* of one blood all *nations* of men, not *evolved races* of men. This goes against the creeds of our Commission."

Her mind reeled in silent protest. *'Creeds?'* When she was first hired, they had no mission statement, no paper trail, no recording. During the round-table job interview, their subtle, deceptive words now echoed in her memories like sea sirens in Greek mythology: mariners mesmerized by their enchanting melodies from afar were lured to their deaths. Blinded to scientific half-truths that are rife in their academic fields, she was hooked by the lure of money and perks.

Phillip continued, "The social construct of race is, by default, inherently divisive. Academics, backed by scientific ideology, have enabled people in power to manipulate nation against nation. We all know about the rise and fall of totalitarian despots and the policies of war-mongers."

This was weighty, inner-circle stuff. They watched Chloe closely to see if she would flinch.

Cold and remorseless, Dawkins chimed, "Confusion creates failures and failures create voids. Voids become vacuums. The void of God creates a vacuum that we fill with our evolutionary theory." Phillip stood from his seat for flair and effect to recite what he knew so well. "Ah, yes, Nietzsche's classic parable of the madman: '*God is dead. God remains dead. And we have killed him. How shall we comfort ourselves, the murderers of all murderers? What was holiest and mightiest of all that the world has yet owned has bled to death under our knives: who will wipe this blood off us? What water is there for us to clean ourselves? What festivals of atonement, what sacred games shall we have to invent? Is not the greatness of this deed too great for us? Must we ourselves not become gods simply to appear worthy of it?*'"

Smirking, Dawkins gave his finishing touch to this parable. "Nietzsche's God-is-dead idea necessitated the rise of *ubermenschs,* above-human, supermen, whose will-to-power fills the God-void. Ubermenschs such as Joseph Stalin, Adolph Hitler and Mao Zedong." Dawkins paused and motioned at everyone around the table. "*We* are ubermenschs!"

Out of uniform, the well-groomed man reminded Chloe of Luke: slightly shorter, rougher looks, more stout and heartless. He became involved with the commission since the missile silo was in its planning stages. Successful completion would result in his access to inner circles of government.

The tone of General Saul Cohen's voice was callous, "One word, Dr. Hansen. Control."

'The nature of God transcends the heights of human intellect; the worship of God in spirit and truth frees people that once hailed deception as truth....' echoed in her memories. Dr. Kyle Pahono slipped this in at one of his symposium presentations. Seen as the inclusion of church at a state-funded event, she thought it was pure gall. Now, for reasons she could not explain, it started to make sense. In context, this Commission's intent was revelatory: man worshipping himself and forging in his image everything he could control.

Phillip applauded, "Well-said, General Cohen. With our indoctrination of a naturalistic worldview, science can be god without the knowledge of God. The Genesis account, or all beliefs that acknowledge a Sky-Father who created the world, is now laughed to scorn by the intelligentsia. Our science dictates human origin: past, present and future; dictate that people evolve. The weak are, and will remain, ruled by the fittest."
"Like all of us here on this Commission." Gordon Zeit blurted as he stood to pour himself another cup of coffee.
Everyone around the table chuckled.
A high-placed government official gone rogue, Gordon spent decades in foreign espionage. The death of his closest allies by CIA operatives hardened him. Not a shred of dignity was left. Anything that breathed could not be trusted—

brown, black, white. Didn't matter. Commission members knew this. Still, his abilities were useful.

For the first time, Chloe felt repulsed as she thought, '*Who in their sphere of influence are involved in this megalomaniacal scheme?*' She voiced, "Conclusions on a wide-range of findings in field research disciplines are often speculative. Attempts to re-create the past are subjective. None of us will ever be able to determine, accurately, the precise thinking of ancient societies. The past can only be recreated from fragments that yield different interpretations from scientists."
Raising her voice, Julie boasted, "Nonetheless, Dr. Hansen, our theory has effectively constructed the alternate worldview of man as an australopithecine."
Phillip mocked, "Was it not Bertrand Russell who said that '*there is something feeble and a little contemptible about a man who cannot face the perils of life without the help of comfortable myths?*'
Dawkins chimed in, "Don't you see, Dr. Hansen. Those who believe in God as Creator have been effectively labeled by academics as *weak-minded*. Intellectuals like us prefer to believe in evolution which has enlightened the masses," he glared at her, "for over a hundred years!"
Some of them laughed at one of many jabs Dawkins was known for. He continued, "If scholars and like-minded scientists can propagate theories about polytheism as fact, then a naturalistic worldview becomes the foundation upon which the pillars of

evolution can support all ideological constructs that argue for man the measure and science the panacea."

Chloe cleared her throat and shifted in her chair.

In smooth tones, Dawkins continued, "Nehune were horded to Kahoolawe. What they did to survive over the generations is politically expedient. Consider, Dr. Hansen, the geo-political consequences: man-over-nature; civilized-man-over-primitive-man; conquest and slavery."

When Kyle and Dana found the Pacific Archaeology Society, it was to counter evolutionary ideas long entrenched in the western mind. That she was tapped to represent the Commission's ideas as true, while sustaining their web of lies, gave Chloe deep pause.

Dawkins continued, "Sir Carlton Lyell's original intent to test the theory of evolution on Kahoolawe has, in our minds, *succeeded*. Where this scientific experiment has *failed* is by the actions of a retired admiral, what's his name, ah, Luke Moresi."

Chloe's expression changed, "I don't understand?"

"While living among Nehune, he learned of a rogue priest who held to the belief in one God. If this belief is rekindled among them, it threatens the sum of Darwin's, Tylor's and Lyell's work. Native peoples from all corners of the globe that have floundered in their belief in a Creator could unite and protest the damage done by evolution on their beliefs. With this kind of momentum, the overarching risk is for the masses to turn from believing they evolved to being created in the image of this one God."

Julie added, "If the world discovers why these people were confined to an island for over a century, reporters will label this as the ultimate racist scheme that could effectively undermine the evolutionary sciences. Tylor's documents will go viral over the Internet. People will realize how deep this racism goes when they read his data showing Nehune natives to be inferior primates."

Tapping his fingers on the table, Saul cleared his throat, "Leveling what they've perfected for over a century and replacing the area with a missile silo will bury all evidence from scientists seeking to affirm news reports of their existence. Once we get them off the island, we can commence with the silo. It will be easy from there to convince the media that they are nothing but a bunch of Hawaiian misfits still pissed off over the shootout at Kanapou Bay."

Chloe asked, "You all seem confident about the constructs of evolutionary sciences. Did I hear all of you right?"

"Yes. You did!" Dawkins admitted. Then, as if the veil of deception lifted off his mind for a brief moment, he said, "Evolution is said to be a theory, because it *is* a theory! To date, we have found no scientific evidence to, for example, link when humans branched off from apes on the evolutionary tree, even if human-ape DNA is 95 to 98% similar. Regardless, this theory had gained so much traction that funding became available to continue with research. Funded research was, and is, political, because we need legislators to enact laws that drive policies to ensure funding. Once steady funding was involved, this missing link was overshadowed by the growing numbers of people that started to believe evolution as fact."

The commission members were aghast, stunned by what he just said. With no reasonable explanation, Dawkins just revealed their closely held secret that exposed the depth of their deception.

Awkward pause.

Chloe queried, "How is Luke Moresi tied to the failed efforts of Darwin, Tylor and Lyell?"

His left brow raised, Dawkins agitated, "He was told by this rogue priest of a secret symbol that has some kind of power to deliver people. We were able to affirm this in Nehune legends. The problem is that this symbol is not just an idea, but tangible proof that this power exists. We can't have proof of this power interfering with the power of an idea that our predecessors, and us, have successfully persuaded the masses to believe in for over a century!"

Part VIII

Follow the Shooting Star

19

The popular espresso café on the beachside of the Royal Hawaiian hotel was Luke's favorite hangout. Given the stressors in life, it was therapeutic to breathe in the commanding view of the ocean with sail boats skimming on the surface against a stark-blue horizon.

Chewing on a custard pastry and sipping his coffee, Kyle pondered on the etchings on the cave wall of a large, single stick figure with three, smaller stick figures below. A line was chiseled from the center figure down to a series of stick figures followed by canoes and other migratory symbols depicting their journey from land and sea---all of which ended with the symbol of Jesus, God our Savior detailed by Luke. Sipping more of his coffee, it became clear to him as he spoke out loud, "The large stick figure is God. The three smaller figures below represent Abraham, Isaac and Jacob. The line from the center figure that connects a series of stick figures represents Nehune, the children of Isaac. Their journey led them here where they hid the symbol that was coded into the end of their cave mural."

"Wow." Dana was lost in her own thoughts as she bit into her pumpkin bread and sipped green tea. Realizing she didn't hear a word he said, Kyle quickly shifted his attention. "Good?"

"Not this. Our experience." Dana rolled her eyes.

Nodding, Kyle said, "Oh. I know. I was blown away. Believing Jesus rose from the dead is one thing, but to see Him like that was powerful!"

Luke walked up from behind. Overhearing them, he quipped, "A fitting experience for scientists. Secularists will have trouble debunking what all of us witnessed as..."

"Myths?" Kyle finished.

Luke sat down, leaned on the table and responded, "Given your reputations, they will think the both of you have lost it. I can see the headline in an Archaeology article titled: *Island Scientists Claim Encounter with God.*

Dana chuckled, "Ha. Ha. Yeah, and an article in Navy Today titled: *Ex-Admiral's Religious Fairytales.*

"So, how are you, Admiral Luke?" Kyle teased.

"Refreshed."

Overhearing Kyle, the waitress asked, "Admiral, the usual this morning?"

Luke winced.

"Oops, I mean Luke."

"The usual."

He turned to them, "She's been here since I was on active duty."

A waiter, facing Tiare, turned and pointed at their table. Walking up to them, she dropped her wallet. Luke scooted his chair out, bent down, reached for her wallet and gave it to her. She smiled, "Thanks, Luke."

Kyle goaded, "Butter fingers."

"Moke!" Tiare playfully smirked.

Chuckling, Dana said, "I knew you would come."

"When I heard your voicemail, I dropped everything to be here for Hanani."

The mood turned somber when they turned to see Hanani approaching from outside the cafe.

The red streaks in her long, dark hair were pronounced in the morning sun that warmed her fair skin. She came to Oahu to get Malia while Kawika and Hoku remained on Kahoolawe. Opening the glass door, loss was etched all over her face. She had little time to process her life with Makoa.

When Dana saw her, she grieved. Here she was sitting with Kyle, and both her friends lost their husbands.

Hanani sat and greeted them.

Tiare leaned close and rubbed her back. "He and Po'o are…"

Stiff response, "I know," she softened, "probably playing ukuleles instead of harps."

Kyle smiled. "Or begging an angelic chef to make sushi and shrimp tempura."

"Don't forget lobster with butter and garlic." Dana chimed in.

The waitress looked up from the adjacent table and came over to their table.

Hanani pointed on the menu and said, "I'll have a tall coconut and macadamia nut coffee combo with whip cream and cinnamon. Oh, and this lemon cake." She opened her purse, pulled out a tissue and dabbed below her watery eyes.

"Whatever we can do to help you through this." Luke offered somberly.

Kyle and Dana agreed.

Hanani requested, "At least attend the funeral." The mention of 'funeral' triggered her encounter at Kealaikahiki.

"We'll be right next to you." Tiare assured her. Tiare's words slowed, faded, as Hanani reflected, trance-like, on that fateful evening….

…The villagers had prepared a hut for her, Hoku and Kawika. The sight of Christ in His beauty strengthened her and the kids to embrace Makoa's death, knowing that his spirit was with the Lord. Finally, after 2am in the morning, Kawika and Hoku dozed off. Hanani knelt, leaned forward with her face low to the ground, and prayed….

Staring at her, Tiare said, "Hanani, did you hear me?"

…After nearly an hour, she heard someone approaching. Sitting up, she saw light piercing through the walls of the hut. The being of light gently pushed the door open and stepped into the hut. Reaching into the side of his radiant robe, taut at the waist with a golden sash, he removed what seemed to be a small scroll and said, "I have come to give you this…"

Tiare pressed, "Hanani?"

…Speechless, she reached out her hand and took it. He immediately turned to leave. She stood to follow him outside, but he had disappeared. She looked down and saw footprints in the sand, the outlines of which glowed. Awed by this encounter, she remembered what she was holding. When she opened her hand, the scroll dissipated. As it did, images of Makoa's burial preparations were clear in her mind, except for a part that left her puzzled…

263

When the waiter placed the coffee combo and a slice of lemon cake down in front of Hanani, it jarred. "Thanks."

Luke and Kyle looked on as Dana leaned over. Hanani lifted her head to meet Dana's green-eyed gaze. "What?"

"Nothing," Dana caught herself, "blown away how the Lord's appearance was so bright that it was blinding. When I looked up, I could see the blue flames in His eyes."

Hanani was in awe, "Words cannot describe His power and authority when we all beheld Him."

Kyle agreed then shifted. "Had no idea angels get that big. He was huge! And his sword!"

Dana mused, "The way Alika died after you yelled at him was crazy."

Luke interjected, "We knew when Alika died that something was happening. We just couldn't see it."

Hanani shivered. "See it?" Hanani shivered, "you could *feel* it! What else would account for the flat stone just shattering and the tree suddenly set on fire?"

"When Kalani's eyes got big as he threw himself on the ground, I thought someone hit him from behind." Kyle confessed.

Luke shook his head, "Numea and his boys? I've never seen such fear in the eyes of men trained to kill. That freaked me out!"

Rapt by their divine encounters, Tiare shook her head. "Gosh, I wish I was there to see it all!"

A hush came over them. Solemn, Hanani said, "When Jesus rose from the dead, there was an earthquake. Some saints came out of their graves and were seen by people in the city. Death has no sting so the grave is powerless. He and those He chooses are neither confined by time, dimension, or the grave."

Brows furrowed, heads wagging, they were still trying to wrap their minds around all that happened.

On the table next to them, the rotund tourist in the Hibiscus-printed shirt and khaki shorts put his fork down. His wife, dressed in a loose fitted muumuu printed with bird-of-paradise flowers, sipped on her coffee. He leaned over and whispered, *"Bunch of religious nut cases rambling about some fantasy encounter. We came here to relax, not listen to this crap!"*

*****

Cliff's labor of love in Aotearoa formed into a ministry called Te Ora, or New Life. It was structured to bridge the divide between Maori culture and pakeha Christianity. Similarly, the ministry of Isle Breaz on the Big Island was started to heal the rifts between Hawaiian culture and haole Christianity. As lava flowed from Kilauea creating acreages of new land, the ministry of reconciliation was like a healing balm on generational wounds inflicted by religion.

Like Te Ora, Isle Breaz came under close scrutiny by church hierarchy. Some condescended out of piety. Others reserved their judgement over the use of native regalia, songs and dances of Polynesia to

265

communicate the message of hope to indigenous peoples.

Cliff's move to Oahu proved fruitful in re-uniting with his extended family. Impressed by Malia's poetic recital on the night of their Waimea Bay reunion, he persuaded Makoa and Hanani to let her join a tour he arranged with Te Ora and Isle Breaz. They agreed. Malia was excited to learn about first-nations people and international cultures in Canada, California, South Africa, Aotearoa, Samoa, Tonga and back to Hawaii. But her tour was cut short while in Aotearoa. Devastated by the news of her father, Cliff let her grieve as he arranged to accompany her back to Oahu so they could be at Makoa's funeral on Kahoolawe.

*****

Kalani was asleep in their hut. Still awake, Nahiena thought of when she had been suspicious of how Makoa and Kyle were elusive while launch preparations were in full swing. When she found Makoa hiding behind palm fronds, kneeling and interceding for Nehune, she knew he was standing in the gap left by her son. Dozing off, she dreamed the same dream back then: Tevake warned her to say nothing about Makoa and Kyle.

Shortly before dawn, she awoke, sat up and pondered on this dream. Light rays peering through the hut openings roused Kalani out of sleep.

Waiting till he was fully awake, she firmly asserted,
"Father breathe in Makoa mouth in cave."
Kalani lowered his head in shame.
Nahiena added, "You not take birthright from
father."
Silence.
"Makoa dead," she grieved. "You now humble to
God, help people."
He remembered telling this to Makoa in Luke's hut.
With Makoa gone, Kalani was left to carry this
legacy forward.

*****

Their best artisans hollowed out a seven-foot long
sandalwood log, deep and wide enough to
accommodate Makoa's six-foot frame, and a cover
made of the same fragrant wood to fit on top.
Hanani instructed them to shape the log into a
canoe-coffin, and then prepare two cross beams that
would be fastened to an outrigger.
No mast, no sail.
Strange request in light of their burial customs, but
they did not question Hanani. Nahiena obliged
Hanani's wishes that Kalani preside over the
ceremony as a priest of God, whose Son Nehune
saw with their own eyes.

Before the burial ceremony, Nahiena declared to her
people, "From Kalani's dream, husband see we sail
new land. He say blood on Kealaikahiki soil from
body sail on water and wind. Go before us."

267

When Alika was struck by lightning, there was no blood. Falling face down to his death, Vanatu did not bleed.

Makoa was the only one that bled.

Nahiena went on, "He tell Kalani dream meaning before die."

Kalani's eyes were locked on his mother as she said Kalani dreamed of a canoe fashioned from fragrant wood and filled with spices and ointments. Tevake knew it will symbolize the star Arcturus. He said in the canoe will lay a man whose death will end human sacrifice among Nehune, a man who reveres Bootes, the Coming Shepherd-King. Kalani saw the canoe suspended for three days upon the sea, alone, abandoned to God. Tevake assured Kalani and Nahiena that Nehune will know when to go and find the canoe on land in the direction they set sail. He said where they find the canoe will be their temporary place of refuge. Tevake was emotional when he explained to them that soon after, Coma, the star that Nehune have known for many generations as the Desire of the Nations, will be the brightest in the sky to guide them back to Kahoolawe for a permanent resettlement and to become a blessing to all peoples.

Tevake's interpretation of Kalani's dream provided the missing piece to Hanani as she pondered, *'Abandoned to God? No wonder I did not envision sails on his canoe.'*

Villagers gathered in a large circle around the sandalwood hull set on bamboo stilts in the center.

Inside, Makoa's malo-clad body had been placed on layers of spiced tapa that hung over the sides, and ti-leaves soaked with awapuhi and pikake oils. Hanani asked Cliff to bring a large bolt of deep-purple cloth he had from Aotearoa, the same material he made his priestly wear for the ceremony on the mound.

"The color of his true heritage," she whispered, teary eyed. She wanted purple to represent Makoa's spiritual royalty from God.

Before the hull was set in place, Cliff and Hanani unrolled and hung the purple cloth loosely along the sides to cover the bamboo stilts like a skirt on the bottom.

Makoa's hands were not folded over his chest, so Hanani took a strip of the cloth, placed it over his heart and tucked it under his arms to cover his bullet wound.

Along with Luke, Kyle and Dana, Makoa's immediate family members from Oahu looked on as Hanani stepped into the center of the circle. True to what was written on the scroll, she held up a half-coconut shell in front of everyone and spoke, "In this," she paused, "awapuhi and pikake oils, like the oil of joy for the spirit of heaviness." She was attuned to Nehunes' sorrow for sinning against the Lord. But joy now availed. She poured the oils over Makoa's face and body to anoint him for his sea-borne journey.

Tiare was pulled back in time…*She was on the beach in the center of the crowd, bullhorn in hand, using a triangular apparatus that symbolized God, man and land…*

Taking a wide, hollowed-out, two feet long bamboo from Kalani, Hanani raised it up and said,
"Filled with rose petals to remind us of Christ, the Rose of Sharon." Tilting the bamboo, she gently sprinkled red and white petals on his face, torso and legs.

Kawika, Malia and Hoku stood close by while tears fell from Hanani's eyes.

Malia teetered weakly, trembling, too choked for words. Then she wept bitterly, drew close to the canoe, swung her arm around Makoa's torso and rested her head on his chest to say how much she loved him.

Hoku walked around to the other side, removed a few rose pedals from his face, leaned close, kissed his cheek and whispered in broken sobs, "I love you daddy." The last she said this, he was still alive. She remembered his response, '*I love you, too, bebe girl.*'

In his guilt, Kawika blamed himself, though it was is friend that squeezed the trigger. He knelt next to Malia, rested both arms across Makoa's thighs, buried his head and cried, "I'm sorry, dad." Sniffle. Then he placed his left palm over his father's beefy left hand. Sniffle. "I love you."

Kawika looked upwards and recalled how the sky, just days ago, were filled with screams. It was a portent, as if a clang of dirges bade him to weigh-in on his ill-intent.

But now that someone he loved lay breathless, someone dear who had been to him what a son would desire of a father, his broken heart felt shattered. He sowed disobedience to the wind, and reaped the consequences of his rebellion.

"God forgive me. Let the fire for your ways that burned in daddy's heart purge me," sobs, sniffles, "and I shall follow you all the days of my life." Hanani was reminded of Makoa, remorse-filled, kneeling next to Kawika as he lay semi-comatose in a hospital bed. She paused from her own pain to comfort her children.

Kalani came up alongside the grieving family. He held a large gourd filled with sandalwood chips that Nahiena whittled. Raising the gourd high, he implored heaven for the preservation and guidance of Makoa's impending plight. He lowered the gourd and sprinkled its contents evenly all over him. Moving away, Hanani, alone, crisscrossed oiled ti-leaves over Makoa, took the loose, spiced tapa cloth hanging over the sides and folded it over his body. As several villagers stepped forward to hand her armfuls of more oil-soaked ti-leaves, she motioned for Malia, Hoku and Kawika to help cover their father completely.

They moved away as another villager stepped out from the circle holding a small gourd which contained a seasoned batch of breadfruit sap. He poured an even line of the natural glue along the grooved edges of the single-hull. Then Numea and another warrior carried the top half of the canoe and pressed it into place for a water-tight seal. Artisans that shaped the canoe-coffin fastened a pair of hau wood crossbeams across the top cover more

than an arm's span apart with sennit and tied each
end to an outrigger.

Villagers broke from the circle and dispersed in a
hushed, orderly fashion. They regrouped into two
parallel, widely-spaced lines with enough clearance
in between for the procession of pall-bearing chiefs
and priests.
Cliff took the purple cloth from the stilts that held
Makoa's canoe and gave it Hanani. She tore the
cloth in half and gave it to Cliff in his brother's
memory. The other half, she placed it over her right
shoulder and wrapped it around her waist several
times then tucked it in place. The length that
remained hung loosely at her side.
Kawika, Malia and Hoku followed closely behind.

The lines formed a westward path that led all the
way up the beach where his canoe was placed on
the waist-high shallows.
The scene was reminiscent of Hanani's dream.
Everyone fell silent for the last time before
releasing Makoa's canoe.
Shaped like a seed pod, it was about to be sown
onto the ocean depths under the watchful care of the
Great Care-giver, with their hopes and dreams in
Christ to reap the reward of their suffering.

Kalani stretched both arms towards heaven and
prayed:
*"God, embrace brother spirit. We set body on
current and swell. You breathe on water, brother
journey across sea he love. Lord, brother die so we*

272

stop kill own people. Guide canoe. We follow place canoe land. There we humble to You, not do bad, seek face. There we pray and You heal people and land!"

20

As the four of them strolled along Kealaikahiki's
shoreline, moon-lit canoe masts reached like
outstretched arms in the quiet night, as if praying
for those who would sail in their hollows.
"I'm going with them," Hanani stated firmly.
Kawika piped, "Me too, mom. With dad gone,
there's no way you're going without me."
Just then, Malia looked up and saw a shooting star.
Tennyson's poem stoked the fire in her mind as she
whispered, "As often through the purple night,
below the starry cluster bright, a bearded meteor,
trailing light…"
Intimate with this poem, Hanani followed Malia's
upward gaze and added, "The shooting star is a sign
that tomorrow's weather will be blue, unclouded,
and the burning flame of the sun a lamp unto our
path."
Malia was destined to carry the pain of her loss to a
lost world in pain. She said to Hanani, "Kawika is
right, mom. I'll feel a lot better if he stays with you.
I have a lot to process. It's best for me to re-join the
tour group with uncle Cliff."
Her mind already set, Hoku said to her mom, "I
know this people well."
"Meaning?" Hanani glanced at her.
"I'm coming with you and Kawika."

*****

Hanani pointed upward as she told Nahiena about a shooting star headed toward the northwest. "What does it mean?"

All that Tevake told Nahiena before he died were alive in her soul. "Another sign Tevake speak. Place of refuge. We sail there. Pray. Do good."

"Where?" Hanani puzzled.

"Land we find where star go."

'Makoa's canoe?' Hanani wondered silently.

Nodding her head slowly, the old woman confided, "Place people learn Jesus we see. Makoa canoe land first."

"Intuitive." Hanani whispered.

Nahiena cupped her ear and said, "Huh?"

"Nothing. Just thinking out loud." An image of Po'o's dust offering on the summit of the mound filtered through Hanani's memories. She heard Makoa's voice, *'a call to the four corners of the winds.'* The cross flashed in her mind. *'Heaven's sword brandished in love; holy implement of war for the souls of men, stained with the blood of the Lamb of God to take away the sins of this world.'* As quick as these came, they left.

Hanani seemed dazed. Nahiena stared at her as she pointed to her own chest. "See *inside?*"

"I...I heard my husband's voice."

Nahiena grinned.

*****

The morning star glistened in the horizon's glow, not a chariot of fire tugging a lassoed sun, but Venus in the dawn's early light.

275

It filled them with awe.

And Hope.

Here, a redeemed people were to be lifted above earthly woes by the Light of the Son who would set the compass of their journey.

In a short period of time, Nehune turned from human sacrifices to the One who sacrificed Himself for love.

They waited, unmoved by the ship that anchored out from shore last night.

Under orders, a Coast Guard Cutter returned on the day after Makoa's body was abandoned to divine guidance at sea. The naval men on board knew only that they were here to escort the flotilla to Niihau. Within hours.

To make way for a weapon of mass destruction: like beating plowshares into swords and pruning hooks into spears; nation against nation because man has not unlearned war.

From the Cutter deck, Captain Frederick Weiss had been observing their activities on shore. He assumed the volume of gourds and leaf-wrappings carried onboard the canoes were gifts for Niihauans upon their arrival. Instead, these provisions were for their stay in the direction of the shooting star.

Somewhere beyond Niihau.

Several nights prior, Kalani instructed a few Nehune to store gourds filled with seeds, along with tools, materials and miscellaneous farming supplies for their envisioned return in a secret, upland cave that his father, Tevake, revealed.

Luke took precautionary measures and left mini radios, a collapsible disc antenna, and fold-out solar panels with Kawika. Monitoring communications and keeping satellite surveillance from his home was critical to their safety and survival.
Returning here to their birthplace would be redefined by their obedience elsewhere, because man who is made from the dust of the earth must first be renewed if the earth is to be restored.

Emotions were high when the Coast Guard Cutter turned its bow north-westward.
On shore, sweat glistened on the throng of brown bodies as everyone engaged in last minute preparations. Uncertain of the distance they would be traveling beyond Niihau, Mau gave strict instructions to insure that their food supply were stored in watertight gourds.
Nahiena assured him that his logistics were sufficient. "Like swift star, journey swift."

The Cutter signaled that it was time to leave.
Kalani prayed for their protection. Many cried over being torn from their land as they boarded.
Mau wasted no time. He signaled for the men to push the canoes into the calm surf. Then they climbed in, picked their paddles up and began synchronously digging their blades in the water until they were far from shore.
Two years of intensive preparations were now in motion.
Women, children and the elderly were unsteady, queasy, choosing to either sit or crouch in a long,

Quonset-like hut built into the center platforms of all twelve, double-hull canoes.

Cutter shipmates marveled at the undulating rhythm of blades appearing and disappearing beneath the ocean surface. Canoe masts with closed sails bobbed under manual propulsion for about a half-hour until Mau ordered the sails opened to increasing northwest trades in the Kealaikahiki channel.

Nahiena and Kalani were onboard the canoe with Mau, along with Hanani, Hoku, and Kawika. Mau had a Hawaiian lead on another canoe in parallel while the other canoes, manned by Hawaiians and Nehune that followed close behind. The trek across the channel was uneventful.

After rounding far out from the south end of Lanai, pass the western tip of Molokai, silhouettes of Oahu's east end came into view on the horizon to their right.

The Cutter escort was careful to maintain a safe distance out at sea.

Sailboats and pleasure cruises gawked at the canoes that followed a Naval patrol. Were they being *escorted* by the military?

Some of the onlookers recalled a similar gathering of canoes when Pacific islanders sailed together from Aotearoa, Tahiti, Cook Islands, etc., to join their Hawaiian kinsmen before anchoring at Kualoa Regional Park on Oahu's east end.

Someone from the commission tipped the media with an alibi that native activists came from all the islands in their canoes to protest the planned construction of a missile silo at Kealaikahiki. Unsuccessful, they were turned back by the Navy to Niihau, where island representatives would mediate their demands.

Nehune moved fast under full sail, cleared Oahu's Kaena point and headed in the direction of Niihau beyond Kauai.
Two helicopters buzzed like hornets high above the koa vessels. They were awed by the hovering machines. Since aircraft never flew in the airspace above Kealaikahiki, the copters looked like giant insects descending from the clouds. Told that strange, roaring objects in the sky would appear, no one could prepare Nehune for the emotional impact. Isolated for generations, disorientation and confusion set in.

*****

Luke Moresi was upset when he found out that Dr. Chloe Hansen did not follow through with the media. Two weeks before Nehune set sail, she was supposed to inform reporters that a rabble of Hawaiians had been dug in at Kealaikahiki to protest the Kanapou Bay standoff. Evicted by the Navy, native sympathizers sailed their double-hull canoes from different islands to assist with their removal.
The commission she served decided on a more effective diversion: make the missile silo public knowledge so native activists would join in organizing their opposition. With these efforts

afoot, any suspicions about Nehune existence would be minimized. They knew that sailboats cruising past the flotilla would recognize Nehune as peculiarly shorter, dressed in native garb, evoking questions and rumors that would go viral. The spotlight off Nehune with Niihau as cover could proceed with minimal complications.

"Chloe!"

She turned from watching the live news coverage on her wall-mounted flat-screen and knew the look on Luke's face as he stormed into her office suite. Calmly clicking the remote off, she leaned on her desktop and nervously folded her hands. She felt her heart flutter when she saw him as she once knew him: clean shaven, well-groomed and neatly dressed.

"Yes, Luke. May I help you?"

"Help me?" Luke growled, "how about keeping your promise!"

She glared at him, "They changed their minds."

Luke's blue eyes seemed to penetrate her soul as he weighed her response. "Reporters are on a feeding frenzy and doing their own investigations."

"I was told to stay out of it!"

Disgusted, Luke grunted.

Chloe remarked, "Besides, when people find out what's really going on, who will believe that human guinea pegs have been harbored there for over a hundred years?"

"You, of all people, should know!"

Chloe bit her lower lip as she turned away. She knew of the legal and socio-political ramifications.

"Human rights groups," Luke bellowed, "will come to the fore demanding answers from our government. Lawyers will be scrambling to offer their services and tying up the courts for years. A slew of scientists will stampede over each other to study..."

"Living artifacts?" Chloe interjected, "and your worst fears, Luke? Religious zealots of different persuasions seeking to, maybe, proselytize them? I heard about what all of you saw---these visitations from heaven."

Cheap shot. She misjudged the significance of their spiritual encounter.

*****

Staff members excitedly walked into Dr. Kyle Pahono's office and said, "Have you seen the news? There's a bunch of canoes being escorted by a naval vessel. They're all double-hulls with huts on the center platforms. And get this, they all have plaited sails!" Shaking their heads in dismay, they continued, "The people onboard kinda look like they stepped out of time. Strange..."

He was expecting it. No one in his employ knew what was really going on, nor did his colleagues and some authorities.

Kyle turned on the T.V. in his office and took out his cell phone, punched in a phone number and let it ring. "Hello?"

"Dana?"

"Yeah, sweeheart?"

"Did Cliff and Malia leave?"

"They're still with me. We were just stepping out for lunch."

"It can wait. Bring them with you to the office. They'll want to see this."

The Pacific Archaeological Society was located on Pier 45 close to downtown Honolulu. Before heading to Aotearoa, Malia and Cliff were encouraged to drop by to explore how their research could augment Cliff's ministry among native peoples.

When Malia entered the Pahono's office, she appeared calm.

"Malia," Kyle explained, "we had nothing to do with these media lies. I was with your father when we helped with their launch preparations."

"I know," she stared at him, "you also saw him die trying to rescue Hoku."

Kyle admitted, "I thought he was struck by a lightning bolt."

Malia sat down. Her countenance was tense. "I just don't understand."

Cliff, unable to make any sense of it himself, sat quietly beside Malia and listened.

"We may never understand," Dana reasoned, "but we have to tell the truth about Nehune."

*****

Back in Aotearoa to rejoin Te Ora and Isle Breaz, Malia isolated herself for several days to fast and pray, struggling that she did not stay back with her

mom and siblings. Cliff and others randomly
checked on her.

One night, she dreamed of strolling alone on the
sand as slow-moving waves ebbed and flowed. She
sensed as if the expanse above her, breathed.
Glancing sky-ward, wispy billows floated amidst
the blue.
"Before you were formed in your mother's womb, I
called you."
Startled, she turned to see who spoke. No one was
there. Slightly shaken, she thought, *'I'm dreaming,
so chill, girl.'*
The breathing above, now surrounding her, was
audible.
Climbing up a sand dune, she paused to rest at the
top. Enraptured by the ocean's sunlit glisten, stirred
by soothing breezes, the sky's cellophane-hued
colors danced. Ballerina-like, it undulated in slow,
shifting patterns to the faint sound of a harpist's
chord.
Suddenly, the distinct sounds of neighing caused
her heart to skip. Casting her eyes downward, she
was startled to see three white, majestic horses
frolic out onto the sands from a grove of coconut
trees.
From this distance, their eyes met.
The horses snorted, hooves scratching the sand,
before slowly trotting upwards toward her.
All three stopped at the top of the dune, their manes
dancing in a gentle wind as their nostrils flared in-
sync with the air they breathed, looking at her, with
penetrating eyes.

The first horse was notably larger than the other two, his musculature more pronounced. Suddenly he faded out of view. The snorts of the other two horses turned her attention on them. She noticed that around the neck of the second horse was a small, gold shield, embossed with a red letter, F, that hung on a gold chain. Similarly, around the neck of the third horse hung a gold chain attached to a gold shield with an embossed letter H, blue in color.

Pondering on the meaning of this dream, the second horse spoke, "I am Faith." Marveling that it spoke, its name gripped her. Slightly bobbing its head and snorting, the third horse chimed in, "I am Hope." All three turned their gaze toward the first horse that, as it snorted and neighed, came into clear view, this time more radiant and grand in appearance. The chain and shield around its neck were also gold, but the embossed letter, L, on the shield was purple. It, too, spoke, "And I am Love."

Then, in unison, the horses lifted their heads up and fixed their eyes over her shoulders. Malia turned to see someone approaching them wearing a long white robe with his face hidden under a hood. As he walked up, all three horses bowed low as he removed his hood.

"Lord!" She gasped, fell on her knees, and bowed her head in reverence. Tenderly placing His right hand on her head, she looked up, tears rolling down her cheeks as she reached for His left hand to stand her to her feet. He kissed her forehead, and said, "I called you back to this land for a time and season to teach you that when men speak, they are like sounding brass and clanging cymbals. Many prophesy, expound on mysteries, glory in what they know, or may even have faith to remove mountains. All of this means nothing, if their hearts are not ruled by My Love. Many relinquish their world possessions to give to the poor; others give their bodies to be burned for just causes." He paused. She peered into His blazing blue eyes and trembled. He continued, "The deeds of human compassion are vain if not done in My Love. Study my Word and learn more of Me. Faith and Hope will guide you. But only Love will ensure that your journey succeeds."

Then she awoke.

*****

Mau had the eye of an eagle. As soon as Niihau was in sight the next morning, he noticed how the Cutter began to merge toward the island.

Mau signaled for the other lead canoe to lower his sails and fall back in with the group behind. Then he called out to his steersman to position their canoe, under full sail, in front of the rest.

Out in open, unfamiliar waters, he already developed a feel of the swells and subtle currents. His eyes were fixed on the exact position of the horizon since yesterday's launch, using tack to maintain true heading against cross-sectional winds. His mind, a natural protractor and compass, factored the height and angle of the sun which indicated that they were on course.

Hanani looked longingly out on the horizon as she observed Mau's silent calculations and short, terse commands to the steersman. Still clear in her mind was the star that shot across the sky in the direction they were moving. She marveled how Mau was about to sail beyond Niihau without blinking an eye. He accurately used the rise and fall their bow, the sun, his hand and fingers, measuring speed by visual timing, and motion sensitivities in and through his body.

No sextant, no navigational tools other than proven, ancient exactitudes.

"Sir, they're breaking away!"
The seaman's voice was excited when relaying this to the officer in charge.

Agitated, Captain Weiss turned in his chair on the command deck and looked out the window. *"What the...? Cutter 421 to Naval Op, this is Captain Frederick Weiss, do you read?"*

"Captain Weiss, this is Admiral Jesse Hansen, I read you loud and clear..."

Frederick stared at the helicopters overhead like aerial hounds following an ocean blood trail. He imagined the repercussions as their cameras continued to track the flotilla sailing past Niihau. He looked down to get a reading on his instruments.

"Admiral Hansen, the natives have initiated their own course, maintaining a northwesterly direction. Please advise."

Admiral Hansen looked surprised when he saw one of his Nam buddies walk into the communications room at Pearl Harbor Naval Operations on Oahu. "Luke! What are you doing here?"

Clean shaven and well groomed, Luke was dressed in his military uniform to make an impression when paying an old friend an unexpected visit. "Jess, we need to speak. In private. Now."

The way the muscles in Luke's jaw locked, Jess knew it was serious.

"Captain Weiss, standby for orders."

Luke followed him into his office. Jesse's mind was flooded with memories of marrying, and divorcing, Chloe. Luke fell in love with her shortly after, creating a brief rift between them. But their unbreakable bond in the brotherhood of war mended this rift.

"I wanted to tell you, personally, Jess, that I've known those natives out there long before my father died."

When Jess heard this, he was taken aback. Luke's father was like a dad to him, but he had no idea that the elder Moresi lived with natives on Kahoolawe.

"They're harmless, Jess," Luke assured him, "don't believe what you've heard on the news. Long and short of it, they have no intention of going to Niihau."

Jess probed, "Then where are they headed?"

"If I knew I'd tell you. But I don't. What I do know is that they are on a quest." Luke was out of the loop. He left right after Nehune placed Makoa's body in a canoe onto ocean paths. Knowing that the launch was imminent, he was preoccupied with returning to Oahu, hoping that his connections with Naval and State authorities would clear any obstacles until they re-settled.

In an unknown land.

"A quest?" Jess brows furrowed.

Luke gave a stern answer, "Yes. And I'm here as their advocate!"

"What do you want me to do, Luke? Captain Weiss is waiting for my reply."

Luke sighed heavily, "I'm asking you to trust me on this, and let them go."

*****

Mau noticed a puny speck on the horizon about three hours sail.

They left Kealaikahiki early yesterday morning and would make landfall before dark.

Nahiena inched toward the bow where Mau stood, statue-like. She pointed and said, "There."

Mau, a man of few words, gracefully accepted the swiftness of their journey since Makoa's canoe was set to sea three days ago.

When Hanani overheard Nahiena, the thought of Makoa was like the breath of the wind passing through her body. At first glimpse of the small islet, her spirit groaned, '*Makoa, my beloved.*'

Mau turned his focus on a squall about an hour away. Pointing to the shadow beneath grey clouds, he said to Nahiena, "Two hours till heavy rain. Winds pick up, waves little rough before we land."

Nahiena did not flinch. Her quiet confidence in God, like Tevake, was steady. Kalani, awed by the Hand of Providence, came alongside his mother and put his arms around her.

When the squall hit, the children cried.
They always loved the rain on land, but now their terra firma was rolling as it poured. The women did everything they could to keep them calm while the animals squawked and cackled.
Menfolk hustled in the driving rain as they managed the lashings and sails while steersmen mimicked Mau's every move: any miscalculation could have widened the gap in their tight formation and set some of the canoes on currents moving far out at sea.

The weather cleared as they got closer to land.
The people thanked Jesus for stilling the waters, otherwise they would have been at risk from being dashed on the reef surrounding…
"Nihoa!" Nahiena's voice quivered as the island's unique topography suddenly became familiar from what she faintly remembered from their legends. "Ancestors leave Kauai, come here!"

As they approached Adam's Bay, Hanani scanned the shoreline for any sign of her husband as they passed over the reef and into shallow water. She felt her pulse increase as the men jumped out and dragged each double-hull canoe up on the shore. When her feet touched the sand at Derby's Landing, she knew Makoa was near. The oneness they shared, their holy bond, seemed to quicken her soul. But there was only enough daylight to start fires in several pits the men needed to prepare food for everyone.

Weary from the day-plus journey on the ocean, women, children, and the elderly slept soundly in the platform huts while the men used mats and tapa blankets to sleep on the sand below.

At dawn, Kalani rose to pray. Finding a place on the beach close by, he beseeched God for Nehune. When he was done, his mind raced, '*Nihoa place people come long ago. We now here to heal?*' His thoughts were jostled by Makoa buried in spices and ointments and confined in a sandalwood canoe-coffin, then set upon the movement of many waters. Recounting how Mau led them here against currents and cross-winds, Makoa's canoe could not have possibly made it here without a sail.
He was borne by the breath of God alone.
He reflected, again, on his father's interpretation of his dream: Makoa's canoe is a symbol of the star Arcturus in the constellation of Bootes, the Coming Shepherd-King---and the star, Coma, that meant the Desire of Nations.
Nahiena came and sat next to him.
After a long silence, Kalani turned to his mother and queried, "When Coma star bright, we go home?"
She looked up, "Yes."
He asked, "Why Coma?"

"Coma star like Jesus. Earth become dark, all
people desire Him. Lead people here. Learn
humble. Pray. Do good before lead people back to
Kealaikahiki."

When Hanani awoke, she saw Nahiena and Kalani
sitting together. Walking over to them, she asked,
"Give me your blessing to look for my husband. Let
me find him alone."
Nahiena nodded approvingly. Kalani was honored
to oblige the woman whom Nehune wrongfully
thought was Sun.
Hanani returned to awaken Kawika and Hoku.
"Stay here. I won't be long."

She strode anxiously down the beach toward the
east until she reached another inlet, known as
Landing, not far from Camp Cave. Breathing
erratically, Hanani had to consciously inhale and
exhale.
The way her heart was beating in her chest, she
almost fainted when she found him.
Kneeling beside the fragrant sandalwood-pod, hot
tears rolled down her cheeks.
Quivering in prayer, her spirit was deeply moved by
the reality of Jesus' resurrection which seemed to
kindle her soul's dim flicker into a steady flame. A
fire, stoked by love so life-giving, that the power of
the grave was without sting.
Makoa lay here. Breathless. Still-form.
Ashes to ashes. Dust to dust.
Yet a body that shall again rise in the same power
of his Lord's resurrection.

She rested in how no one, nothing, could persuade her against the Light who came into the world as the Resurrection and Life. In Whom could hope otherwise be realized and made overwhelmingly alive?

Makoa's passing only served to remind her that he was asleep in the arms of his Lord.

In her deep mourning, she was tempted to pry the lid open and awaken him.

Hanani longed for warmth to return to Makoa's body.

And for his eyes to open.

That her beloved would rise from his requiem and reach over to embrace her with his strong arms.

And kiss her.

21

"His canoe is here."

Nahiena wiped the tear from Hanani's cheek, took her by the hand and sat her down. "Me and Kalani happy you and children with us. You not die, help people know Jesus."

Kalani faced Hanani squarely, "Jesus change people when come. We want know Him."

She wished that Makoa was alive so *they,* together, could lay Nehune's spiritual foundation. His blood was sown as seed; the Word in her heart was Light. Now she was to help the seed of Tarani return to the Light of God.

With Kawika at her side, she led some men to the Landing inlet. When they got there, they carried Makoa's canoe back to the settlement and placed him in her hastily built hut.

*****

Days ago, when the pilots from different news stations returned to refuel their helicopters, they were abruptly ushered into debrief. Station managers wanted to avoid being embarrassed from what they learned were misleading reports on the flotilla they were filming from the skies.

Fragments of what was going on had piqued the interests of others that launched their own investigations.

Admiral Hansen refused to release an official statement until he found out what was going on. Local mediators, unwittingly hired through channels linked to the shadow commission, were tight-lipped when they returned from Niihau, saying only that their meeting with the Kealaikahiki *evictees* was canceled.

*****

"Nihoa?" Chloe look startled.

On the other end of the cellphone, Dr. Julie Glen tersely said, *"Yes!"*

"Hmmm." Chloe hung up and stared at Luke across the restaurant table. He said, "I heard. About 120 miles northwest of Niihau. Except for the federally governed island of Midway, all of the islands in the archipelago that stretches northwest from Kauai to the Kure atoll are owned by the State of Hawaii."

"What are you saying?"

"Nehune are still on native soil."

Chloe agreed to rendezvous with Luke at Toney Loma's in Waikiki for dinner. He remembered the look in eyes when they last met. Since then, he wanted another excuse to be with her.

"I like your clean shaven look." She put her cellphone in her purse, pulled out his favorite-color lipstick, cosmetic mirror and freely applied more on her already glossy lips. Her compliment and subtle, feminine move caught him off guard.

Luke rubbed his beardless cheeks. "Oh. Ummm. Thank you."

She wore a beige-fitted dress, deliberately enhancing her lovely figure. Her perfume, Luke's favorite, tugged at his heart. She folded her hands under her chin, turned to look out the window, and sighed.

"Thanks for coming." Luke said.

"I'm glad I came." She made sure their eyes met. More signals. What was happening? Old feelings come alive? Was she having a change of heart? Luke shrugged it off. They were here on business.

The waiter brought a loaf of onions rings with a bowl of sauce dip.

"May I take your order?"

"Yes." Chloe said, "I'll have the baby back ribs with a small green salad and blue cheese dressing"

"And you?"

Luke said, "The same, all the way around." When the waiter left, he was more precise, "They've been on Nihoa for several days at Derby's Landing."

She looked at him suspiciously. "They were supposed to land on Niihau."

He retorted, "They were supposed to be left alone!" Luke calmed down. "Jess managed to pull some strings. So far, the navy is hands-off."

His name made her cringe. Their divorce was bitter and the rift between him and Luke was difficult before things mended.

"Interesting." Her response was terse.

"And you with the media?" Luke asked.

She leaned back and sighed, "The commission needs time to think this through," she paused, then revealed, "Nehune will be forced back to Niihau."

"Forced?"

Chloe said too much, but felt relieved that she did. Then something inside of her broke. "Dr. Dawkins had his sights set on Niihau several years back. This *lost tribe*," she rolled her eyes, "would blend with the locals there by adapting their culture. Second most isolated island in Hawaii, so it's plausible, you know, because it's privately owned? Suspicions would be assuaged as media coverage fade into oblivion. In several decades, Nehune would be fully assimilated with Niihauans as if they never existed." Unfazed by what she said, Luke took a bite of the ribs, chewed, sipped his drink and stared at her.

"You knew about this?" Chloe pressed.

Luke nodded affirmatively.

"From whom?"

"You're forgetting who Jess re-married after your divorce."

Chloe's eyes grew wide. "Jenna Robbins! The same family that *owns* Niihau!?"

Luke changed the subject. "This Dawkins guy is a piece of work."

She grits her teeth, "I heard him yelling when I was on the phone with Dr. Glen."

Luke surmised, "Nehune confinement on Kahoolawe will inevitably go viral."

Her resolve to break from the commission would put her at-risk. It no longer mattered as she looked forlornly at him and said, "If you knew how this commission thinks, Nehune are not safe. I'll tell you what you need to know to ensure their safety."

Even after the damage she had done, his guts told him to trust her. Moved by the fear in her eyes, he assured her, "They will not harm you…" When Luke said this, he held her hands firmly in his. A tear fell from Chloe's eye.

*****

Their first day at Derby's Landing was spent on logistics. Food and water would be rationed until a survey of the island's provisions could determine their long-term survival.

Mau instructed Kalani, "Build huts for three canoes. Use for practice. Other canoes sail later."

The remaining nine canoes were dragged high up on shore and into a shade of trees. They built stilts to suspend them from the ground to avoid rot. The hau masts were disassembled and placed in the hulls. Nothing could be done to preserve the plaited sails so they were removed from the mast and used to cover the canoes. Nihoa yielded enough lauhala to weave new sails at the appointed time. Coconut and kukui nut trees were also in abundance to provide for sennit cord and oil to message into the koa hulls and hau masts for preservation.

At the break of dawn on the second day, work began in earnest. They cut branches for framing and gathered piles of palm leaves for their roofs and sidewalls. Lashings were made in advance at Kealaikahiki to expedite their temporary settlement here.

While canoe and residential huts were assembled and earth ovens hollowed, women and children wasted no time tilling, seeding and fertilizing with fresh fish cut in small pieces and mixed with the dirt. Kawika was careful to load the communications equipment from Luke into his hut.

Nehune City of Refuge was an area the chiefs planned to designate for restitution once they resettled. They were eyewitnesses to Makoa's death at Kealaikahiki that was immune from state law because it was still under military jurisdiction. To assuage his conscience, Kawika wanted self-imposed penance, so he subjected himself to Nehune justice. Luke agreed and, providentially, was able to negotiate with naval judges to clear Kawika's friend from manslaughter charges.

Nehune law enforcement was one of Kalani's first points of order. He and two chiefs scouted the coastal areas and chose to build their City of Refuge at the Landing inlet. Not far from where Makoa's canoe had settled, the bordered confines would allow offenders to weigh their offenses, make restitution and be released back into the tribe.

Upon its completion, Kawika had agreed to solitary confinement. Two natives were assigned to keep a 24/7 watch and supply him with drink, food and tools for survival.

Days turned into weeks. Plunged into silence, Kawika's existence felt like another dimension. Unfurled thoughts joined with the haunting calls of owls and hawks. The earth breathed, its erratic winds vibrated on waters. When preparing for cooked meals, hypnotic pulses of fire became a time-tunnel that pulled him into past memories. Cadence of sun-lit days and moon-lit nights synchronized with clouds and stars. Rise and fall of constellations played the scenes of Malia citing her poem to their uncle Cliff at Waimea Bay that night.

At dusk, Kawika stepped out of his small hut for a quick stroll around the perimeter as part of his routine exercise. As he was walking, he saw the backside of one of the native watchmen sitting and looking out at sea.
Getting closer, Kawika greeted him as he passed by. "Hi."
Without looking up, the man responded, "Hi, boy."
'Boy? Gosh, he sounded like dad!' When he turned, the man was staring at him. Kawika stopped in his tracks, mouth agape, "Dad?"
Makoa smiled. "How you, boy?"
A swell of emotions overcame Kawika as he stood speechless.
Makoa motioned for him to sit. "It's me, son. It's okay."
Slowly, he sat next to his father.
Makoa felt the pain of his son's agony in not forgiving himself. "In the cave, Tevake explained that rebellion was the tip of a spear that would pierce my heart. Nehune rebelled against God by killing their own. You rebelled against mama's counsel, even if you meant well in saving Hoku and me. When I tackled Numea, everything went dark. Then Light appeared. I saw the Lord and have been with Him since. He explained to me what happened

and allowed me to come here and tell you that His love for you remains."

Kawika buried his face in his hands and wept. Makoa placed his hand on the back of his head, massaged his neck and encouraged, "Where I am now is glorious beyond what people have described."

Kawika lifted his head, his face wet with tears. "You and mom spoke of heaven when we were growing up."

"From what the scriptures say, yeah. But to be there, boy," Makoa's expression lit up, "whoa, major beautiful!"

Silence.

Makoa intoned, "You didn't pull the trigger, remember?"

Kawika lowered his head.

Makoa consoled, "The Lord heard your prayer at my funeral. He has forgiven you. I forgive you. Stop blaming yourself from what you told your friend to do. No worries. What is more important now is your opportunity to live for Him and move forward in life," leaning closer, staring, "and help this people."

Kawika looked surprised, "You wuz there?"

"Lord let me watch."

"Nah?"

"Yup!"

"Whoa, dad, tight."

"For real kine tight. He created time with beginnings and ends. Eternity has neither a beginning nor an end, so He dwells outside of time."

Kawika tried to comprehend this.

"Kinda cool, boy, how mom told them to soak the ti-leaves. I could smell the awapuhi and pikake oils. Where do you think she got the idea?"

"Huh? Oh, she said in a dream."

With tender eyes, Makoa smiled gently, "You're doing it now."

Kawika looked puzzled, "Doing what?"

"Dreaming."

Kawika awoke, sat up quickly and looked at the entry to his hut. When he stepped out, it was dusk. The light in Makoa's eyes, and his smile, were still impressed in Kawika's mind.

Strolling around the perimeter, he longed to see his father.

*****

6 months later

"Look!" Kalani pointed to the sky object that emitted a slow, pulsating buzz. Nehune gawked at the low flying helicopter moving slowly over Adam's Bay.

Shaking his head, the pilot quipped, "Man them monkeys down there don't waste anytime digging in!"

"Monkeys?" the sole passenger guffawed, "too funny."

The pilot focused on a clear patch of green at Derby's Landing, not far from the recently constructed village.

Nahiena watched suspiciously as the mechanized hornet descended for a landing.

"Wait here," Hanani assured them, "I'll see what they want."

Kalani had just walked up to her, "I go with you."

Kawika protested, "Mom!"

"Stay back, boy."

Kawika ran to his hut and radioed Luke, *"Kawika to Luke, do you read?"*

Luke heard his cellphone beep. It had an app to intercept incoming signals from Kawika's radio, 24/7. He pressed an icon on his screen. *"I read, Kawika. Everything okay?"*

"No! Some dudes just landed in a helicopter and it looks like trouble…"

The blades spun at low speed as the pilot idled his engine.

Four casually-dressed men in shades emerged from the insect's belly and stepped onto Nihoan soil.

The leader's cool, professional manner reflected the shadow commission: people who lived a lie and needed facades.

Three thugs stood next to him.

Hanani and Kalani approached them and stopped several feet away.

Gordon Zeit was here to do business. Speechless, he gave a hand signal. Two of the men seized Kalani and tied his hands behind his back.

Hanani screamed, "What are you doing! Leave him alone!"

Gordon grabbed Hanani and shoved her to the ground.

Alarmed, Nehune warriors grabbed their weapons and moved toward them.

The thugs pulled out their guns and pointed.

"Not a good idea, tough guys," Gordon smirked and said to Hanani, "Tell them to put their weapons down or we shoot."

Scrapped from the rocks and in pain, she turned and signaled for them to pull back.

Nobody was paying attention to a warrior that was out of sight with a stone in his sling. After several revolutions, he released one end.

It struck Gordon hard on the side of his temple. As he fell unconscious, his men turned and fired on the native, killing him.

When the other warriors saw this, they yelled and lunged forward.

Boom! Boom! Boom! Boom!.....

They were hit by volley of shots. Nehune and Hawaiians brave enough to jump into the fray were also shot.

Wounded and dead were strewn on the ground.

Witnessing the horror, the others ran to their aid.

The men dragged Gordon and forced Kalani at gunpoint into the copter.

While Hoku stood crying, Kawika knew where the chiefs kept his rifle and ammo. In the fray, he had time to load and lock the magazine, chambered a round, turned and aimed.

303

Blades accelerated in sync with the engine's high-pitched whine as the hornet ascended slowly upward.

Kawika was careful not to hit Kalani when he fired.

Boom! Boom!

Gordon was hit and a thug was struck in his right arm.

It happened fast. The other two yelled at the pilot to turn around so they could shoot back.

"No!" He turned to see Gordon bleeding heavy out of his left side and the man holding his arm. "We must get them back!" he pointed, "the first-aid kit is in that compartment. Patch them up now!"

As the copter buzzed away, Nehune wailed and mourned in shock.

Grief-stricken, Nahiena fell on her knees.

*****

The pilot said over the phone, "As I was lifting off, Gordon was shot. He didn't make it."

Dawkins fumed, "He's dead? Bastards!"

His forehead wrinkled with tension, General Cohen grunted, stood up abruptly and left. With the death of Gordon, he moved fast. From a contingency plan refined and approved months ago, he arranged for two UH-1 Hueys, pilots, gunners and a fifteen-man team of well-armed mercenaries for a ground assault.

With no media footage on Nihoa, it would be quick and decisive. Instead of Hotchkiss guns used by the

7th Calvary Regiment to mow down a Lakota tribe at Wounded Knee, or the British using Gatling guns to kill several thousand Zulu warriors at Khambula, Nehune would be in sight of M-240 machine guns mounted on two Hueys. Fleeing survivors would be picked off by the ground assault team.

Dr. Chloe Hansen arrived and walked into the middle of the commission's lair. Here to confront members about Kalani, she had no idea what General Cohen was planning. "I hear Gordon was shot on Nihoa," pause, "after he took Kalani hostage! I don't know what this is all about, but I want out. I resign now!"
Dawkins stood violently, causing his chair to roll back and hit the wall. He kicked the leg of the table and shouted, "You are not going anywhere! We hired you to cover our trail!" He slipped, but told the truth. She was hired to address *areas of concern* and other *logistics*.
Chloe protested, "Cover your trail?"
The others were startled, waiting for his response.
He yelled, "IF THE PUBLIC FINDS OUT WHO THESE PEOPLE REALLY ARE, THE REPERCUSSIONS WOULD EXCEED DAMAGE CONTROL. BETTER TO INFLICT DAMAGE NOW BEFORE WE LOSE CONTROL!"
No one around the table witnessed his rage like this. Chloe looked into his bloodshot eyes. "You intend to *harm* them?"
The language of tyrants is often veiled in euphemisms.

Dawkins lowered his voice, "We intend to make them...disappear. And when we do, you will be the public face to speak on our behalf. Julie and Phillip will help Bonnie spin the transcripts. When we tell you to read, you go on air to read. When we tell you to shut up, you keep your mouth shut until suspicions subside and people forget."

Disgusted that she was treated like this, much less by a well-reputed pillar among the intelligentsia of American society, Chloe stormed out of the room.

*****

The sound of their dirge pierced the air as Nehune mourned their dead and treated the wounded with Nihoan herbs.

With no clear explanation, Hanani insisted that the priests have their kinsfolk buried up on the ridge. Mau and Hawaiians took the bodies of their fellow islanders, wrapped in tapa cloth, with them back to Oahu on one of the training canoes left afloat. Nehune assured him that they could sail the remaining canoes back to Kahoolawe when the sky-sign of Coma appeared.

Resting against a palm tree, Hanani wondered if Nahiena was wrong about the direction of the shooting star. Their restoration on Nihoa was uneventful for months, then the sudden, violent interference by Gordon and his men.

Did their holy encounter at Kealaikahiki set them on a path of redemption, or demise? Many are the journeys of those who have been given divine direction. In their euphoria, the looming mountain posed no challenge to climb, yet they found themselves in a valley of despair. Fatigued, she dozed off. Then she heard a voice, *"Obedience is learned through suffering. When humbled, they will depend on Me."* She pondered on how the Son was affirmed by the Father when the Spirit alighted upon Him after baptism. Compelled by the Spirit, Jesus endured severe fatigue and hunger for forty days in a lonely desert. At His weakest, the enemy of our souls tempted Him. He resisted by clinging to the word of God. Self-righteous religion mixed with the poison of politics led to his His tortuous demise. When Jesus Christ rose from the dead, the path to eternal life was sealed forever.

*****

"Hope for people, for you." Kalani was sweating profusely from the blinding lights. Generators were shipped in to provide for powerful tent lamps in a remote area on Niihau. He had no understanding of interrogation techniques designed to break the will of informants.

Phillip Bolten was unmoved. "You take us as fools? Once belief behind this stupid symbol takes root, it will crack our foundations. Redemption from this Jesus will render the salvation of our lie null and void."

"Salvation of lie?"

He studied Kalani and intuitively knew Tylor's findings were unraveling.

Phillip explained, "Don't you see? We have managed to make people believe that priests like you are nothing more than a façade for a God that never existed. This lie is *our* salvation from the existence of *God* so we can be left to our own devices. We are free to live without a moral law you pukes speak of so we can create our own morality based on beliefs we say are true. "

"Ummphh!!" Kalani breathed rapidly after being punched in the gut by a thug that accompanied the professor.

Philip yelled, "WHERE IS IT!?"

Silence.

When some know, they hurt you to get you tell them...his father's words in the cave echoed in Kalani's soul as he endured more beating. Hunched over in pain, he refused to tell them where the symbol of hope was located.

Back at the commission's office, Dawkins became more delusional, convinced the symbol held a power he could harness and control.

Once unleashed from its earthen crucible, the hope it represented could shift the evolutionary tide that had deceived millions.

It, too, would have to be destroyed.

*****

Shaking and crying, Chloe wasted no time telling Luke everything.

A planned slaughter of Nehune was, in her mind, unthinkable. Never again would money, prestige and privilege pull her into the vortex of evil.

While Luke was pressing the numbers on his smart phone, scenes of Hueys neutralizing Charlies in Vietnam ran through his mind---but to rake down Nehune? What was this commission capable of?

"Jess?"
"Who is this?"
"Luke."
"Hey, bud. What's the latest?
"Ever heard of General Saul Cohen?"
"Nope. Name doesn't ring a bell. Why?"
"He's arranged for a small strike force: two UH-1 Hueys with mounted M-240s and a ground assault team to take out Nehune on Nihoa in about," he looked at his phone, "48 hours!"
Shocked, Jess offered, "What can I do to help?"
"My contacts have their own weapons and are ready to mobilize. We need ammo, portable equipment and a boat to get us there by *tomorrow morning*!"
Silence.
"Jess?"
"I'll get you what you need."

Luke's contacts were his Nam friends.
Retired from Special Forces.

22

"Nahiena! Nahiena!" the villagers cried aloud.
The sudden death of their matriarch was more than
they could bear. Kalani's abduction and watching
some of her people die was too much for her weak
heart.
Shaken by her passing, Hanani honored the request
of the chiefs and priests to bury her on Nihoa.
Knowing they would someday leave the island,
their dark horror would be illumined by the
presence of her guiding virtues of courage and
compassion.

*****

Luke slammed his fist on the wall in his living
room. He was hoping his contacts could mobilize
the Superferry overnight to move the over 300
natives off Nihoa. Out of operation for some time,
upstart maintenance and fueling would take too
long.
His Intel confirmed General Cohen's strike force
was set to engage in 24 hours. As expected, Jesse
supplied ammo, equipment and a chartered boat to
land his team on Nihoa to set up defense positions.

*****

Malia was on Oahu when she heard of the grim
news. Her spirit groaned; her emotions, unhinged.
On this hot afternoon, she sat in her living room to

besiege the Lord in prayer. Hours passed. Twilight
crept in until night fell. As she sat silently, waiting
on the Lord, she heard a distant, familiar sound. The
slow, in-cadence trot became louder as it drew
closer until a white horse stepped into the room.
By the red letter on the gold shield, she knew it was
Faith. Bobbing its head slightly, mane swirling,
Faith flared its nostrils and said, "Fear not, child.
Trust in the Lord with all of your heart. Take no
other thought," bobbing its head again with a faint
snort, "but to lean on Him."

*****

Before going to Nihoa, Luke was having coffee
with one of his Nam buddies. "You and the boys
ready for this?"
Frank nodded, "A little rusty, but we've been
brushing up at the range."
Luke stared at him.
"What?"
"Your quick thinking kept me alive on that hill."
"Vietcong was coming in hot," Frank leaned back
and folded his arms. "Heard a zinger past my head
as I was patching you up."
Silence.

Watching them for a while, the man stood and
walked over. "Are you Luke Moresi?"
Frank eyed the stranger suspiciously.
Luke was defensive. "Who are you?"

My name is Feyman. I know what happened to Nehune on Nihoa. I hear you guys are looking for action."

Luke's hackles were up. "Who's your source?"

"I'm a former FBI agent. A friend in CIA knew Gordon Zeit. He was shot dead on Nihoa and Gen. Saul Cohen is sending an attack team to take out Nehunes."

The details were enough for Luke to open up. "How can we help you?"

Feyman shook his head. "I want to help *you*, but you guys need to equip me."

After they left the coffee shop, Luke vetted and verified Feyman's background, including his active fund for survivors and being homeless at one time. He contacted Frank that Feyman was legit.

After Feyman's encounter with the Lord on Opu Iwi, he checked himself in with a rehab program on Oahu to detox and get back on his feet. He found work to make ends meet until he was able to rent an in-law unit in downtown Honolulu.

Kyle protested when Luke informed him about Feyman. After confronting Feyman, Kyle was satisfied that his remorse was sincere.

Boarding the boat, Luke, his Nam team and Feyman were accompanied by Kyle, Dana, Tiare, Cliff and Malia.

Feyman's healthy appearance got Cliff's attention. "I almost did not recognize you."

Studying Cliff's face, Feyman replied, "You're the priest on the mound that prayed for me."

Cliff smiled. "Yes."

"I, ah, cleaned up after God touched my heart,"

"And here you are. Why?"

Feyman responded, "Penance."

In his guilt-stricken conscience, Feyman knew that Jesus forgave him. Still, he was unable to forgive himself. It is in this kind of turmoil that many people seek penance in various forms, any of which can be a misguided proxy to Christ's redemptive power. Because Feyman could not bring himself to believe that Jesus' blood cleansed him from perpetrating bloodshed, augmenting his restitution money with his life was the only way he knew how to ease his conscience.

*****

When they arrived at Nihoa, they anchored at Derby's landing about 50 yards from the shoreline. They lowered two large, inflatable boats, loaded up people and supplies, and paddled right up to the sand.

Malia jumped out of the boat and ran toward Hanani. She hugged her and cried. "Mom, are you okay? Is Kawika and Hoku alright? We heard what happened yesterday!"

"How?"

"Dr. Chloe Hansen," Dana said as she walked up and gave Hanani a long hug. "She called out of the blue, apologized for past wrongs, told us what was going on and offered any help she could."

"*Gosh...*"

313

"Soooo good to see you're okay, girl!"

After removing some gear from the boat, he walked up to Hanani. As he did, she fought back tears because he reminded her of Makoa. "Cliff, good to see you!" They hugged.
Cliff said, "Malia and I were pretty flipped out when we got the news. Luckily, Isle Breaz was performing on Oahu when we heard. Luke contacted all of us to come here. I made sure Tiare joined us."
"Tiare? Where is she?"
Tapping her on the shoulder, Hanani turned. Their embrace was long. "Haven't seen you for a while!"
"Too long," Tiare responded, smiling, "glad Cliff got ahold of me. Didn't hesitate to come."
Observing Nehune from a distance, Dana and Tiare marveled at the sight of them.

Another man walked behind Hanani and tapped her on the shoulder. Turning, she smiled and hugged him. "Kyle!"
"Hello, Hanani. Miss you sooo much! Dana and I felt sick in our hearts when we heard."

Hanani got her bearings and focused on the men and equipment they were carrying: backpacks, black rectangular cases and stuff. For what?
"All of you came at the *same time.* And those men...what *is* goin' on?"

Kawika and Hoku ran when they saw Malia. Hugs and smiles. The greeted their uncle Cliff, Kyle and Dana.

After the distraction, Hanani pressed them further. On cue, Kyle and Cliff asked Kawika and Hoku to help them with offloading communications equipment, including a portable disc that could link directly to a GPS satellite. Cliff marveled when seeing this lost tribe for the first time, as were the men on the boat that were briefed as to who, exactly, they were here to protect.

"Mom," Malia said with tears, "you, Kawika and Hoku have to come back with us when Luke leaves."

"Luke?"

"I'm here."

Hanani glanced to her right and only now recognized him. "Luke! I'm sorry I didn't see you earlier." They hugged.

"We're very concerned for you, the kids and for all of you!"

Forehead wrinkled, Dana said. "Hanani, this is serious. You and the kids have to come with us."

Tiare interjected, "Very serious. We came to plead with you to come back with us."

Nehune had no idea what was happening as they watched the retirees versed in the art of war hike with their gear up the mountain slopes above them. Hanani stared at him. "Luke, talk to me, what is happening? You said nothing about all of this over the radio to Kawika."

315

Dana and Tiare fidgeted as Luke locked his blue eyes on Hanani. "No, I did not. Panic would make matters worse," pause, audible exhale, "an attack force will be here tomorrow."

"To do WHAT?"

Kawika and Hoku heard their mother yell and turned back to see if she was okay.

Avoiding a direct response, Luke pointed to the men climbing the slopes. "They're here to protect all of you."

Watching from a short distance away, Cliff and Kyle turned back to help convince Hanani.

Approaching, Cliff said, "Kyle and I will stay back to help. Please listen to Dana, Tiare and Malia---and leave."

Alarmed, Hanani looked left and right along the shore of Derby's Landing. Treacherous waters pounded the rocks on both sides of their settlement, leaving no room for escape. Climbing the steep mountain sides to reach further inland would be too dangerous for the elders and children.

Cliff pleaded, "Will you, Kawika and Hoku *now* come with us?"

Turning to Luke, Hanani protested, "I watched many of them die. I am bound to them, come what may."

Knowing he, or anyone, would be unable to budge her, Luke gripped Hanani's shoulders and looked her in the eyes. "You take care of yourself and the children. We'll do our best to keep everyone safe."

Luke tried to get as many Nehune women and children onboard as he could. No one was willing to leave their loved ones behind. Frustrated, pressed for time, he jumped in the boat, started it and motored away. Skimming along Adam's Bay until he was far out at sea, he disappeared on the horizon toward Oahu.

*****

"Johnny, do you read?"
"Roger, Frank."
"Two o'clock, about two clicks out."
Johnny peered through his binoculars, *"We got ourselves two bogeys."*
"Yep. They're on time." Frank mic'd in his headset. *"You guys are on this?"* Seven others that were situated at strategic, well-camouflaged positions on the mountain side facing Derby's Landing grabbed their binoculars and mic'd in code, *"P1: I'm on it. P2: on it. P3: got it. P4: let's do this. P5: roger that. P6: roger. P7: roger."*
Frank mic'd to all, *"If we lose comm, hand signals."* He and Johnny, serving as lookouts at higher elevations from different positions, turned to see the six men and two snipers down below go through the rehearsed sequence of hand signs in timed intervals.
"Looks good, boys," Frank mic'd.

Frank radioed to the portable command center set up in Luke's living room, *"Luke, they're landing. What's goin' on?"*
Luke radioed back, *"Not in our intel. My guess is they know you're there."*

317

"Counting fifteen boots on the ground." Frank radioed.

Johnny confirmed his count on the mic.

Frank mic'd to his men, *"Battlefield contingency. P1 to P7, heads-up. Fifteen men spread, moving in our direction. Assume they'll stay under cover and shoot from a distance. Snipers 1 and 2, do you read."*

"S1: roger."

"S2: roger."

"Take out the Huey gunners before they get too close."

"S1: do our best, Frank."

"S2: no worries."

"Frank," Luke radioed. *"You take it from here. I'll stay on the horn and chime in if needed."*

Chloe, anxious, sat next to Luke.

"Roger, Luke." Then Frank mic'd to his team, *"Nineteen against ten, boys. Almost two-to-one: fifteen mobile, 2 gunners, 2 pilots against us old fogeys. Let's show 'em what we got."*

Johnny mic'd, *"Age before beauty."*

"Ha. Ha."

His rifle ready, sniper 1 mic'd, *"S1 to S2, left Huey is mine. You take the right."*

Sniper 2 returned comm., *"S2: roger that."*

The villagers were awakened by the familiar, distant sound. Scanning the skies and seeing nothing, they nervously went about their daily chores.

The two Hueys lifted off from little over a mile away and headed in their direction.

318

"Sound louder!" a village child looked wild-eyed at Hanani, her own eyes bloodshot from being up all night praying for their safety.

Frank mic'd, *"S1, S2, fire if you see the gunners pointing the M-240s in their direction."*
"S1: roger."
"S2: roger."
The ten man team on Derby's Landing mountainside watched as the Nam-era copters got closer.
"M-240s ammo belts in," Frank mic'd to S1 and S2, *"but unmanned. Weird. Heads up."*
Huey-1 circled wide around, turned and headed toward Huey-2 that remained hovering at a lower elevation until Huey-1 hovered a short distance above Huey-2 facing in the opposite direction. Nervous, Jonny mic'd, *"Frank, any idea what they're up to?"*

Huey-1 pilot radioed in, *"H1 to command center, scanning for a signal."*

Alarmed, Frank mic'd, *"They're locking on our positions! Turn ALL electronics off!"* Not knowing what to expect, the men trained their M4s and AR-15s with .223mm, 30 round clips on both copters.

"This is H2. I have a lock on their positions."
From his command center in the commission's conference room, General Cohen blared over the radio, *"H1 and H2, give them everything you got!"*
"Roger that."

319

"Ellison, you copy?"
"Yes sir."
"Close in your ground force to 50 yards before firing."
"Roger, sir."

Both pilots gave hand signs. Huey-1 gunner appeared and unloaded his M-240 from left to right while the gunner in Huey-2 below jumped behind his mounted machine gun and fired from right to left.
Rat Tat! Tat! Tat! Tat! Tat! Tat!...
Rat Tat! Tat! Tat! Tat! Tat!...

Cowering from the sky hornets suspended right above them, Nehune panicked at the sound of fire sticks.

Frank hand signaled his men to turn all communications back on as both Huey gunners laid cover fire to allow for the mercenary team on the ground to close in on the villagers.
Hampered by a wall of bullets, Frank watched as nine red lights turn green on his unit and yelled in his mic., *"FIRE! FIRE! FIRE!"*
They fought with semi-automatic weapons.
Boom! Boom! Boom! Boom!...Boom! Boom!...Boom! Boom! Boom!...

The foot soldiers closed their distance, remained hidden in tall bushes and picked off the villagers, one-by-one.

Nehune scattered when bullets zinged past them and struck many down. Wailing and distressed panic ensued. The wounded whimpered and bled; puddles of blood marked the silent dead. Amidst horror and chaos, Hanani, Malia and Hoku rushed to help carry screaming children. Dana, Tiare and village men hurried to assist the elderly.

Kawika kept his rifle by his side as he stayed close to Hanani.

Numea and his warriors, armed with their hand-made weapons, acted as human shields.

Feyman's very presence evoked Kyle's memories of the shootout on the mound. Shaking it off, Kyle focused on Feyman's weapons skills and Cliff's defense training in New Zealand to assist Frank and his men on the mountainside.

Earlier, Cliff had them pick green leaves off a tree, soaked them in water and mixed dirt in for a paste effect. With the right texture, Cliff instructed, "Now we rub it all over our bodies and shorts for camouflage."

Kyle quipped, "Makoa and I had to tan our butts for several weeks to blend with Nehune."

With his flashback of Makoa running down the mound and being shot by one of SWAT's snipers, Feyman said nothing.

Cliff replied, "Just days ago, I was telling people about God."

Feyman looked at Cliff. "When I was on my face at the foot of the cross, you said that *I* must cry out to God to forgive me."

Kyle was surprised to hear this.

Cliff remarked, "If you both know anything about the Black Robe Regiment during the American Revolutionary War, you would understand my dilemma. Makoa's family needs defending from paid lowlifes. Not happening. They're cowards for picking on women and children!"

Cliff saw guilt etched on Feyman's face and knew why. "God has forgiven you of your past."

Feyman responded, "I told you I came for penance. I think you now understand."

Fully armed and blending with the plush landscape, Cliff, Kyle and Feyman hid behind rocks along the cliff bottom to right flank the incoming ground force.

"S1 and S2," Frank mic'd, *"Fix on their ground positions and take those bastards out."*

Desperate, the snipers gazed down their scopes to detect muzzle flashes or movements in the bushes down below.

Boom! Boom! Boom!

"Got one!" S1 mic'd S2.

Boom! Boom!

S2 mic'd, *"Make that two!"*

When the ground force started taking fire from the right, Ellison tasked four of his men to deal with it. Cliff, Feyman and Kyle waited until they got close.

Boom! Boom!...Boom! Boom!...Boom! Boom!

Two of the mercenaries went down: one dead and the second wounded.

The third and fourth men ducked, crawled and stood behind trees. Kyle laid cover fire as Cliff and Feyman split off in two directions to rear flank them. As the third man fired back in Kyle's direction, Cliff closed in from behind him, wrapped his hand around his mouth and shoved his blade in the man's side. Buckling from his wound, Cliff broke his neck, a Maori tactic as the enemy fell. The fourth man kept rear guard further back behind a tree, swinging and pointing his rifle at anything that moved. Feyman managed to get far enough behind him. The second mercenary that was wounded had been watching Feyman's moves. Feyman was already in his crosshairs as Feyman raised his pistol for a clear shot at the fourth soldier. Feyman was shot.

P1 hand signaled P2 about 20 yards away: *aim at the gunner in the Huey above.* They timed when the left-to-right, right-to-left sweep of both M-240s would pass the mid-point and create a clearing. P2 kept an eye on P1 as his left hand went up in the air to fold his thumb down until he folded his pinky finger down to end a 5-second count. *Boom! Boom! Boom! Boom!* *"Got 'em!"* P1 and P2 whooped in their mics. Huey-1 gunner flew back with blood splattering on the wall of the copter.

Cliff and Kyle watched Feyman drop. Kyle had the second soldier in his sight and shot him. In the fray, neither Cliff nor Kyle saw the fourth soldier crawl behind another tree. With Kyle having no positional

323

fix on him, the fourth man waited till Cliff approached Feyman to render aid.

Boom!

As Cliff fell, Kyle saw where the shot came from. He swung his rifle and waited. The fourth man crawled out from behind the tree for another position. Kyle saw him, aimed, and took him out.

"H1 to command center, gunner down."
"Get outta there!" Gen. Cohen barked, *"H2, hold your position!"*
"Roger, sir."

Cliff was gasping and holding his side when Kyle got there. "Brah, no way!"
"Yes, way!" Cliff grunted and sighed. "Don't think it's too bad, eh?" Losing a lot of blood, his breathing was heavy.

Familiar bushes were in sight. Kyle ran to gather a handful of herbs, crush it in his hands and apply several pinches to Cliff's wound. "Don't move." He ran to break off some palm fronds and tied them together to hold the herbal patch. "My Asmat friends from Iryan Jaya taught me this. Those boys can name over a hundred different herbs."

Cliff managed a slight grin, felt dizzy, flung his head back and winced in pain.

Kyle then went over to check on Feyman about 15 yards over. When Kyle got there, he reeled back and knelt. Lowering his head for several seconds, he prayed, "Lord, I thank you that you gave me the strength to forgive him."

Watching blood pour from the side of Feyman's head was grievous enough than to have held against him what God had already forgiven.

When Huey-1 copter banked hard right for an evasive maneuver, P3, P4, P5, P6 and P7 concentrated their aim.
Boom! Boom! Boom! Boom!...
Several of the .223mm rounds pierced the cockpit window and wounded the pilot.
Huey-1 went into a tail spin as he struggled toward the ocean for a water landing. Unable to control his craft, the pilot plummeted back toward some fleeing villagers on the shore.
Frank, Johnny and the men watched in horror as the crippled copter hit the sand and burst into a ball of flames. Several dozen natives were killed, many of whom were children.
There to protect all of them, Nehune fell as victims in the fog of war.

Luke radioed, *"Frank, what was that? It sounded like an explosion!"*
Silence.
"FRANK? TALK TO ME!"
"We took down a Huey, Luke." Frank was not one to mince words with his close friend. It was he who put a tourniquet on Luke's waist after being shot through his side on the hill they held overnight in Nam. *"It hit a crowd of villagers with lots of children as they were running for cover."*
Chloe covered her mouth, held her stomach, bent over, stood and ran to the bathroom to throw up.

Huey-2 radioed to command center, *"Sir, H1 gunner and pilot down! Advise on continued action."*

Disgusted, General Cohen radioed back, *"H2, swing back to drop-off point."*

One of the mercenaries on the ground radioed. *"Sir, ten down. Only five of us left."*

"Pull back and meet H2 at drop-off!"

"What about our dead?"

"You were given orders to pull back. NOW!"

Once he sold his soul to the commission, Gen. Cohen dismissed a cardinal rule of war: never leave any man behind. Military ethics and ethos are null and void when evil dictates and schemes avail.

Several warriors waited in ambush as the mercenaries retreated. Mock combat training turned real as Numea ripped a soldier's jugular vein with his shark teeth club. Another warrior swung his stone-head club and missed the soldier that ducked and stabbed him. The other soldiers opened fire and killed Numea and his men.

Under heavy fire, it was miraculous that no one on Frank's team was injured.

"Luke, counted five left from the ground assault team. They stopped firing and pulled back. Heard shots about a hundred yards from retreat point--- not sure why. Looks like Huey-2 is headed back where boots were dropped off."

"Roger, Frank. I expected Gen. Cohen to take it all the way."

326

Chloe returned to be at Luke's side as he lowered his head, reached deep in his gut and asked. *"How many villagers?"*

Grimly, Frank radioed back, *"Too many. Not looking good."*

"Can you see Hanani, Dana and Tiare? Malia? Hoku and Kawika...anywhere?

Frank surveyed the scene below through his binoculars.

Emerging from the bush, Feyman was slung over Kyle's right shoulder. Cliff's right arm was locked in Kyle's left arm as he limped and pressed Kyle's herbal patch on his wound to slow the bleeding. The threesome hobbled back to the shambled village.

Luke turned to look at Chloe, put his arms around her and radioed for a response, *"Frank?"*

"Negative, Luke."

Part IX

Desire of Nations

23

In the setting sun, Kalani faced northwest to the distant island of Nihoa from a hilltop on Niihau. His spirit groaned and travailed in prayer for the plight of his people. After nearly two weeks of captivity while Prof. Bolten tried to figure out what to do with him, he escaped before dawn that morning. This gave him enough time to gather food and drink in the wild and find refuge on this hill to seek the Lord.

During a peaceful night of sleep, he dreamt of a faint light hovering above the sea. A dark, lingering shadow on the ocean surface slithered in its direction, opened it gapping maw and clamped down on the light. As he watched, the shadow began to writhe in agony, heave and regurgitate the light, now more luminescent, back onto land. When he awoke, he knew that the light given to his people would pass through the bowels of darkness and emerge stronger, brighter.

The next day seemed surreal. In the warmth of the rising sun, morning breezes brushed gently over the emerald heights and cascaded downward, causing the tall grass below to undulate like ribbons of silk flowing in the wind. Kalani spent the day in meditation and prayer, rising only to take little food and drink.

As the day waned, twilight draped over him like a fragrant veil. Gazing upwards, the stars became clearer. His attention was drawn to a brilliant light in the sky.

It was the constellation of Coma.

Shaken by the spectacle, Kalani whispered in awe, "Desire of Nations," a tear fell from his eye, "lead us home."

He turned when he heard footsteps coming up the side of the hill to the top clearing of his hideout.

He recognized the thug that beat him when he was being interrogated by Bolten. The man took out a Ruger .22 cal. and shot Kalani several times in the chest.

On his back from the force of the shots, Kalani lay bleeding, profusely. The cold stare of his heartless killer peered through the descending darkness.

Kalani turned his eyes toward heaven and uttered softly, "Jesus, not hold this to him. Forgive," lips quivering, "forgive him."

Some of the Niihauans carrying their tools from the farm field below heard the shots. Alarmed, they looked up but could not see where Kalani was gunned down.

Kalani's body was dragged into tall bushes and left there.

The gunman casually brushed himself off and walked away into the dark of night.

*****

No one on the outer islands would have imagined what happened on Nihoa.

330

Seeing the village dead lying on the beach when they came down from the mountainside, the Namera defenders went to work. They radioed Luke, who came immediately to help with recovery efforts. Hanani insisted to bury them on the ridge next to the others that fell. Digging graves for over a hundred bodies high up required intensive labor too burdensome for the weak and shocked survivors.

Luke went through Feyman's pockets and was surprised to find a letter he wrote before boarding the boat:
If I die on Nihoa, it would be my honor to be buried with the natives that we came here to defend.
Luke discussed this with Frank. They decided to fulfill his death wish. Once back on Oahu, Luke would reach out to the organization that managed Feyman's fund for survivors to handle post-mortem logistics.

Kyle, Dana and Tiare worked side-by-side with Hanani and her three children. Mild to severe injuries were treated with aloe and herbs. The Asmat herb patch Kyle placed in Cliff's wound helped. His healing was hastened by remedies he learned from Ngati Kahungunu iwi that were similar to herbal concoctions used by Nehune.

When it was time for Luke and his men to finally bid their farewell, Hanani urged Kyle and Dana to board with the defense team and get back to their work on Oahu.

331

Cliff and Tiare opted to remain.

*****

Still bruised from the air and ground assault, Hanani awoke shortly before dawn to brave the rocks and breaking waves. She achingly reached the southern tip of Dog's Head Peak and slowly inched her way several yards up, sat, and wept.
Silent for several moments, a bright light in the sky caught her eye. She looked up and realized it was the constellation of Coma. Exuberant, she sensed that wherever Kalani was, he, too, witnessed this longed-for sign. Her joy, however, was mixed with a gut-feeling that something happened to him. No one knew where he was taken or how he faired. Reeling from this grief, she bowed her head and prayed.

Malia opened her eyes from a deep sleep. Glancing around the hut, she noticed that Hanani was gone. Kawika and Hoku were fast asleep. She mozied out of her cot and stood. Stepping outside, the sun peered over the horizon. Birds tweeted and chirped. Palm fronds swayed.
Aggrieved from the recent mayhem, she felt a surge of encouragement fill her heart. It slowly rose inside. Then she was alerted to a *thump-thump-thump-thump* sound in the sand not far away. Listening closely, the thumping, in cadence, got louder. Startled, she saw a white horse trot from around a nearby hut and turn towards her. Around its muscular neck hung a gold shield embossed with

the letter H, blue in color, dangling on a gold chain. She whispered under her breath, "Hope."

Its mane swirled as it nodded its head and neighed. Awed by this real-life encounter, Malia watched with bated breath as Hope knelt in the sand. A voice in her spirit said, *"Get on."*

Trotting slowly, Malia marveled as Hope's mane danced in a gentle wind, and its smooth, white, powerful body carry her away to Dog's Head Peak. When they arrived, she looked up to see Hanani's head resting on her knees.

The white horse stopped and knelt so Malia could get off. It stood and said, "You must not lose hope for what is to come." She watched as it trotted away and turned around boulders jutting from the sand toward the ocean.

Brows furrowed, Malia hurried over to the boulders. While in prayer, a surge of hope filled Hanani's heart. It was so tangible that she opened her eyes. Looking down, she saw her daughter looking perplexed and shouted. "Malia! What's wrong?"

Dazed that the white horse was nowhere to be found in the shallows of the mildly rolling surf, Malia looked up and responded, "Mom! Nothing. I'm okay!"

Joining her mother up on the rocks, Malia, transfixed, surveyed the ocean below. Sensing something was amidst, Hanani said nothing.

Tiare showed up on the sand below. "Hanani, Malia!"

They both looked down to see her.

Hanani answered, "How did you know we were here?"

"I woke up and," shrugging, "I just knew that I would find you two here."

As Tiare climbed up to where they were, Malia cautioned, "Careful, aunty, the rocks are slippery."

"No worries." Tiare looked up and smiled.

Up on the rocks together, they conversed about all that had happened.

Suddenly, they felt a slight rumble. It was strong enough to cause small, loose rocks to fall into the ocean. The tremor startled them—and awoke others still asleep in their huts.

Hours after, sirens were blaring on all of the islands. The first time sirens blasted in Hawaii was on the USS Enterprise when Japanese pilots attacked Pearl Harbor in 1941. Surprised that the ship's radar was picking up blips that looked like crawling ants on their screen, the ship's radioman received a coded message that this was no drill: they were under attack. The quartermaster pulled the general quarter's alarm. It blared 17 times while men scrambled to their battle stations.

Alarmed newscasters from all channels scrambled to warn the islanders. One reporter from Channel 4 stated, "*An 8.0 earthquake struck just minutes ago. The epicenter is said to be approximately 200 miles south of the Kure atoll. All islands in Hawaii are on a major tsunami alert. Emergency evacuations from all low-lying areas are currently underway. Niihau and Kauai will be hit first in approximately 18 hours.*"

Luke radioed, *"Kawika, do you read?"*
Silence.
"Luke to Kawika, do you read?"
He jumped up from a deep sleep in his hut to radio back, *"I read."*
"Do you know about the earthquake south of Kure Atoll?"
"I thought I was dreaming when I felt the ground move."
"A tsunami will hit Nihoa by mid-afternoon...."

The chiefs moved fast when they heard this grim news. They made a head count and ordered only five of the nine canoes removed from the stilts and dragged to the shore. Men and women worked hard to keep the children calm while they hastily hauled all of their supplies onboard. Others loaded the two canoes anchored in the shallows. On one of them, Cliff, Kawika and several men carried Makoa's canoe pod and secured it to the center platform. Nehune had little time to fill the hulls before they set out to sea. Slightly weathered and worn from months of exposure, the sails were rigged back to the masts. If torn while seaborne, they had extra sails from the canoes left behind. Paddles were ready if needed.

*****

Once Nehune left Kealaikahiki sometime ago, General Saul Cohen immediately followed through with plans by the commission to level the village and replace it with a missile silo. Civil engineers bulldozed the entire midland and shoreline areas where the village once stood. The uplands were left unscathed.

Channel iron, concrete bags, rebars, steel beams, copper wiring, conduit piping, and other materials were shipped from Oahu on a barge and transported over a 100 yards inland from the shoreline. Building that close to the water should have factored in worst case weather scenarios. It did not matter. The object was to replace the entire village layout as if it never existed.

Pallets of rebars, tie wire and plywood sheets were placed along the edges of a massive, arch-shaped trench dug ten feet down and five feet wide. Workers would shortly begin setting and tying the rebars, securing sheets of plywood to shape the inner and outer walls, then pour cement into the forms. Once built, the 50-feet high seawall was designed to protect the silo complex from storm waves.

Back hoe operators dug two massive cylindrical pits deep down into the soil. The shallow pit was 60 ft. in diameter and 40 ft. deep for a manned, launch operations unit. The second pit, about 20 ft. in diameter and 90 ft. deep, made way for an ICBM missile.

An underground boring machine was hauled down a carved-out road to hollow out the earth for blast tunnels. Hauling trucks used this road to remove tons of material from below.

Gen. Cohen kept a close watch on logistics during the various phases of construction. "How much longer?"
The head engineer assured, "Projection was for 2 years. Looks like we're on schedule."
"All of this may be for nothing."
"Sir?"
"Haven't you been listening to the radio?"
"Oh, the tsunami?"
Grunting, "Yes."
The engineer, non-chalant, shrugged. "We've had tsunami warnings before, but nothing to worry about. We've had false alarms before. Guess we just have to cross our fingers."
Gen. Cohen glared at him for this stupid remark.

*****

Hanani reminisced on the fateful sign of Coma on that morning when she sat alone on the shoreline rocks before Malia and Tiare joined her. Again, it lit up in her soul like fire: the long awaited sign for Nehune to return to Kahoolawe. Now, here they were, forced to leave because of an earthquake, but on an ocean path the navigators were trained for--- back to Kealaikahiki!

The ocean level rose gradually as waves continued to roll in and around Nihoa. Nehune watched as the powerful tide crept slowly into Adam's Bay until their village was inundated and all of their canoes were afloat. With the village now underwater, Hanani's insistence to bury everyone on the ridge was the Lord's prompting to preserve the bodies from being unearthed.

As the flotilla started to move, many Nehune questioned if God had abandoned them. Encouraged by Hope, Malia remained steadfast.
In seven double-hull canoes, men were positioned at the sterns and bows. They called out orders to man the sails, gave directions to the steersmen to hold their headings and trained their eyes on the horizon, sun, clouds and swells.

Favorable winds carried the canoes in full sail on rolling seas for several hours. Studying the horizon, the lead canoe navigator strained to confirm what he was seeing at a great distance. He yelled, "Look!" he pointed in a northeast direction, "clouds angry." Navigators on the other canoes saw him pointing excitedly toward the faint, gray-topped rain curtain heading their way. Veering off-course to avoid the storm would risk a detour from the path Mau trained them on. Deciding to hold steady in the tempest ahead, the lead navigator signaled the other canoes. "We go through!"

Drawing closer to the storm, tempest winds churned the ocean. When hit by the full force of its fury, the waves tossed the canoes like rudderless matchsticks.

A signal was given to pull in all the sails so the flotilla could ride it out. More men were ordered to help the steersmen stay on course.

Women stayed in the platform huts and held on to their children. Many of them vomited from being violently tossed. Gale winds whipped open some of the doors on the huts and spilled supplies.

A heaving, treacherous sea; like the rise and fall of a giant's chest breathing deeply. High above the obscured horizon, dark clouds billowed and rolled by the forces of wind and rain.

Hanani held onto Makoa's canoe-coffin tied to the platform in back of the center hut.

Tiare, holding a sail line, stood nearby.

In pain, Cliff gritted his teeth and grabbed chords of sennit rope, cut it to length, and shouted above the waves crashing on deck. "Hanani, Tiare, tie this around your waists and to the railing! Malia, you and Hoku do the same!" He moved back to the stern to help the steersman.

Hanani, thinking that Ateo was on one of the other canoes, noticed that he was onboard. The native teen had grown close to their family by hanging around Kawika's hut and learning how to operate the radio. Tall, dark and sinewy, his strong legs could not keep him steady while being tossed on deck. He clung to the sail lines and rails, but Hanani knew it wasn't enough.

"Ateo!" Hanani yelled. "Take rope, tie around you," she pointed to her own waist, "like us, and tie to rail!"

Ateo was stubborn. He wanted to brave the canoe just like the other men onboard as it jerked, rose and dropped. Shaking his head, he held on to the rail and moved astern to find Kawika.

A massive wave was building and heading toward them. The steersman, Cliff and Kawika tried to angle the canoe for a diagonal climb up the wave, to no avail. Left with no choice, everyone ran to hold on the rails and mast poles.
Kawika shouted, "ATEO! HANG ON!"
When the wave struck, the brunt of the impact was astern.
Ateo was flung overboard.
Drenched, Hanani, Tiare, Malia and Hoku were shaken, but tethered securely in place. The hut buckled under impact, but remained intact.
Everyone inside and on deck survived.
When Tiare stood up to assess the damage, her eyes grew wide with fear when she saw the storm-tossed youth flailing and kicking to stay afloat. She screamed, "ATEO! ATEO!"
Hanani hollered at Kawika, "ATEO IS DROWNING!"
Malia and Hoku looked on in horror. Buckled over, Cliff held his side as he whipped around to see the navigator on their canoe waving his arms and shouting, "No! Not safe!"
Watching the fear-gripped teen struggling to survive, Kawika tied himself to the rail, made a large loop at one end of the line and threw it out to him. Nobody saw it, but a divine hand reached for the rope, still far from Ateo's reach, and placed it

firmly in his hand. Thinking it was he, alone, that grabbed ahold of the rope, he put the loop over his weak body and held on as Kawika and Cliff pulled him in. Once the frightened teen was safely onboard, Cliff fell on his knees from the stabbing pain in his side.

Kawika yelled, "Uncle! You okay!?"

"I'm," grunt, "fine."

The other canoes were tossed and dashed, but avoided the massive wave that crashed on the canoe Hanani and her family were on.

In these violent waters, the lead navigator relied on his training to listen to his body and feel a swell lift and lower his canoe. As he counted, other swells followed the same lift-lower timing and direction to lead them out of the storm.

Over an hour passed before the ocean fury abated. Triangulating his position using his hands and fingers, he was elated that all the canoes remained on course.

Cries from the children turned to calm. Women picked up toppled supplies. Some stepped out of their beaten huts and threw tethered gourds over the side to fill with water to wash vomit off the hut floor. Menfolk smiled and whooped that they steered their families safely out of the belly of the beast.

What they would later understand is that the grace and mercy of God carried them safely through troubled waters.

After some time, Niihau came into sight.
Once they had a fix on this landmark, they could
retrace their path back to their beloved homeland.

*****

The tall, bearded man with blue eyes and curly hair
stood where Kalani lie. He knelt beside His
precious servant, leaned over, and gently blew on
his face.
Kalani opened his eyes to find himself flat on his
back in tall bushes and looking at clouds floating in
a blue dome.
Alone.
He remembered being shot and sat up quickly.
Anxious, he felt his chest. Blood and bullet holes
soiled his garment. When he ripped it open, he
marveled that his chest wounds were healed.

*****

Tsunami damages along southwestern coasts were
devastating. Niihau was hit hard. Several occupants
in a large boat close to the Niihauan shoreline rode
out incoming waves. As the distant flotilla of
double-hull canoes sailed pass them, the captain
onboard steered the boat to follow them.
On Kauai, emergency sirens worked briefly, then
malfunctioned. Locals and tourists there thought it
was just a drill. Unaware of breaking news, they
were curious when the tide pulled far back from the
shoreline. Foolishly, some of them ventured out to
exposed reefs. They thought nothing of the far-off

waves, until long, white crests drew relentlessly closer. When they realized something was wrong, they ran. But it was too late. The impact of incoming swells swept them off their feet. All of them drowned.

Water levels on Oahu reached higher than the picnic park front across from Ala Moana Shopping Center. It rushed in to fill the center's parking stalls and spilled into shops and the popular food court.
Hotel swimming pools close to the Waikiki beach were replaced with saltwater and debris.
The people at Kaunakakai on Molokai suffered great losses, as well as those on Lanai.
At Lahaina, Maui, ocean tides destroyed well-known storefronts and restaurants.
Cars, buses, bikes, motorcycles and anything that could be moved along the affected areas of each island were lifted from their places and became part of the powerful streams that flowed mercilessly inland.
News reporters in helicopters were stunned by scenes on each affected island.
Next to impact zones, plans were in motion to set up FEMA workers and volunteers from charity organizations to aid the wounded, search for signs of life under the rubble and bury the dead.
Emergency crews tried to evacuate everyone on each island to higher ground. Those that lingered and strayed were caught in the grip of the waves.
Hospital rooms overflowed with patients needing emergency treatment.

All island coasts suffered cataclysms of
undetermined magnitudes.

Though slighted buffeted by swells emanating from
the quake's epicenter, full sail and normal winds
propelled Nehune forward. When they reached
Kealaikahiki by day two, the tsunami left natural
debris, along with sparse remains of steel, conduit
pipes, wood, etc.
Powerful tide surges had washed most of the
construction material and all of the operating
equipment into the long, seawall trench and into
both massive holes dug for the support facility and
the ICBM missile.
Sand and rock mixed with tons of cement bags on
pallets from the force of the swirling water
miraculously filled the trench and holes completely.

Lamenting over the loss of everything they knew,
their *lulululul* wails reached a haunting crescendo.
A boat pulled slowly alongside the cluster of canoes
a short distance away. The wailing subsided as they
all turned to watch the priest dive off the side and
swim to shore. Shocked, Nehune pointed excitedly,
jumped into the water, swam, ran over and
surrounded him. "Kalani! God bring Kalani back
us!"
Jenna Robbins-Hansen heard that one of the local
farmers found him wondering around, bloodied, but
peculiarly joyful. She contacted her husband,
Admiral Jessie Hansen. A family member on Niihau
had a boat and solicited help from locals to bring
Kalani home.

Part X

The Son Sets in the West

24

Kalani told Hanani of the secret cave, hidden somewhere in the upland forest, where he had some natives store seed and other resources before they left. "We take Makoa in cave. I told do this by father before he die."
Hanani looked perplexed. "Tevake?"
"Yes," Kalani nodded
"Why?"
"He tell me rebellion kill Makoa. Secret cave mean rest. Rebellion kill us if we no rest in God."

The tsunami-altered topography impacted their Kealaikahiki village layout on Kahoolawe. Still, their hearts steady flame stoked their efforts to rebuild. Once huts and other constructs were built, the midland areas were topped with reddish soil carved out of the hillsides by the waves, leaving rich nutrients for farming.
The land was trenched to retain and divert rain water for crops. Upland areas were left unscathed, leaving an abundance of trees for felling.
Aquafarms on Oahu supplied them with seafood for their fishponds.
Big Island locals brought pigs and other livestock, including boar and deer for reproduction and hunting in the wild.
Kauai farmers helped plant papaya and mango trees and herbalists from Molokai grew a variety of medicinal plants.

Native practitioners committed to Christ taught dance, song and chants as purer forms of worship to God. Children learned different crafts by artisans. Nehune's assimilation of the English language improved communications.

Displaced locals on the other islands were astonished when they heard what was happening on Kahoolawe. They came in droves to see and help a people lost in time: from living in nylon tents on beaches and parks, and eating packaged and canned foods, to grass huts on a remote beach and eating food grown and hunted. This simple lifestyle transition improved their health.

*****

Self-governance efforts on Kahoolawe faced daunting hurdles. Chiefs and priests listened to what Nainoa had to say. "Lahui o Pono was formed to correct what the Hawaiian Kingdom did not do, and what the U.S. government is not doing. If we seek justice and righteousness, our lives will fare better." Recalling the dictates of Vanatu, one of the chiefs cautioned, "People high up not want this way." He correctly discerned that corrupt politicians in the State of Hawaii would resist Lahui o Pono for several significant reasons. For example, the recent exodus of homeless natives to Kealaikahiki on Kahoolawe could become an example of solving the long-standing problem of homelessness on Oahu. It would be good reason for sovereignty groups to lambast the government for being incapable and inefficient, and demand that funding to uphold the homeless apparatus be diverted toward their efforts to form an independent government. It could embolden splinter groups to force their nationalist agendas. If so, the state of Hawaii would be under pressure from global governments to take control over Kahoolawe. Such is the way of well-oiled, government machines on all corners of the globe.

Kalani was more forthcoming, "We not want Hawaiian kingdom; not want Ame-can gov-ment. We want follow Jesus, King, seek His Kingdom." Weighty words.
Kyle and Dana flew in from Kauai where they hosted an annual luncheon. They sat next to Hanani. At her right, Cliff remembered his global quest when he was younger. He said, "People were subjects in kingdoms of pharaohs, emperors, caliphs and monarchs. Peace was plagued by war; religious battles of swords and guns affirmed power and rule. The blood of innocents lies in the wake of history. These people desire," he looked around, "Jesus and His Kingdom where the greatest are those that serve and lay their lives down for others."
Kyle gave him the shaka sign.
Knowing Luke's body language well, the chiefs encouraged him to speak. "Kalani not wanting anything to do with the American government is understood. But we must remember that its present form of corruption and control over the people was never intended by our founding fathers."
"And mothers." Chloe interjected.

"Yes," he rubbed her arm, "as a former naval officer, I swore to uphold and defend the constitution from foreign and domestic enemies, a constitution rooted in biblical statutes that were intended to reflect precepts of God-bestowed decrees."

Shaking her head in agreement, Hanani intoned, "If *only* American leaders and the people feared and honored the Lord, what *is* broken *can* be fixed."

Politicians listen to lobbyists and special interest groups while the voices of people fall on deaf ears. Numbers strategists obsessed with polls and trends to feed the election cycle have little regard for what matters to God. Disinviting Him from government, public schools, the sciences, etc., was taking its toll. Abortion, homosexuality, pornography, human trafficking, murder, etc., were abominations deserving of judgement *if* the Lords' repeated calls for repentance through the voices of true prophets were ignored. Repenting from our evil ways and honoring the Lord would release America into a greater vision and destiny.

Nehune's return to their homeland was setting this kind of precedence by humbling themselves, turning from their wicked ways, seeking God's face and praying. They were eager to see Him heal the land of Kahoolawe. Broken and contrite prayer would welcome the presence of the Lord in their midst; patience and kindness would fill their days. If envy, boasting, pride, self-seeking, and being easily provoked to anger took root, love would not

349

flourish. Truth, protection, trust, hope and perseverance were stalwart virtues of their restoration. Fearing the Lord was the beginning of wisdom that would keep them from folly that led, and lead, to the fall of all nations.

Kalani remembered when Hanani taught them the Beatitudes on Nihoa. "Pure in heart, they see God. People mourn, He comfort them." He gestured for Hanani to continue.
She said, "All who are meek will inherit the land. They that hunger and thirst for righteousness, will be satisfied. The merciful will receive mercy. Peacemakers will be called children of God. For us who are persecuted for the sake of righteousness, ours will be the Kingdom of Heaven on earth, under the rule of Jesus."
"See," Kalani said, "she say Jesus Kingdom, not man kingdom."
Hanani turned to everyone on the council. "Jesus said our reward will be great in heaven," lips quivering, "Nehune gunned down on Nihoa are in heaven with Him."
Long silence.
One of the chiefs turned to Nainoa and asked, "Lahui o Pono gov-ment, how look?"
Feeling his insides stir, he had no stomach to counter the simple devotion to Christ that they desired. "Leaders will not be allowed to declare genealogical descent from ancient bloodlines. They will not be masters, but servants in word and deed---and earn respect by giving it."

Almost on cue, all of the chiefs lowered their heads. They knew the weight of their task was crucial in restoration.

Hanani emphasized, "Knowing the Lord will be foremost."

Cliff added, "The troublesome, meddler and power-seeker that have no regard for prayerful counsel will be asked to leave the island."

One chief responded, "What Hanani teach Jesus and you say, good."

Dana's anthropological wheels were turning in her mind: Hawaiian navigators came here to study stone configurations that depict star patterns for wayfinding. She pointed to the sky. "With all of Nehune struggles that brought them back to their homeland, I find it interesting that our ancients used Hokupaa, the North Star, and Hanaiakamalama, the Southern Cross, to navigate. In my heart, the North Star represents the Lord who is higher than human luminaries seeking to exalt themselves, so all men are drawn to Him alone. The Southern Cross speaks of our Lord's redemptive sacrifice for all mankind."

Hanani sprung up and declared, "The Spirit of the living God has guided Nehune back home as we all, together, rebuild this place to honor Jesus our King!"

Everyone could feel the breath of revelation in Hanani's words.

Sitting silently next to Hanani, Tiare added, "Evil leaders deceive the masses with false hopes. We will honor Jesus with our lives and speak of true hope that is in Christ alone."

*****

Several years passed. Tiare remained close to
Hanani and the children. Cliff had gone to the
mainland to marry Tonya. When he brought her to
Kealaikahiki, she was delighted to be with the
people.

As a priest, Cliff was asked by Hanani to preside
over Luke and Chloe's marriage ceremony. Aside
from a traditional script, he was free to articulate
wedding vows to be repeated by groom and bride.
Dressed in his admiral attire, Luke stood in front of
Cliff. Nehune insisted on his military uniform to
honor his service in the navy. Chloe stepped onto
the dirt pathway lined with flowers on each side.
Her father came to escort her down the aisle. She
wore a white, knee-length gown that revealed her
tanned legs, with a magenta scarf loosely wrapped
around her shoulders. Woven by an elderly
Hawaiian woman, her headdress was made with
maile leaves and bright flowers. Native youth
weaved her sandals from pandanus leaves with
intricate, tight patterns that made for surprising
comfort when she tried them on.

Among those standing on both sides of the aisle,
Luke's Vietnam buddies that protected Nehune on
Nihoa were also dressed in full military regalia.
Admiral Jesse Hansen, still on active duty, chose to
keep a low profile and wore a floral-print shirt,
jeans and slippers; his wife Jenna wore a floral
muumuu and slippers.

Hanani and Tiare both wore white plumeria-print, pink-colored pareos around white tee-shirts, jeans, slippers and pikake leis around their necks. Kawika, Malia and Hoku were dressed in tunic-like garments made by Nehune women for this special occasion: beaten tapa was soaked in water, died with plant and berry extract, cut to modern design, and hand-sewn with fine sennit. Woven ropes were made to use as belts loosely tied around their waists.

Kyle and Dana wore floral-print shirts, plain-colored shorts and slippers and stood close to where Chloe was walking. As Chloe passed by, Kyle teased, *"Psssstt. Buk! Buk!"* His part-Filipino heritage was the same as hers. Dana elbowed him to be nice. Overhearing this, Tiare glared playfully at Kyle. Chloe smiled and mouthed in jest, *'Shut up'* and waved her clenched fist at him. When Kyle looked at Hanani, she aligned with Chloe and made a clenched fist at him.

Dana leaned her head on Kyle's shoulders, pressed her lips close to his ears and whispered, *"We've been married for almost 30 years. I love you more now than ever."* He whooped a little when she pinched his butt while no one was looking.

Luke and Chloe stood, held hands and smiled as Cliff went through marriage protocols. Shortly after, Ateo, now a fine, young, muscled man, lifted the small silk pillow loaned from Chloe's mom, with two gold rings, one studded with diamonds that glistened in the sun.

After placing their rings on each other's fingers, they knelt in front of a handmade bowl with two small pieces of breadfruit. A coconut shell with a little wine brought for this occasion was placed next to the bowl. In their communion with God, they vowed their communion with each other for life. A food-filled reception followed and went down in everyone's memory as the first holy matrimony on their home soil.

*****

"General Cohen, this is Delta 13, do you read, over?"
"Roger that, D-13."
"Target 5 miles and approaching, sir."
Dawkins sat next to the military officer, sick and emaciated. In a few, short years, his obsession to destroy Nehune led to the loss of his mind. Like Friedrich Nietzsche, Dawkins rant against God infected his intellect that could no longer reason; a reprobate mind that called good, evil, and evil, good. When Prof. Bolten stood up in their conference to recite, verbatim, Nietzsche's parable of the madman that celebrated the death of God, Dawkins felt high, drunk with the wine of hubris. The increasing frequency of his psychobabble, twitches and strange behavior left commission members concerned for his mental welfare. Unaware that he accidentally hit the com. switch, one of the pilots on the charted C-130 joked about the sound of the mound's name. *"Oh-pu-ee-vee. Sounds like poo poo wee wee."* he teased. *"Ha ha ha heee heee...."*

"D-13, what the hell is going on?" Gen. Cohen radioed, irritated.

"Sorry sir, didn't mean for this to transmit. Just an inside joke up here."

"Stop messing around and stay focused."

"Yes sir—copy that."

Com. switch off. *"These names baffle me. Them people are strange folk."*

"I heard that Neh—hu hu—ne ne named the mound."

More laughter.

When scientists learned of the cave's location, they swarmed, as predicted, inside Opu Iwi and conducted a series of studies to determine the existence of Nehune clan as first settlers, and to affirm the petroglyphic symbol: Jesus Christ, God our Savior. Some of their findings were published in journals, sparking outrage from commission members, particularly Dawkins. What was most unexpected is that a few of the more reputable scientists turned their hearts to God and became convincing defenders of what they once hailed as pure myths.

Midland mansions, Club Mez and the marina at Kanapou Bay were heavily damaged by the tsunami. Shocked and scared, most of the residents fled to higher ground in the Kula area. Those that ignored or mocked the warnings, perished.

Dawkins was able to convince politicians in Hawaii that the area was unfit for re-habitation. He bribed actuaries to payout insurance in amounts higher than assessed values of destroyed property, with the

355

difference coming from his contacts in investment and banking. These moves were to ensure zero risks for collateral damage: Gen. Cohen needed the freedom to have a bunker-busting bomb destroy the symbol in the Opu Iwi mound, the belly of Mother Eve.

Humiliated when Nehune descendants were exposed and enraged that they flourished, Dawkins was left with the only option: destroy what was dearest to them.

"Delta-13 verifying target in sight. Permission to drop package, sir."

Hunched in pain, Dawkins drooled on the side of his mouth. His hand shook violently as he reached for the button on the radio.

"Per..mis..sion...gr..granted."

Both pilots looked curiously at each other.

"Gen. Cohen, sir, is this you? Please verify."

He radioed back with his deep, rough voice, *"We had some static. Permission to drop. I repeat, permission to drop package."*

"Roger that, sir."

BOOOOOMMM......

The ground tremor was felt by everyone at Kealaikihiki.

Hanani held her chest and gasped, "What was *that*?" She and everyone else were startled.

Kalani pointed eastward. "Sound come from there!"

356

25

30 years later

It was a time of peace for Nehune.
Though physical evidence of their Messiah in Opu
Iwi was destroyed, the symbol that represented
Him, now etched in their hearts and minds,
remained their sacred legacy.

The coalescence of Nehune, Hawaiian and other
cultures endured many challenges. People from
different corners of the globe were welcomed with
open arms. Eventually, some demanded that the
ways of God give way to eastern mysticism and
other esoteric protocols toward enlightenment.
Others found biblical teachings on adultery,
divorce, keeping oaths, being salt and light, etc., as
ascetic nonsense. Realizing that Nehune would not
compromise their simple devotion to Christ, people
left in droves. If others became contentious and
disruptive, Cliff had arranged for trusted people to
oversee their departure.

The remnant that remained was of one heart and
one mind. With no technology to interfere with their
quiet, labor-intensive, contemplative lives, they
were more inclined to think on things that were
pure, noble and right. Things that were admirable
and excellent were praised and held in high regard.
Disagreements were inevitable. Through prayer and
fasting, the word of the Lord provided them road

maps out of tension, strife, or encroaching disunity.
Loving God with all their hearts, minds and souls,
and their neighbors as themselves, became the
capstone of their lives.
However imperfect, the kingdom they lived for was
real.
The presence of the Lord among them was felt by
all.

Hanani and Tiare aged gracefully and remained as
matriarchs among Nehune and Hawaiians.
Kawika came and went, but mostly stayed close to
his mother and sisters. He married his childhood
friend and had children and grandchildren.
Malia and Hoku remained steadfastly at Hanani's
side: Malia married an island native from Maui;
Hoku fell in love with and married a man from
Texas. Both sisters also had children and
grandchildren of their own.
Ateo was adopted into their family, bringing many
challenges that were overcome by love. He married
a woman from his tribe and had a son.

*****

Late one afternoon, Malia, now in her late 40s, sat
alone on the shoreline as her husband and
grandchildren visited with Hanani. Pondering on
what Nehune had endured to come into this time of
peace moved her deeply. As dusk fell, she became
preoccupied with the memory of her encounter with
Hope on Nihoa that carried her to Hanani's side.

Then a sudden, familiar stirring surged within her. There, far away, a shadowy figure was moving in her direction. Coming into focus, she watched as a man, his head covered, was dressed in a white flowing robe and sat on a white horse. As they drew closer, she recognized the horse by its majestic size. Around its neck hung a gold chain and a purple letter on the gold shield.

"Love!"

Turning her attention to the white-robed man, her heart raced wildly. She stood and ran over to them, fell on her knees, and exclaimed, "Lord!"

Looking down at her, Jesus pulled back His head covering and said, "Though they cannot see Me, they know My presence as I ride among them, because they seek My face." His countenance was pure peace as He continued, "I am their first love." When Jesus said this, Love lifted up its powerful head, its mane frolicking, and neighed.

Jesus's blazing, blue eyes pierced inside the depths of Malia's soul. Trembling in awe, she bowed her head and did not realize that the Lord came down from the horse and stood next to her. As she looked up into His face, a tear rolled down her cheek. The Lord let it fall on the sand. "Their valley of tears is now a spring. Love covers it with blessings. From strength to strength this island surges, appearing as Eden before Me."

*****

The pudgy girl looked at her with piercing eyes. Since Kawika's daughter-in-law gave birth, there

359

was something peculiar about his granddaughter's far away stares, as if she possessed knowledge beyond her years. "Can I sit in your lap, tutu-ma?" The villagers made a rocking chair for Hanani. Her long hair turned white as she advanced in years. Ever active and forward moving, her body became weaker, her olive eyes, dimmer. She smiled, patted her lap and said, "Of course, sweetheart." Her head drew back. "Do you know what your name means?" Eliana settled down and shook her head, her bright eyes and cherubic smile waiting for an answer. "It means my God has answered. He has answered grandma's prayers. You remind all of us that God has answered our prayers."

The young boy ran up and tried to muscle Eliana. Malia scolded her grandson, "No, be nice to your cousin. She asked first. What have we been teaching you about manners?"

He looked at Malia, pouted and turned to Hanani. "I'll be nice to Eliana." His tone made them all chuckle.

Hanani patted her other leg, "You can sit here." Manasseh gladly climbed on her lap. "What does *my* name mean, tutu-ma?"

"Oh, that's easy. It means God has caused me to forget my troubles."

"Am I in trouble?"

"No, silly. You're too cute to be in trouble," she giggled and glanced at Malia, *"now."* She squeezed his cheek. "With all that tutu-ma has been through, when I see you, I forget all of my troubles."

Hoku's grandson saw his cousins from a distance. His jovial, effervescent ways brought joy to everyone. He ran and tried to get up into the rocking chair with them. "Me too, tutu-ma."

"No," Hoku cautioned, "grandma's lap is full."

Hanani offered, "You can stand right here, hold the arm of my chair and rock us *very* slowly."

Ephraim was glad to participate. He shifted his weight and tipped-toed to rock them. "What about my name?"

"It means fruitful."

"Like how we eat papayas and bananas for breakfast?"

"Like how the fruit of our peace is joy, the way you bring joy to tutu's heart." She kissed the tip of her right finger then touched the tip of his nose.

*****

Luke and Chloe lived a happy marriage and settled in a plush, verdant area in Hawaii. His war buddies blended back into island life and remained active in rotary and other clubs to give back to their communities.

When Admiral Jesse Hansen decided to retire, he and Jenna left for the mainland and settled there.

Drs. Kyle and Dana Pahono resorted to light lecture schedules in Hawaii and abroad, ever vigilant to discuss science as thinking God's thoughts after Him: tangible and intangible phenomena emerged from unseen realms, defined in part by quantum physics. Big Bang was debatably a point of ignition that channeled what was invisible to all that is now visible; all things now known and measurable merely crossed over from the veil that separates us

361

from eternity. Age took its toll, forcing the archaeologist and anthropologist to live their remaining years peacefully and quietly on Oahu.

By trial and error, Hanani's and Tiare's labors among Nehune yielded much. They all witnessed God's faithful interventions on many fronts. Adversaries bent on disrupting their way of life for the last thirty years were thwarted at every turn. Eventually, there was enough pressure from the world community that forced the State of Hawaii to sign all of Kahoolawe over to Nehune and Hawaiians to govern as they pleased. No monetary or other support were pledged with hopes that it would eventually send the natives groveling back at their feet for assistance and force a renegotiation for power and control of the island.
God was in control.

Seafood was in steady, abundant supply. Because the soil was left fallow every seven years, farmed crops were consistently high in yields. Game animals multiplied, providing all-year hunting in set quotas to allow for reproduction cycles. Their health and vigor drew attention to doctors sent to study their lifestyle, much like centenarians in agrarian parts of earth untouched by pollution and population density.
In all, the religious and medical communities observed the decades-long drama unfold on this island. Miracles occurred where herbs and other interventions failed. An equal distribution of

resources met the needs of everyone, so there were no poor among them.

*****

Sleeping sound and peaceful in the night, Hanani heard the Lord's voice, *"Faith, Hope and Love. The greatest of these is Love."*
When she awoke, the wisdom of His words encompassed all that had transpired over the long, painful decades. In addition, several more passages from the Word burned in her heart. Later in the day, she asked Tiare to gather the people together in one place.

When they all were gathered, Hanani slowly stood and cited from the Book of Psalms:

"Surely His salvation is near to those who fear Him,
That glory may dwell in our land.
Mercy and truth have met together;
Righteousness and peace have kissed.
Truth shall spring out of the earth,
And righteousness shall look down from heaven.
Yes, the Lord will give what is good;
And our land will yield its increase.
Righteousness will go before Him,
And shall make His footsteps our pathway."

On Hanani's cue, Tiare turned the pages to read from another passage in Psalms:

"God be merciful to us and bless us,
And cause His face to shine upon us, Selah
That Your way may be known on earth,
Your salvation among all nations.
Let the peoples praise You, O God;
Let all the peoples praise You.
Oh, let the nations be glad and sing for joy!
For You shall judge the people righteously,
And govern the nations on earth. Selah
Let the peoples praise You, O God;
Let all the peoples praise You.
Then the earth shall yield her increase;
God, our own God, shall bless us.
God shall bless us,
And all the ends of the earth shall fear Him."

When Tiare was done reciting the scriptures,
Hanani collapsed beside her.

Kawika ran over, "Mom!"
Alarmed, Malia and Hoku hurried over and knelt
beside her. "Mom! Nooo…"
Tiare was in shock. She knelt and whispered, "Lord,
please…"
Ateo knelt next to them, shaken, confused.

Hanani lifted her head up and saw a bright Light.
"Bebe."
Intense, ambient colors were bathed in radiant
luminescence. The power of Light and Life
permeated this awe-filled, eternal realm. Though
she could see only little, with crystal clear vision,

she sensed it was vast beyond comprehension and filled with indescribable wonders.
She looked up to her right. A youthful, stunningly handsome Makoa had a big smile on his face. "I've missed you, sweetheart."

Eliana, Manasseh and Ephraim came alongside and started to cry, "Tutu ma! Tutuuumaaa…!"
Nehune, their children and grandchildren gathered around her in disbelief that they were losing the matriarch they loved.

Hanani noticed her long hair was black, emitting a soft glow. Her wrinkleless skin shone like a newborn child. The garment she wore was pure, brilliant white.
"Is that the Lord?"

They noticed the subtle expressions on Hanani's face as she lay still on the ground. Having seen Makoa in his dream, Kawika knew something beautiful was happening. Malia, Hoku, Tiare and Ateo sensed it, too. The great grandkids, sniffling and wiping the tears from their eyes, looked on.

He gently nodded, "Give me your hand, bebe. He said I can take you to Him. He's waiting."
Makoa helped his beloved to her feet. When she stood, renewed, vigorous strength that had waned over the years pulsed through her body. All of her pain was gone. She was conscious of every deep breath and how strong her legs were.

365

Focused on the Lord, Hanani felt an unspeakable peace as she drew closer to Him. The power of His presence caused her to fall at His feet and worship. Gently lifting her up, she stood there, in awe, gazing on His beauty. Then Jesus smiled and said, "Good and faithful servant, enter into My joy...forever."

They placed her body in a canoe pod, alongside Makoa, in the uplands secret cave where he lay. Their bodies remain there to this day.

Pronunciation/Translation

Makoa: *Mah-ko-wah (brave)*
Hanani: *Hah-nah-nee (God is gracious)*
Kawika: *Kah-vee-kah (David)*
Malia: *Mah-lee-yah (calm)*
Hoku: *Ho-ku (star)*
Ateo: *Ah-teh-yo*
Po'o: *Po-o (head)*
Pahono: *Pah-ho-no*
Tiare: *Tee-ah-reh (fragrance)*
Aloike: *Ah-lo (presence) ee-keh (knowledge)*
Olapa: *O-lah (life) pa (yard)*
Nainoa: *Nah-ee-no-wah (protector)*
Lopaka: *Lo-pah-kah (Robert)*
Kapena: *Kah-peh-nah (Captain)*
Kaopua: *Kah-o-pu-wah*
Kaipo: *Kah-ee-po (caring)*
Tutu Pani: *Tu-tu (grandparent) Pah-nee (fill a breach)*
Akau: *Ah-kau (north)*
Ikaika: *Ee-kah-ee-kah (strong)*
Tevake: *Teh-vah-keh (character named after one of the greatest Pacific navigators of the twentieth century)*
Nahiena: *Nah-hee-eh-nah*
Kalani: *Kah-lah-nee (heavenly)*
Numea: *Nu-meh-yah*
Vanatu: *Vah-nah-tu*
Alika: *Ah-lee-kah*

Hawaiian Islands

Oahu: *O-ah-hu*
Maui: *Mau-wee*
Kauai: *Kah-wah-ee*
Kahoolawe: *Kah-ho-o-lah-weh*
Niihau: *Nee-ee-hau*
Lanai: *Lah-nah-ee*
Molokai: *Mo-lo-kah-ee*
Big Island: *known as island of Hawaii*

Pacific Islands
Nihoa: *Nee-ho-wah (known as Bird Island, an atoll northwest of the Hawaiian islands)*
Aotearoa: *Ah-o-teh-ah-ro-ha (New Zealand)*
Rapa Nui: *Ra-pah Nu-wee (known as Easter Island)*
Nuku Hiwa: *Nu-ku Hee-vah (largest of the Marquesas Islands in French Polynesia)*
Tahiti: *Tah-hee-tee (largest island in French Polynesia)*
Raiatea: *Rah-ee-yah-teh-yah (second largest island in French Polynesia)*
Samoa: *Sah-mo-wah: (South Pacific island)*
Savaii: *Sah-vah-ee-ee (located in Samoan islands)*

Tribes
Nehune: *Neh-hu-neh. Fictional derivation of Menehune (Meh-neh-hu-neh), a legendary race of small people*
Nana Ulu: *Nah-nah-u-lu (clan known to have settled Hawaii)*
Ulu Ohana: *U-lu O-ha-nah (clan known to have settled Hawaii)*
Sourced Bibilical Geneaology: Lua-Nu'u, (*Lu-ah-nu-u*), Mihakulani (*Mi-hah-ku-lah-nee*), Ku-Nawao

(*Ku-Nah-vah-o*), Ahu (*Ah-hu*) and Taranimenehune (*Tah-rah-nee-meh-neh-hu-neh*)

Ancient land-based System

Ahupuaa: *Ah-hu-pu-wah-ah (ancient Hawaiian land-based system)*
Uka: *U-kah (upper forest area of ahupua'a)*
Kula: *Ku-lah (midland crop area of ahupua'a)*
Kai: *Kah-ee (coastal area of ahupua'a)*
Aina: *Ah-ee-nah (land)*
Kauila *(Kau-wee-lah)*/ulei *(U-leh-ee) (trees used for spears and a variety of handmade tools)*
Hau: *(used for sail masts)*
Olona: *O-lo-nah (cordage used for their fishing lines and nets)*
Mamo (*Mah-mo*), Elepaio *(Eh-leh-pa-ee-yo),* Iiwi *(Ee-ee-vee),* Oo *(o-o) (birds whose feathers were used to make cloaks for chiefs)*
Iliahi: *Ee-lee-ah-hee (sandalwood tree)*
Tapa: *Tah-pa (bark soaked and beaten to use for clothing, etc.).*
Wauke: *(Wau-keh)*/ Mamaki *(Mah-mah-kee) (native trees/shrubs used to make clothing, etc.)*
Kukui trees: *Ku-ku-wee (nuts used for oil)*
Pili: *Pee-lee (grass)*
Kalo: *Kah-lo (taro)*
Awa: *Ah-vah (root, also known as kava [kah-vah]. Its juice is used for ceremonial drinks)*
Milo *(Mee-lo)* and Kou *(Ko-u)* trees (used to make bowls)
Pohuehue: *Po-hu-eh-hu-eh (plant native to Hawaii).*
Maile: *Mah-ee-leh (native shrub)*

369

Lauhala: *Lau-ha-lah (Pandanus tree)*
Ti: *Tee (plant leaves used to wrap and cook food)*
Pili grass: *Pee-lee (grass, when dried, used to weather-proof huts)*
Pikake: *Pee-kah-keh (fragrant flower)*
Plumeria: *fragrant flower*
Awapuhi: *Ah-vah-pu-hee (ginger plant)*
Limu: *Lee-mu (seaweed)*

Chiefs/Rulers
Chief Ka'eo: *Kah-eh-o (ruled Kaua'i and Ni'ihau)*
Chief Kahahana: *Kah-hah-hah-nah (ruled O'ahu and Moloka'i)*
Chief Kahakili: *Kah-hah-kee-lee (ruled Maui, Lana'i and Kaho'olawe)*
Chief Kalani'opu'u: *Kah-lah-nee-o-pu-u (ruled Hawaii).*
Kamehameha: *Kah-meh-hah-meh-hah (Rose to power as the first Hawaiian King)*
Keopualani: *Keh-yo-pu-wah-lah-nee (high ranking wife to King Kamehameha I)*
Kaahumanu: *Kah-ah-hu-mah-nu (favored wife of King Kamehameha I)*
Liliuokalani: *Lee-lee-u-o-kah-lah-nee (last reigning Hawaiian Queen)*
Kalakaua: *Kah-lah-kah-u-wah (last reigning King-- and brother of--Queen Liliu'okalani)*
Paao *Pah-ah-o* and Pili *Pee-lee (ancient rulers that came from Tahiti to Hawaii)*
Kahuna: *Kah-hu-nah (Hawaiian priest/navigator)*

Geography
Keoneoio Bay: *Keh-o-neh-o-ee-yo (Maui coastline)*

Kanapou Bay: *Kah-nah-po (Kaho'olawe coastline)*
Kamohio Bay: *Kah-mo-hee-yo (Kaho'olawe coastline)*
Puukoae Bay: Pu-u-ko-ah-eh (*Kaho'olawe coastline)*
Ule Point: *U-leh (on Kaho'olawe)*
Halona Point: *Hah-lo-nah (on Kaho'olawe)*
Kealaikahiki: *Keh-ah-lah-ee-kah-hee-kee (Kaho'olawe coastline)*
Waikahalulu Bay: *Wah-ee-kah-hah-lu-lu (Kaho'olawe coastline)*
Lae o Kuikui Point: *Lah-eh o Ku-ee-ku-ee (Kaho'olawe coastline)*
Kaena Point: *Kah-eh-nah (Oahu coastline)*
Alalakeiki Channel: *Ah-lah-lah-keh-ee-kee (channel separating the islands of Kahoolawe and Maui.*
Kure Atoll: *Ku-reh (Northwestern Hawaiian island)*
Mauna Ala: *Mau-nah Ah-lah (Fragrant Hills. Place in Nu'uanu valley of the Royal Mausoleum of the Hawaiian ruling class)*
Wao Kele O Puna: *Wah-o Keh-leh O Pu-nah (Southern district on the Big Island)*
Haumakua: *Hau-mah-ku-wah (Northeast district of Big Island)*
Waikiki: *Wah-ee-kee-kee (Oahu coastline)*
Ala Wai Canal: *Ah-lah Wah-ee (Two mile long waterway located in Waikiki district)*
Waimea Bay: *Wah-ee-meh-ah (Oahu coastline)*
Naalehu: *Nah-ah-leh-hu (Big Island community)*
Kealakekua: *Keh-ah-lah-keh-ah-ku-wah (Big Island community)*
Manoa: *Mah-no-wah (Oahu community)*

Waimanalo: *Wa-ee-mah-nah-lo (Oahu community)*
Kaneohe: *Kah-neh-o-heh (Oahu community)*
Hawaii Kai: *(Oahu community)*
Makapuu: *Mah-kah-pu-u (Oahu beach)*
Nanakuli *(Nah-nah-ku-lee)*, Maile *(Mah-ee-leh)*,
Waianae *(Wah-ee-ah-nah-eh)*, Makaha *(Mah-kah-hah)*---West Oahu communities
Makawao: *Mah-kah-wah-o (Maui community)*
Moanalua: *Mo-ah-nah-lu-wah (Oahu community)*
Aina Hina: *Ah-ee-nah Hee-nah (Oahu community)*
Waikahalulu: *Wah-ee-kah-hah-lu-lu (beach on Kaho'olawe)*

Mountains
Puu Moaulanui: *Pu-u Mo-ah-u-lah-nu-ee (mountain on Kaho'olawe)*
Koolau: *Ko-o-lau (mountain range on Oahu)*
Moaulaiki: *Mo-ah-u-lah-ee-kee (Kaho'olawe mountain where Polynesian navigators trained in the arts of celestial navigation).*

Volcanoes
Kilauea: *Kee-lah-weh-yah (active, Big Island)*
Mauna Loa: *Mau-nah-lo-wah (inactive, Big Island)*
Mauna Kea: *Mau-nah-keh-yah (inactive, Big Island)*
Hualalai: *Hu-wah-lah-lah-ee (inactive, Big Island)*
Diamond Head *(inactive, Oahu)*

Legend
Papa: *Pah-pah (mythical female ancestor of Hawaiians)*

372

Wakea: *Wah-keh-yah (mythical male ancestor of Hawaiians)*
Lono: *Lo-no (harvest deity in ancient Hawaii)*
Kane: *Kah-neh (male; husband, also lead deity in ancient Hawaii)*
Hina: *Hee-nah (known as moon deity in Hawaii)*
Nanawahine: *Nah-nah-vah-hee-neh (derivation of sun deity in ancient Hawaii)*
Opu Iwi: *O-pu (belly) Ee-vee (bone) fictional mound symbolizing the womb of Eve, the first woman*

Pidgin (Island slang)
da: *the*
dis: *this*
cuz: *cousin*
kine: *kind*
whateva: *whatever*
neva: *never*
kea: *care*
wuz: *was*
wen: *when*
wea: *where*
pau: *finish*
ono: *delicious*
fut: *fart*
opala: *trash*
huki: *to pull or tug*
goin: *going*
bebe: *baby*
mo betta: *more better*
da kine: *the kind, in reference to something*
neva mine: *never mind, or, pay no attention*

373

small kine: *small kind, or, trivial; nothing to worry about*
booyah: *gotcha*
bruddah: *brother*
brah: *short for brother*
sista: *sister*
moke: *guy with an attitude*
tita: *girl with an attitude*
fo: *for*
shaka: *hand signed used by Hawaiians to greet or to bid farewell*
hanabutta: *nasal mucus*
dunno: *don't know*
gotta: *got to*
howzit: *how are you?*
kinda: *kind of*

Miscellaneous Hawaiian
Hokulea: *Ho-ku-leh-ya (Double-hull canoe built with modern materials using ancient design and launched its maiden voyage in 1976 from Big Island to Tahiti)*
Mau: *in reference to a navigator from Micronesia who taught celestial navigation to the crew of Hokulea in preparation for its maiden voyage in 1976)*
Hawaiian Renaissance: *successful voyage (Big Island to Tahiti using celestial navigation) of Hokule'a that influenced the rebirth of a fading culture.*
Kualoa: *Ku-wah-lo-wah (Regional Park on Oahu's east end)*

374

Kanaka Maoli: *Kah-nah-kah Mah-o-lee (full blooded Hawaiian person)*
Kupuna: *Ku-pu-nah (grandparent; elder)*
Ha ina ia mai ana kapuana: *Ha-ee-nah-ee-yah-mai-a-nah-kah-pu-wah-nah (and so the story is told; let the echo of our song be heard)*
Ua Mau ke Ea o ka Aina I ka Pono: *Ua-mau-keh-eh-yah-o-kah-ah-ee-nah-ee-kah-po-no (the life of the land is perpetuated in righteousness)*
Iolani Palace: *Ee-yoh-lah-nee Palace (built in 1882 by Hawaii's last King, David Kalakaua)*
Kawaiahao Church: *Kah-wah-ee-ah-hah-o (Historic church in downtown Honolulu, Oahu)*
Iokaha: *Ee-yo-kah-hah (to soar…like a hawk)*
Iwakauikaua: *Ee-vah-kau-wee-kau-wah (known as an ancient law inherited by the Queen through her parents).*
Hokupaa: *Ho-ku-pah-ah (North Star used for ancient navigation)*
Hanaiakamalama: *Hah-nah-ee-yah-kah-ma-lah-ma (also known as the Southern Cross used to navigate)*
Pahu: *Pah-hu (Hawaiian drum)*
Ipu heke: *Ee-pu heh-keh (gourd used as Hawaiian instrument)*
Lahui o Pono: *Lah-hu-ee o Po-no (fictional name for activist group seeking Hawaiian independence)*
Hooponopono: *Ho-o-po-no-po-no (protocol for healing and reconciliation)*
Lokahi: *Lo-kah-hee (said to be the triangular harmony between God, man and land).*
Ha: *Hah (breath; life)*
Pau: *Pah-u (Finish)*

Moolelo: *Mo-o-leh-lo (talk story)*
Kapu: *Kah-pu (ancient Hawaiian laws and regulations)*
Pilikia: *Pee-lee-kee-yah (trouble)*
Auwe: *exclamation of wonder, surprise, fear, pity or affection*
Haku lei: *Hah-ku leh-ee (head garland)*
Koa: *Ko-wah (hardwood tree)*
Keawe: *Keh-ah-veh (topical mesquite brought to Hawaii in 1800s)*
Aa: *Ah-ah (slow moving lava)*
Pahoehoe: *Pah-ho-eh-ho-eh (fast moving lava)*
Lanai: *Lah-nah-ee (patio--same spelling as the island Lanai)*
Ohana: *O-hah-nah (family)*
Kane: *Kah-neh (man)*
Wahine: *Wah-hee-neh (woman)*
Maikai: *Mah-ee-kah-ee (good; fine; well)*
Aloha no: *Ah-lo-hah No (farewell or greeting)*
Hula: *Hu-lah (Hawaiian dance)*
Pareo: *Pah-reh-yo (sarong used to wrap over a bathing suit--or casual wear)*
Malo: *Mah-lo (loincloth for men for ceremonial occasions)*
Shaka: *Sha-kah (hand salutation using thumb and small finger)*
Haole: *Hah-o-leh (foreigner)*
Ehu: *Eh-hu (red)*
Puka: *Pu-kah (hole)*
Mahalo: *Mah-hah-lo (Thanks)*
Moemoe: *Mo-eh-mo-eh (sleep)*
Hoomoemoe: *Ho-o-mo-eh-mo-eh (put to sleep)*
Pueo: *Pu-eh-yo (owl)*

'Io: *EE-yo (Hawaiian Hawk)*
Muumuu: *Mu-u-mu-u (loose fitted dress)*

Miscellaneous Maori, Polynesian, Native American, Other

Te Ora: *Teh O-rah (New Life)*
Tangata Maori: *Tahn-gah-tah Mah-o-ree (person of Maori descent)*
Ngati Mutunga Maori iwi: *N-gah-tee Mu-tun-gah Mah-o-ree ee-vee (person of Maori descent)*
Wairarapa: *Wah-ee-rah-rah-pa (north island of Aotearoa)*
Ngati Kahungunu iwi: *N-gah-tee Kah-hun-gu-nu ee-vee (person from Wairarapa)*
Te Rangi Hiroa: *Teh-rhan-gee Hee-ro-wa (doctor, military leader, health administrator, politician, anthropologist, museum director, member of Ngati Mutunga).*
Te Matorohanga chant: *Teh Mah-to-ro-han-gah (known as a creation chant)*
Taikama: *Tai-kah-mah (mentioned in the Te Matorohanga creation chant).*
Tupuhorunuku: *Tu-pu-ho-ru-nu-ku (mentioned in the Te Matorohanga creation chant).*
Io: *Ee-yo (Maori Supreme Being)*
Marae *Mah-rah-eh (Maori longhouse)*
Tahunga: *Tah-hun-gah (Maori priest)*
Te Puna Mātauranga o Aotearoa: *Teh Pu-nah Mah-tah-u-ran-ga o Ah-o-teh-ah-ro-ah (National Library of New Zealand)*
Te Ope Kaatua o Aotearoa: *Teh O-peh Kah-ah-tu-ah o Ah-o-teh-ah-ro-ah (New Zealand Defense Force).*

377

Pakeha: *Pah-kee-hah (foreigner)*
Haka: *Hah-kah (Maori ceremonial dance)*
Te lapa*: Teh lah-pah (Underwater lightning--
bioluminescent streaks from an island's volcanic
activity that can shoot out up to 125 miles out at
sea.*
Hua hoa dele tai: *Hu-wah ho-wah deh-leh-tah-ee
(Ocean swells used to navigate without sextant or
compass).*
Rapa Nui: *Rah-pah Nu-ee (Easter Island)*
Moai: *Mo-ah-ee (Statue...in the form of stone heads
on Easter Island)*
Birdsman tribe: *known as a cult on Rapa Nui—or
Easter Island*
Asmat: *Ethnic group from West Papua, Indonesia*
Wahunsenacawh: *Wah-hun-sah-nak-kah-weh
(father of Matoaka-- Mah-tah-o-kah-- better known
as Pocahontas).*
Wahhabi: *fundamentalist movement within Sunni
Islam*
Wayfinding: *Ancient celestial navigation restored
by Mau Piailug, in Hawaii, in the 1970s.*

Made in the USA
Monee, IL
08 July 2023

38354074R00213